Widow of Escondido

The Tale of Two Dancing Hearts

By Emme Rocher

Hidden Shelf Publishing House
P.O. Box 4168, McCall, ID 83638
www.hiddenshelfpublishinghouse.com

Copyright @ 2024, Emme Rocher
Hidden Shelf Publishing House
All rights reserved

Editor: Kerstin Stokes

Artist: Megan Whitfield
Graphic design: Rachel Wickstrom

Interior layout: Kerstin Stokes

Library of Congress Cataloguing-in-Publication Data

Names: Rocher, Emme, author.

Title: The widow of Escondido / Emme Rocher.
Description: McCall, ID: Hidden Shelf Publishing House, 2024.

Identifiers: LCCN: 2024912866 | ISBN: 978-1-955893-45-9 (paperback) | 978-1-955893-46-6 (ebook) | 978-1-955893-47-3 (Kindle) Subjects: LCSH Marriage--Fiction. | Divorce--Fiction. | United States--20th century--Fiction. | Romance fiction. | Historical fiction. | BISAC FICTION / Family Life / Marriage & Divorce | FICTION / Friendship | FICTION / Historical / 20th Century / Post-World War II | FICTION / Romance / General

Classification: LCC PS3615 .O34 W53 2024 | DDC 813.6--dc23

Printed in the United States of America

Table of Contents

Part I

Part II

Part III

Dedicated to Bob Gaines.
Thank you for the inspiration and wisdom.

Part I

Chapter 1

THE UNEXPECTED

My work week had been fierce. By Friday, I needed sleep and some mental peace. No one protested when I left early.

Once home, I collapsed into my chaise lounge and immediately drifted into a deep sleep ... until a startling ring. Fumbling for my phone, my alertness was disturbed by a limp voice.

"Lori, this is Ethelene Narramore."

"Who?"

A louder reply struck my eardrum, "It's Ethelene, Lori."

Ethelene is my aunt's best friend in Lillian, Alabama. She never calls.

"Ethelene, is something wrong?"

"Yes, there is." She seemed distraught. "I'm afraid I have some very bad news for you. It's about your aunt. I found her unconscious at the cottage. She wasn't breathing, so I called 911. It's awful, Lori."

Her startling words ziplined directly to my heart; my breathing seemed to stall in an off-and-on-again, light-switch pattern, numbness invading all muscles.

"Ethelene, Aunt Lorea has died?"

"Yes, dear." She choked on her words. "I'm sorry."

"Oh, my Lord. Why? How?"

"I don't know what happened, Lori. It's hard to believe. Old age?"

"What did the medical team say?"

"Possible heart failure. They didn't say much. All I know is they couldn't revive her."

I paused, trying to process.

"When was the last time you talked with her?"

"Well, she called on Sunday afternoon to ask me if I would come over to help her weed and plant in the garden. It's hard at our age, but I was thrilled since she has not cared about doing anything over the last few months. I thought maybe her listless mood might be changing."

Ethelene continued to recap what had transpired with a shaky voice, as if the ground was moving beneath her.

"Since I was going to visit relatives in Mobile earlier in the week, we set an early morning work time for today to avoid the intense heat and humidity that we are experiencing right now. I called to touch base with her first thing this morning. She didn't answer, but I thought maybe she might be sitting outside by the bluff enjoying her breakfast tea."

My attention drifted. Images of Aunt Lorea's daily ritual—sitting on the bench by the bluff overlooking Perdido Bay—floated through my mind.

With a strong pinch to the bridge of my nose, my attention cycled back to Ethelene who was still recalling what happened.

"Well, anyway, when she didn't answer, I just drove on over to the cottage. When I arrived, I noticed she was not sitting by the bluff. I went in the house and called out to her, but there was no answer. I decided to check the art studio. The door was unlocked, and I found her on the divan."

Ethelene was crying so hard I was unable to discern her words.

"Ethelene, you don't have to tell me all this right now. Just take a few minutes to calm yourself."

Ignoring my plea, she continued, obviously feeling a need to immediately reconstruct the whole thing, but my mind had released me from the present. Wonderful memories of Aunt Lorea engulfed me again. She was a special person. After my father died, I spent some time each summer with her as my mother was too consumed with oiling a rusty social life to fulfill her parenting duties.

"Lori, are you still there?"

"Yes. I'm sorry, Ethelene. What were you saying? Please, go ahead." I rubbed my hand across my forehead.

"Well, she was gone. It was horrible to find her like that. I called you as soon as I could."

I bit my lip and bowed my head. Once again, words stalled, train-wrecked in my throat.

"Ethelene, I know this is hard for you. The two of you were such close friends."

"Lori, there are no words for my feelings right now. I should have called to tell you how she had been acting lately. Maybe if I had called, she would be alive today. I feel so responsible."

"Please don't go there, Ethelene. You are certainly not responsible for her death."

"Yes, I hear you, my dear," she said, her voice reflecting a trembling rage, "but that doesn't help me at all right now."

What? I threw my free hand up towards the ceiling, wanting to scream. I'm the relative. She should be comforting me right now. Plus, I have turmoil in my own life currently ... divorce. And she's wanting me to deal with her self-imposed guilt trip?

"Ethelene, please try to calm yourself," I politely responded, stifling the urge to lash out. "We have other things that we need to think about right now. You said something about how she had been acting lately. What exactly was she doing?"

"I'm not sure. She became more and more reclusive, especially over the last few weeks. She was showing no interest in anything, not even pampering the orchids in the greenhouse, and you know how she loved her orchids. That's why I was pleased when she asked me to come and work in the garden."

I tried to fight back another rush of tears.

"Lori, when can you get here? I need you to get down here," she begged in a syrupy Southern voice, eliminating the razorlike edge from her earlier tone. "Funeral arrangements have to be made."

"I know, Ethelene. I know. As soon as I can notify work, I'll be on my way. I'll be there tonight."

"Please be careful. You know how dark it is on the back roads getting here. I'll meet you at her cottage."

"I'm totally familiar with the roads, Ethelene, even in the dark. I've driven them many times." I paused, taking a deep breath silently begging for patience. "In the meantime, I need you to do something for me. See if you can contact David Lee. He needs to be notified since he's her only other living relative besides me. We have not communicated in years, but I'm sure Aunt Lorea has his number somewhere in the cottage."

"I'll see what I can find. If something turns up, I hope it's current because you're right. He doesn't come around anymore."

"Doesn't surprise me at all, Ethelene. David is a drifter. There's no telling where he is or what he is doing, but he needs to know. Also, see if you can find any documents like a will or a deed to the property. I'm going to need those."

"I'll do my best, Lori."

The worst phone call I've ever had was over, and I just collapsed into a chair at the kitchen table, blankly staring at the coffee pot. I needed a cup, but I couldn't move. Recollections of summers with Aunt Lorea at Escondido, her cottage in Lillian, created a mental swell like the Mississippi River overflowing in the spring. The hold on my tear ducts released, and I began sobbing uncontrollably.

Wasn't it just yesterday that we painted for hours in the art studio, designed costumes for the Pensacola Mardi Gras, caught crabs at night at Pensacola Beach, listened to classical favorites, picnicked at the old unfinished hotel at Perdido Bay, and dressed for our make-believe *Moonlight Ball by the Bay?* Powerful memories filtered through the grief. Losing her slammed me in the stomach like a bad belly flop from a high diving board.

I paced the floor thinking about what I needed to do, running my fingers through my curly auburn-colored hair that needed taming before I departed.

I had never made funeral arrangements or settled an estate for a loved one and had no idea where to begin. Surely, there was a will, and surely, she had a lawyer. Confusion, grief, and sadness crisscrossed and tangled my rational thinking as I drove to Lillian.

As expected, Ethelene greeted me at the door. We embraced like wrestlers. I eventually broke the grip by turning my body in another direction, permitting me to move towards the living area. I circled the room like a surveyor. Everything was just as it had been since my last visit, only Aunt Lorea wasn't sitting in her chair. How was I going to get through this return to the cottage without her being here?

Much like a runaway, wind-up toy, Ethelene began briefing me on what she had accomplished since our earlier conversation. Wiping her face with a cold towel, the verbal onslaught began.

"Lori, I have searched high and low for a will. I can't find a thing. I can't even find papers showing that she owns this place. I do know that she wanted to be cremated with a simple memorial service here at the cottage. She was adamant about her ashes being spread below the garden on the side of the bluff overlooking the bay. I'm not so sure about the legalities of doing that."

Stopping to thread her ringless fingers through her cap of silver hair, she paused as if to regroup her jumbled thoughts.

I took advantage of her momentary lapse and glided slowly into Aunt Lorea's chair, fussing with the throw pillows that emulated her Evening in Paris perfume. A cream-colored pillow with amber fringe reminded me of her mellow-colored complexion. I touched it softly as if it were her face.

With continued kinked energy, Ethelene regained momentum and began verbally motoring once again.

"Believe it or not, I was able to contact David Lee. He

expressed his sympathies but can't come. He told me, to tell you, that you would have to take care of things—but he did mention something about an inheritance." She pointed a determined finger at me. "Lori, this is where the lawyer comes in. I have taken the liberty of contacting Bill Marks. He's a lawyer. Lorea and I have known him for years. I left a message with his secretary. I have also called as many friends as I could to convey the sad news and have drafted an announcement. Plus ..."

Ethelene's rambling provoked unwanted dizziness. I knew she was trying to help, but between the shock of Aunt Lorea's death, nighttime driving, and being submerged in layers of emotions now that I was in the cottage, her talking depleted what was left of my physical and mental energy.

Nevertheless, her rant ensued. I smiled, nodded, and made eye contact as if she had my full attention. My mind drifted. Once upon a time, Lillian was a very sparsely populated, sleepy little area, but time changed that. Condos emerged, and even though the locals knew this would bring revenue to the area, they also knew it would bring traffic and crowded conditions to the beach communities. Although Lorea and Ethelene were far from being antisocial, this insurgence was disturbing to them. They preferred the quiet, secluded, and unadulterated environment that characterized Lillian when they first moved there. Since they were both divorced, they kept their status a secret because of the negative image imposed on divorcees of their generation. Neither remarried, both maintaining independent lifestyles.

Social occasions for them would last all day as they needed time to catch up on local gossip and share interesting books over several glasses of champagne, my aunt's favorite alcoholic beverage. Once a month, planned outings generated opportunities to shop and sightsee, the latter being of high importance as new content was needed for gossip.

Aunt Lorea had expensive taste and spent large sums of money on clothing. She was especially passionate about hats, and local merchants would order special ones in anticipation of her next visit.

When hurricanes threatened the area, daily phone contact occurred between them to share weather news. Evacuation was never an option. They simply boarded up and waited out major storms. They had the strength of southern oaks.

No longer able to sustain the information barrage that was audible in the background, I diverted her attention.

"Hey, Ethelene. Did I smell coffee when I came in? On second thought, do you think there's any red wine in the cottage? I think I've had enough coffee."

"I doubt it, Lori. She only drank champagne. You know that. Would you like a glass? I'm sure there is a bottle somewhere?"

"Find it!"

Shortly, Ethelene returned with champagne iced down in a container, but she refrained from personal indulgence. I, on the other hand, took advantage of obtaining a smoother passage into what was left of the night.

"Ethelene, not trying to be ungrateful or rude, but I can't process any more information right now. I need to be alone. I'm going out to the garden by the bluff. You are welcome to stay at the cottage tonight with me, but right now, I just need some quiet time with my memories."

Signaling her understanding with a nod and a shoulder pat, she located her car keys and promptly left.

Even though the air on the bluff was sticky from the heat of the day, I closed my eyes and let the sounds of the evening and champagne soothe me. My body surrendered to the moment.

As tears flowed, I whispered, "Aunt Lorea, I know you are here."

Chapter 2

ARRANGEMENTS

Daybreak ushered in the realities at hand. A thorough search of every conceivable place in the house did not produce a will or papers of any kind. Ethelene and I couldn't even find utility bills. Momentarily, however, we were out of time. Preparing for the memorial service impeded search efforts.

We decided on a sunset service at the cottage overlooking the bay. Ethelene went to her church to see if we could borrow chairs, tables, and tablecloths. Even though the humidity would be intense, we counted on the breeze from the bluff to make it bearable.

Friends and neighbors arrived throughout the day bringing the usual foods for such an occasion: potato salad, chicken salad, cucumber finger sandwiches, fried chicken, pies, and pound cakes served with gallons of iced tea. The tradition of placing the grieving family with the responsibility of hosting a gathering after a death irked me. Nevertheless, for Aunt Lorea, we would do what was customary.

A stonewall-faced funeral director from one of the funeral homes in Foley, Alabama, made final arrangements for the cremation, and Ethelene's minister, Reverend Thomas Beasley, agreed to conduct the service. Even though Aunt Lorea did not attend formal church services in town, he knew her well and was aware that her favorite place of meditation and worship was at her Escondido Cottage on the bluffs overlooking Perdido Bay. She particularly loved quiet evenings sitting on the garden bench by the bluff. After sunset, flowers partnered with gentle breezes for dance recitals, using the peach and blue horizon as the backdrop for the stage.

The setting reminded me of her paintings capturing the beauty of the garden as well as vibrant summer sunsets. Even though most of her completed canvases had been sold or given away over the years, her favorites remained in the cottage.

Standing in the sunroom looking towards the bay, my thoughts suddenly diverted to things less aesthetic.

Why would she not leave a will, especially at her age? Where was the deed to the property? Why had she become so reclusive and despondent? What had been her source of income? How had she been able to maintain Escondido Cottage as well as her standard of living? She had not worked for years. At one time, she did mention inheriting money from her parents' estate. Did that source of income enable her to purchase the land and build the cottage? Discussions of that nature never occurred between us. She never said anything, and I had never asked. Therefore, I knew nothing of her personal affairs. In hindsight, I should have invaded that space. I was both frustrated and annoyed with myself.

To escape the cavern of confusion that blocked saneness, I lowered my head for a moment of peace. Ethelene's loud voice forced me to the surface.

"Lori, you must be starving! You've not stopped to eat all day. Here, I brought you a plate of food. Believe me, we have plenty in the refrigerator."

"You're right. I do need something to eat. Thanks, Ethelene. You know I couldn't do this without you."

"Say no more, precious. This whole ordeal has been terrible for both of us. Unexpected death creates upheaval. Funerals, even small ones, cost money. Without access to Lorea's bank accounts, I'm guessing you have no cash flow to cover expenses. I'm prepared to help with my personal funds, but I may know a better source. Lorea always kept a large, emergency cash fund hidden in an old paint jar in the art studio with 'friviloot' painted across the bottom."

"Friviloot? What is that?"

"Yep. Funny, isn't it? It was her nonsense name for frivolous money anytime she needed it. She would not call it mad or emergency money. It was friviloot!"

"Money hidden in a paint jar?"

"Lorea put money aside for anything that fancied her. Once, she used it for us to go to Chicago and visit the Museum of Art. We stayed at the Drake, had high tea in the afternoon, and took a boat ride on Lake Michigan. I don't know if she still has it, but it's worth a try."

The practice of hiding money amused me. Why didn't she just put money earmarked for special occasions in an account in the bank? Why so secretive? It was not as if she were married and had to shave money from the household account to buy something outside of the budget, like another pair of shoes or an expensive hat. What was it about this older generation that caused them to hide money?

My grandmother once told me about her friend, Pearl. When Pearl died, her children found a roll of one hundred-dollar bills tied with twine dangling at the end of a long string that had been wrapped around a nail on the back of her chest of drawers. My Grandmother said that type of thinking was caused by the Great Depression.

Our search was productive. Hidden amongst the paint cans on an old art table was a glass canning jar with electric colors dabbled on the outside. A round piece of polka dot cloth secured the mouth with a rubber band. There was quite a bit of cash inside the jar, but not nearly enough to cover all funeral expenses. At least it would buy us some time until we had more information about the estate.

* * *

The next evening, guests began arriving at six. I remembered some names from my childhood years at Lillian, like the McQueens, the O'Neals, Sam Pendleton, and especially Perry

Frederick. All of them had been longtime friends and were much older now. If they were still living, I knew that their attendance was guaranteed.

Laughter and light conversation characterized the mood of the incoming crowd which made it seem more like a reunion. I thought it was somewhat disrespectful. As a child, I was taught church and funeral manners—reverence and somberness prevailed. Apparently, the locals observed a different ritual. Nevertheless, I would be the gracious hostess, even though I dreaded the repeated explanations of when and how she died.

"Oh. You're Lorea's niece," said the first of the onslaught. "I am so pleased to meet you. How nice you look, just like your aunt."

"Thank you. And you are?"

"Doris. I'm Doris, honey," her coarse smoker's voice proclaimed.

Doris towered over most females. Her tall and lanky body was outfitted with a large, loose-fitting black dress which matched her full-bodied, teased-and-sprayed black hair. I laughed to myself thinking that if she fell off the bluff, she could use her dress and bouffant hairdo as parachutes.

I was unable to hear what came after her introduction as we were interrupted by a smartly dressed elderly gentleman who had been working the crowd like a politician.

"Lori, Sam Pendleton here, longtime friend of your aunt's. I remember seeing you as a child."

His thick white hair, crystal green eyes, and toothy smile made him stand out in the crowd. I was particularly amused with his two-toned saddle Oxford shoes, a total throwback from earlier decades.

"Yes, I remember you too, Mr. Pendleton. It is nice to see you again even under these circumstances."

"I was so sorry to learn about her death, Lori. It was a real shock. Had she been ill?"

"I don't know. Ethelene and I were not aware of any apparent illnesses, but it seems that she was very despondent."

"Well, sweetie, you just let me know if there's anything you need. I'm a retired investment broker if ..."

Before he could finish, a tearful woman with a handkerchief over her mouth engulfed me in a bear hug. She was traditionally dressed in a light blue suit adorned with a string of pearls. Her silver-grey lacquered hair fought the wind.

"It's just terrible, just terrible. And you had her cremated? People are doing that now, submitting their ashes to the water or land. I guess that's what she wanted, right?"

"Yes. Ethelene knew she wanted to be cremated. And you are?"

"Forgive me, dear. My name is Maggie O'Neal."

"Yes, of course. Mrs. O'Neal. I didn't recognize you at first. You own O'Neal's Store. I remember shopping there when I was younger. Are you still in business?"

"Oh, Lord no, sugar. My husband and I retired long ago. Your aunt and I go way back. She was such a sweet and gentle person and to think she was cremated is horrible. What happened to traditional burials, for goodness' sake?"

Her question forced a pop-up question on my radar screen. I was also used to traditional burials. Had I really thought about the act of cremation? Dismissing the invasion of that thought and not wanting to think on it, I consoled Mrs. O'Neal.

"Yes. It's been difficult, Mrs. O'Neal, especially since it was so sudden."

Without commenting further, I stroked her shoulder and moved away as quickly as possible only to be confronted by another guest.

"Lori, I'm Loretta McQueen. I've known Lorea for a very long time. My husband and I just live right down the road. You've probably seen the McQueen sign out on the road. Howard and Loretta McQueen. That's us. I remember you in your younger years. It's been a long time, hasn't it?"

I blinked several times. The aging process is not kind to some people.

"Well, I'll be. Mrs. McQueen. Yes, it has been a long time.

How are you?"

"I should be asking you that. So, tell me. How are you holding up?"

"I'm okay at the moment, Mrs. McQueen."

"That's good. Howard and I are saddened by the news. Even though we know that we are very old now, it's hard to accept it when one of us dies. Is it true that she died in the art studio?"

Before I could answer, she waved to a familiar acquaintance, beckoning his attention.

"Bill Marks! Over here," she summoned. "You're looking well, I must say."

"Thank you, Loretta. It has been a while. And you, dear lady, just never change. Same old Loretta that we all know and love."

I pressed my lips together to keep from bursting out loud with laughter, which would have been so inappropriate for me under the circumstances since she was as round as she was tall.

"Lori, it's a real pleasure, a real pleasure to meet you, even though the circumstances are bad. We were all saddened to hear the news. Say, why don't we step over here a bit to fend off the biting flies," he whispered in a hiccupped giggle.

"Sounds great to me," I emphatically stated as I welcomed his diversion from unwanted, nosey inquiries.

"Excuse us, Loretta. I need to speak to Lori, privately. You don't mind, do you?"

"Of course not, Bill. Under the circumstances and all. But please come back my way. We haven't talked in ages."

Mr. Marks looked middle-aged. His Southern accent was thick, and his short and substantially overweight figure was a replica of Loretta McQueen. With his fat, rosy cheeks, protruding mid-section, and jolly personality, he could easily portray Santa in the local Christmas parade. I grabbed his arm and turned away from Loretta who was still chattering to anyone in close proximity to her.

"Mr. Marks. How glad I am to see you for many reasons.

First, thanks for the timely rescue. I needed to get away from all of these well-meaning but inquisitive guests. I don't mean to be rude, but I simply can't answer all these incessant questions or make polite conversation, even though I know that's what I'm supposed to do. I'm just exhausted."

"Of course. Let's find somewhere we won't be interrupted."

A lengthy conversation, however, was not possible as Ethelene began directing everyone to be seated, and the planned service promptly began.

An appropriate ceremonial canvas was created by selecting a Bible verse from Ecclesiastes, reading poems from Elizabeth Barrett Browning and William Shakespeare, and playing classical music, all artistically delivered.

Even though I was aware that the ceremony was taking place, I only heard the gentle sound of trickling water from the pond. I only felt the hot breeze darting in and out of the pine and palm trees. I could only smell the soft fragrances coming from the flowers. I only saw the urn which I held tightly in my hand.

The moment was surreal.

Was this it? Just a container filled with her ashes? Cremation brought on a different emotion, one that I had not anticipated or experienced before. I was used to a body in a coffin being laid to rest in the ground. Even though you knew the person's soul was no longer present within the body, tangible objects remained behind. A corpse, a coffin, flowers, and a gravesite offered something earthly, tempering the sense of loss.

I understood Maggie O'Neal's reaction that cremation was an awful practice. The reality of it hovered worse than the humidity. Aunt Lorea had burned. Since she was such a gentle person, this seemed so cold, impersonal, and harsh. But that is what she wanted.

A hand on my elbow signaled that it was time for the final part of the service. I looked up to see Reverend Beasley smiling through his moving lips, although I heard nothing. Going through the motions, I stood up, walked to the edge of the bluff, opened the container, and whispered the traditional words may you rest in peace. I turned the urn upside down and let the breeze decide the final resting place. Her remains were gone in seconds. It was done. She had been laid to rest at her sanctuary by the bay. So be it.

My legs trembled as I returned to my chair. Her gentle spirit hovered, and my senses once again controlled my thoughts.

Chapter 3

LEGALITIES

Several of Ethelene and Aunt Lorea's friends returned early the next morning to help with cleanup from the memorial service which allowed me to focus on other important matters.

Mid-afternoon, Bill Marks returned. Ethelene escorted him into the sunroom where I was rummaging through a stack of old books. His seersucker jacket was unbuttoned which he immediately removed due to the heat. His straw hat, once removed, revealed his shiny, bald head saturated with perspiration. From his back pocket, he took out a handkerchief and wiped his brow and neck. Instead of coffee, Ethelene quickly revived him with a tall glass of lemon iced tea as he tossed his weathered briefcase on the table which I hoped was filled with information about the estate.

"Lori, let me express again how shocked and saddened I was to learn about the death of your aunt and once more extend my heartfelt sympathies. Is this a good time to talk?"

"It's fine. Please, have a seat. And thank you again for the rescue yesterday."

"I'm glad I could assist. I know how these gatherings go around here. Sometimes, people aren't clearheaded about proper protocol. Now, tell me how I can help?"

"Ok, Bill. I have never done this before, and I know absolutely nothing about the legal process involved. We can't find a deed showing ownership of the property, and a will has not surfaced.

Do you know where I might locate these documents?"

He wiped his brow again and stood up. His body language reflected courtroom behavior as he paced back and forth stating the facts.

"Even though I am an attorney and a friend, I regret to tell you that your aunt did not consult with me about anything legal. She was a very private person. I am sure that you find that unusual and almost unbelievable, but she shared very little personal information."

"Actually, I'm now learning that about her," I interjected.

"Well, that might help you understand when I tell you that I can't confirm the existence of a will. When I spoke with her about establishing one, she avoided the subject entirely. If she has one, it's most likely to be somewhere in the cottage. The reason I say this is because I encouraged her to keep important documents in a safe deposit box at the bank, but she continuously refused. She just wouldn't budge on the issue."

With my elbows resting on the table, I lowered my head into my hands and sighed heavily.

"This is just so hard to believe."

"I understand, Lori. Do you need me to come back later?"

"Later won't change things, Bill. We need to move on this. Can you tell me anything else that you might know about her financial situation?"

"Not really. The only thing I can add is that I tried to offer my help many times in preparing her tax returns, which she rejected. Therefore, I refrained from further offers. Some people are just well-guarded about personal affairs."

I snatched up a stack of grocery store receipts that Ethelene found in a junk drawer in the kitchen and flippantly tossed them on the table. Looking directly into Bill's face, a tense tone governed my reply as mounting frustration consumed my rational posture.

"That's a little hard for me to fathom, Bill. I agree that some individuals embrace privacy concerning personal matters, but people generally have a Last Will and Testament in place to provide direction for the estate handlers. All we have is a stack of useless receipts from the local grocery. I want answers, and I am not getting them. I'm not faulting you for that, but this whole sad situation has been unnerving, frustrating, and very mysterious."

"You're right about that, Lori. When I got the message about her death, Ethelene mentioned the fact that vital documents were missing, and I immediately began inquiring and searching. Even with the contacts that I have in the Tax Assessor's Office and the County Courthouse, I came up empty-handed. For some strange reason, there are no records in your aunt's name that I can find, and that's puzzling. And yes, very mysterious like you said."

"Well, it's just hard for me to believe that Aunt Lorea would have let this happen. I don't understand."

"I know. Dealing with a lack of information on top of her death has to be difficult for you. For right now, though, all I can tell you is that the estate will go to probate court. After that, if no liens are filed, the court will decide what happens next. The entire process can be very lengthy."

"Well, that's just great," I stated angrily. "In the meantime, what do we do?"

"We keep on searching and digging. That's what. Information on the property should be in the records somewhere even if it's not in her name."

"Well, Bill. Hopefully something will surface soon. I do thank you for your time and effort."

With that said, I grabbed my notepad and moved to the kitchen to review the notes that I had jotted down thus far and to indulge in memories of mealtime conversations sitting at the vintage kitchen table with Aunt Lorea. Reminiscent thought eventually succumbed to reality and irritation returned. Slamming my pencil down on the table, I stood up, walked over to the refrigerator, opened the door, and let the cool air soothe my flushed face. Taking a deep breath, I moved about the kitchen; eventually pausing at the window to gaze at the panoramic setting.

The small cottage was quietly nestled in a wooded and serene locale. The property, however, was sizeable. A narrow but long stretch of land connected the county road to the bluffs which was only accessible via a sandy road that had been formed to accommodate automobile passage. Huge picture windows in the main living area provided a magnificent view of Perdido Bay. It was pristine.

To claim Escondido Cottage and the property without a will, David Lee and I would most likely have to jointly purchase the property. Ethelene had mentioned that similar estates in the area were selling for over a half a million dollars based on current market values. Neither of us had that sum of money. Therefore, we would lose everything unless we could produce legal documents naming us as heirs to the property and the cottage.

Bill and Ethelene continued to talk, but I engaged in a selective hearing mode as I tried to unscramble the myriad of thoughts filtering in and out of my brain. What's missing here? Why were legal issues neglected? She might have been a private person, but pertinent documents had to be somewhere. It felt like I was in a spin cycle in the washing machine.

I revisited the memorial service by flipping through the pages of the guest register. Some names were not familiar. The ones I expected to come that I knew for several years attended the service, except for Perry Frederick. He was always present during my summer visits, but the cottage was void of any male clothing items. Therefore, I assumed that he was just a good friend that entertained cottage guests with scenic boating excursions. However, maybe there was more. As a young person, you just don't ask certain questions.

The last time I recalled seeing him was the summer before I left for college. Even though Aunt Lorea and I continued corresponding, it was intermittent, and she never mentioned Perry Frederick. During a holiday visit to Lillian, I asked about him, and there was an immediate mood change. Her smiling face faltered. Disengaging in eye contact, she looked at the garden, gripping her fingers together so tightly that her knuckles whitened. Color disappeared from her face, and her wrinkles were more pronounced. It was almost as if she were aging right before me. Standing up and moving away from me, she compressed her arms across her stomach. After a few moments, she stroked her graying hair, wiped her eyes, took a deep breath, and returned inside the cottage.

My inquiry had changed her total demeanor, and it was obvious that the mere mention of his name was a source of anguish. Sporadic tears rolled down her cheeks like rain on a window. As I approached her and took her in my arms, the rigidness of her body was like a corpse. She pulled away and took refuge in her bedroom.

Obviously, something gut-wrenching had happened. Maybe he had died, and she just couldn't speak about it. Maybe they had a difficult romance that ended harshly. I refrained from delving further and never brought it up again.

Now, at the time of her death, I'm wondering what happened to him. At one time he was active in her life. Ethelene had not brought up his name at all. Why? Could he be a part of the mystery? I remembered occasions when she came by to visit when he was at the cottage. They were obviously well acquainted as no introductions were necessary. Since he had not attended the memorial service, I was certain that he was probably deceased as he was older than Aunt Lorea. So, I decided to probe to see what information I could uncover.

"Hey, you two. Aunt Lorea had many friends in and around Lillian that attended the service. I am curious about one friend that did not, though, Perry Frederick. Whatever happened to him?"

Ethelene's rapid-fire response put her into a top-notch flamethrower category.

"He's dead. Automobile accident. Doesn't have any bearing on this situation. So just drop it."

I was stunned at her aggressive response. I thought it was just hot outside. The real scorcher was inside. I retreated to the kitchen to get a glass of iced tea. Her curt derailment of my inquiry was interesting, provoking deep thought for me.

"Lori, are you listening? Bill is leaving. Do you have any further questions for him?" she tersely belted my way.

"No, I am so confused at this point that I don't know what to ask. Wait. There is one more thing. How long did you say probate would take?"

"Maybe several months. It can be a long process. I'll just have to stay in touch to update you on developments."

"Thanks, Bill. I will appreciate any information you can provide."

After he left, my internal inferno strengthened as I began pacing the floor. Everything seemed to be a mystery. Aunt Lorea was a smart person and would have certainly known what the estate was worth, as well as the legal parameters involved with inheritance. Stuck on the thought of her being so negligent, I simultaneously juggled anger and sadness which catapulted into another search fueled by emotional inflammation. Nothing surfaced.

Totally frustrated, I packed the car. However, before leaving, I had some unfinished business to address with Ethelene.

"Ethelene, let's walk outside. I want to look at the view from the bluff before we temporarily close the place down."

We filled two glasses with mint iced tea and made our way to the garden bench.

"It's hard to leave with so many loose ends. There's got to be something we're overlooking. Let's talk more about Perry Frederick. What's up? You were very terse with me earlier."

"Nothing, Lori. Perry was her friend. What does that have to do with anything?" she replied with a returning element of curtness.

"Maybe a lot indicated by your reaction. I think there's more. So, what is it?"

Ethelene sprang up from the bench, knocking over her drink. Fidgeting like a child waiting for a shot in the doctor's office, she moved several paces away from me.

"Lori, Bill told you how private your aunt was. I don't think it is my place to share information that may be extremely personal, but I will say this. Perry died a few years ago in an automobile accident."

"Yes, you shared that. Were they lovers? You're being much too guarded with all of this, and your reaction possibly confirms that."

"I don't feel that I have the right to comment, Lori."

"Right to comment? Why are you in this protective mode? She's gone. A little help here, please."

I was pushing back and pushing hard.

"Stop right now. You know I will help you in any way that I can, and I don't mean to be unpleasant about this, but I am not going to have this conversation with you. Is there anything else you need me to do before you leave?"

I studied her body language. Agitation was apparent. Slapping her right hand on her right leg, she walked around the bench gritting her teeth which was detectable through the muscular movement in her jawbone. I was right. There was more, a lot more, but she wasn't budging.

"No, Ethelene. I'm sorry to have put you on the spot. I meant no harm, but there's so much at stake here, and I was merely trying to find a thread that might connect all of this. I don't understand why you are not helping me."

With that said, I stood up abruptly, gave her a stern look and power walked towards the cottage.

"Lori, wait. Some questions are never answered and sometimes things are not understood. It's just part of life."

"Well, it may be, Ethelene, and I would like to say that's okay, and smile a philosophically, 'that's life' smile, but I'm about to lose Escondido Cottage which means so much to me, and I am groping for anything that might unravel this mystery. I just don't know what is going on, but you seem to be sworn to some kind of secrecy. Maybe you want the property and the cottage for yourself. You know I can't afford to buy it if it goes on the market. Maybe Aunt Lorea and you had some kind of secret about the place that you are hiding.

Whatever, I'm leaving. I just need to be done with this."

"Lori, please don't go like this."

"I am, and I'm beyond anger. If you know something, tell me something that may help me unless it will benefit you, of course."

"I've told you what I can, Lori, and this is not about me. I'm not trying to take away what should be yours. I do know how important this place is to you. However, I don't think that anything I know would make a difference in whether you inherit Escondido Cottage and the land it sits on. Even though Lorea and I were best friends, some things were personal to her. All of us respected that."

I looked at her stubborn face and offered a volatile, parting comment.

"I hope withholding what you know makes you the proud, loyal friend to the end even if it means that I lose everything. Aunt Lorea would hate you for that."

Momentarily stunned, she gasped, placing her hands over her mouth. Eventually regaining her composure, she looked at me and said, "Things will work out. You'll see."

"Is that what you think, Ethelene? Then you must believe in miracles. Be sure to lock up when you leave," I snarled as I left her standing by the art studio.

This whole situation reminded me of a movie that you see or book you read where you're left hanging in the end, disgruntled and hackles raised because the desired closure was not obtained. I needed something, anything to provide some shred of resolution.

As I opened the car door, I noticed the Escondido Cottage cornerstone. I paused to look, and a question surfaced.

"Ethelene, Perdido means 'lost.' What does Escondido mean? I've never really thought about it until now. It's such an odd name for a cottage on the bluffs at Perdido Bay."

"Escondido mainly means *hidden*."

I stood there in silence.

Chapter 4

SECRETS AT THE COTTAGE

Ethelene and I talked minimally during the next few months. Conversations with her were guarded and lacked openness. Bill called a few times to assure me that he was vigilant in his continued search. Conversations with him were void of emotion, typical of the preferred distance relating to the appropriate legal posture with a client. Eventually, he called with some news.

"Lori, Got a minute? I have a few things to share."

"Good morning, Bill. Sure. What's new?"

"The estate has miraculously cleared probate court in record time, but don't get excited. Mystery still engulfs this whole ordeal. I simply can't find information on your aunt other than the fact that she worked in a dress shop in Pensacola long before she moved to Lillian. No income tax records, no bank accounts, no deed, and no will have been found related to the cottage. I can't even establish that she paid for the utilities on the property. It's just unbelievable."

"Well, I am not surprised at anything. It's like she never lived there other than in a caretaker's capacity."

"I know, but I do have some interesting information from my investigations. A few weeks ago, a deed to the tract of land that she lived on was discovered in official records at the county courthouse. It appears that a man by the name of Woodrow Smith purchased the property in the early 20's. Obviously, he could not still be alive, but oddly enough, there's not a record of his death anywhere, including cemetery burials. Nevertheless, the taxes on the property have been paid each year under his name through some anonymous source. That includes the entire time your aunt lived there. No one seems to know the identity of the benefactor. All information pertaining to Escondido Cottage and the property appears to be heavily protected."

"I don't know what to say, Bill. I'm baffled."

"Me, too. After your aunt died, no one came forth with any information until a few weeks ago. Judge Arnold, the probate judge, shared a letter with me that was delivered to him by a courier service. It specified that the sale of the estate belonging to Woodrow Smith could now be forthcoming, supervised by the law firm of Little and Harville in Pensacola, Florida, once it cleared probate court. It's my guess that the expedient process through probate was due to this letter. So, I checked with the law firm. No one there has the liberty to share anything about Woodrow Smith, the letter, or anything concerning the estate. I've never experienced this in all my years in practice."

"So, what does that mean for me at this point in time?"

"It's hard for me to say this, but since nothing was in your aunt's name, you cannot claim inheritance. So, unless you can buy the place outright, it will go up for sale within the week. One last thing, Lori. Since I knew your aunt and have been investigating this on your behalf, Judge Arnold appointed me as the Executor, and the law firm has agreed to that."

"Ok. That's fine. Your appointment is not a problem, but I'm still confused about how this happened. She knew how much my cousin and I loved Escondido Cottage. Something is missing."

"I know. I'm convinced you're right about that. This whole situation is shrouded in mystery."

"So, Bill, let's recap what we know. She lived there all those years after she left Pensacola, and someone paid for the expenses and supported her entirely, but that person's identity is not known nor who owns the property."

"Right. It does appear that she had a source of total care from someone, and that person's identity was apparently guarded ...protected ... until her death."

"So, what are we supposed to do with her personal belongings?"

"The court is not concerned with her personal belongings, just the property and the cottage. Ethelene and I will help you with that when you come back to Lillian. I'm so sorry about all of this."

"It's not your fault, Bill. I've been preparing myself for this even though I never lost hope. However, with what you just shared, I just need to move on."

* * *

I dreaded going back to Lillian for many reasons, mainly because of the absence of Aunt Lorea and the multitude of memories that would return like a seasonal weather pattern. Ethelene and I had not parted on a pleasantly symphonic note, and I wondered what kind of mood would prevail. Our limited conversations were like rice without salt. My question was soon answered when I returned.

"Welcome back, Lori. Don't you love this colder weather?" Ethelene said with arms extended as she greeted me at the front door. Surprisingly, she was void of any animosity, and my response was cushioned with a light-hearted greeting.

"Compared to this past summer with record breaking temperatures, you better believe it."

"So, tell me, Lori, what has happened with the estate? You seem perplexed."

"A lot. Allow me to summarize: Bill informed me that no liens were filed, and everything cleared Probate. The court has appointed Bill as the Executor since he knew Aunt Lorea. I could not be established as a legal heir since nothing could be found in her name, not even utility bills. Can you believe that? So, the property will go up for sale soon handled by a law firm in Pensacola."

"So, that means that you are not eligible to inherit the property?"

"That's right, and there's more to it which I will explain later, but for now, I can share that nothing about her existence here legally can be found."

"I don't believe it, Lori. She just couldn't have lived here all those years without records."

"Apparently, she did. So, let me ask you something. When the two of you moved here from Pensacola, do you have any idea how she managed to live here all alone with no job? She had to have some source of income. Did she ever mention that to you?"

"No. Since I moved here after she established residency, there was no reason for me to ask about things like that. However, since the cottage was already here and in bad shape, I assumed that she possibly used money from her family inheritance, settlement money from the divorce, or money she saved during the time she worked at the dress shop to buy the cottage and make repairs. It's certainly puzzling. So, what's next, Lori?"

"You and I are going to assist Bill in disposing of her possessions except for the ones that you or I may want. Since he is the executor, he is authorized to make that decision. He contacted David Lee, and he wasn't interested in anything since there was no money involved. Why am I not surprised? So, we go forward if you are willing to help."

"Of course. Be glad to do what I can."

"Well, we need to get busy. The real estate people will be here soon."

"I think they are already here, Lori. Someone just drove up and is getting out of the car with a FOR SALE sign."

Amidst the real estate traffic, Ethelene and I began disposing of personal items. Boxes packed with kitchen utensils, household items, clothes, and other odds and ends were gifted to a shelter. Bill arranged for a local antique dealer to come and pick up some old pieces of furniture that we didn't want. I decided that a few of the paintings probably should remain in the cottage as historical artifacts for the next owner, but I could make a final decision on that after everything had been assessed. However, there were two paintings that I wanted to give to Ethelene that Aunt Lorea painted soon after she moved to Lillian. One was an abstract version of the garden overlooking Perdido Bay with two figures sitting on the bench in the garden. The composition was softly expressed in a palette of black, white, and cream-colored oils. I was sure that one of those figures was Aunt Lorea. Artistic caricature of the other figure revealed someone wearing a safari hat and boots. Faces were hidden. The other painting captured sunsets from the bluff in rich tones of orange, red, aqua, and brown.

She adamantly refused both, insisting that the abstract painting remain strategically placed above the mantel in the sunroom adjacent to the garden, and the sunset painting should maintain its current location in the sunroom on the west wall.

I was a bit startled at her strong convictions about the two paintings remaining in their current locations for now, but there was no reason for me to disagree. I didn't want to pick up where we previously left off, so I deferred asking.

It took a couple of days just to dispose of general household items before tackling personal possessions, most of which I was permitted to keep. Special care was given to the vintage clothing and hat collection from the thirties and forties that I treasured. Each piece resonated with the words *remember me?*

A small oil painting that I painted one summer at Escondido Cottage would be going home with me. It was similar in style to Van Gogh with mounds of oils in hues of violets, blues, and greens capturing the beauty of the lilacs and hydrangeas in the garden.

Mounted on one wall in the bedroom was a unique piece of art that appeared in the studio my last summer there. I decided to keep it. Even though it was not initialed, I was sure it was Aunt Lorea's creation because of the way the oils were expressed on the canvas. The composition included a man and a woman sensually embracing while sitting on a red divan. A beautiful shawl, worn by the woman, was the only visible piece of clothing. Swirls of different flower patterns and textures in vibrant colors of wine, aqua, yellow, and purple were detailed on dark green silk squares that were framed with the same color of velvet. Long black fringe gently teased the woman's breast. Delicate white flesh set against the rich, red velvet texture of the sofa added seductive delicacy to the mood. I never knew the identity of the couple.

After clearing the house, we began the process of dismantling the art studio which was not nearly as neat as the house. Touching familiar items stimulated memories. Pottery, artificial fruits, cloth, flowers, old chairs, tables, rugs, pillows, driftwood, baskets, glass jars, books, and a variety of other odd pieces collected over the years and used as props, consumed every inch of space in the 600 square foot studio. As usual, I could smell turpentine. I smiled at the thought of her, thinking that the scent of the turpentine was sometimes more invigorating than her French perfume.

The divan in the studio was an antique piece that had once been used for courting and conversation. When Aunt Lorea inherited it, she moved it to the art studio, and restored it in a plush red velvet. An array of artsy pillows adorned the corners. When hot weather moved in, we relocated inside to the divan to listen to classical music. It was where we talked about life and the importance of being confident and self-assured. It was where we cried after reading sad stories. It was where I sat and talked for hours with a boy named John who lived nearby. He came by regularly to help Aunt Lorea with garden tasks and to join in our summer get-togethers. She treasured the divan and gave it renewed life. It was now like a shrine. Keeping it preserved memories. How was I going to get it home?

On a table by the divan, a framed message to all visitors rested on a small easel. It read: *Memories only survive by those who treasure and preserve them. Never let them die.*

She had a special worktable that housed tubes of paints and a variety of brushes. Canvases were propped in every vacant space. In one corner of the room, two pieces of art were carelessly tossed aside. I wondered why. At one time, they were hung in Aunt Lorea's bedroom. One was a watercolor called *Pond at Escondido Cottage*. The other was a Gauguin-like oil with people in a tropical setting as the center of the composition. Even though the mediums were different, both were so distinctive of her personality and lifestyle. I decided that they should remain at the cottage in their original locations because of the special sentiments associated specifically to Aunt Lorea and the cottage.

Two large windows in the southwest corner allowed the needed light for painting. Lightweight sheers were rolled up and tied at the top of each window casement which could also be rolled down for privacy. Two slip-covered, overstuffed chairs were strategically placed under the windows with an old iron table between them. A unique pole lamp with a rust-colored silk shade and black feathers around the rim provided evening light with flirtatious ambiance.

Opening the doors to an old chifforobe revealed a variety of shawls hanging from satin hangers. I was immediately drawn to one as the colors and the fringe caught my eye. Removing it from the hanger, I wrapped it around my shoulders and paraded around the room, pretending I was getting ready for the *Moonlight Ball by the Bay*. A mirror on the wall provided a quick, portrait-like snapshot. Instantly, I recognized it as the shawl the female was wearing in the abstract painting in the bedroom and immediately knew the identity of the female. It was Aunt Lorea. And the male?

A few top shelves on the right side of the chifforobe were stuffed with journals. Oddly enough, I didn't know she kept them. What did she write about? I browsed quickly. The first one highlighted her early years when she was a young woman. Another journal from a different stack chronicled her ideas for writing and painting. They were fascinating, but time constraints prevented further review for now, I would have to come back to them later.

Fashion magazines from the thirties, forties, and fifties were neatly stacked on lower shelves. Hidden behind the magazines on the bottom shelf was a man's pair of boots covered up by a safari hat. Didn't Perry Frederick wear boots and a hat like that when he visited? Was he the other individual in the abstract painting? That must be why she saved them.

Another item hidden at the back of the bottom shelf was a locked strong box with no key. Finding it in the art studio would be impossible. There was a piece of paper taped to the top with the word PERSONAL penned in black ink. Had I at last found the documents? Maybe the key was on the key ring that Aunt Lorea kept on a hook beside the kitchen door. It was a lottery moment.

"Hey, Ethelene! Bingo! I found a locked box in the old chifforobe. With a little luck, if it is what I need, I still might have time to save the house and the property. We need to get her key ring from the kitchen."

Not one key worked. Rather than rummaging for hours through the art studio to no avail, it would be easier to take the box to a locksmith. Being quite anxious about the contents, I immediately drove to Tom's Lock and Key in Foley before Ethelene could stall me into another unproductive search.

It was a small store that looked more like a shack than a reputable business. However, that didn't matter. I just wanted access to the box. A bell rang as I entered.

"Howdy there ma'am. Can I help ya?"

"I need your help with the lock on this box. Somehow, I have lost the key. I am studying genealogy and need to retrieve some old pictures."

"No problem, ma'am. That's what I do best. I'll have it opened for ya in a flash."

Within a minute, I had access. It was filled with old pictures. The faces were totally familiar. It was Aunt Lorea and Perry Frederick. Black and white as well as colored photos indicated a time period spanning several decades. I wondered what Ethelene would say about this enlightening discovery! I pondered sharing the contents of the box with her but changed my mind since her initial reaction to my inquiries about the duo had been hostile. Therefore, I decided to keep the information to myself until I had more time to sort through the entire contents.

Luckily, when I arrived at the cottage, she was busy visiting with neighbors who were picking up discarded items. Even though my curiosity was nothing short of a herd of horses running wild across the Western plains, I refrained from saying a word since I wanted exclusive rights to my find. Therefore, I hid the strong box in the back seat of the car and returned to the studio to continue packing. When the visitors left, Ethelene probed.

"Did you get it opened? What did you find? Any pertinent documents?"

I maintained my composure by smiling and just sticking to the facts.

"Yes, the locksmith opened it, but it was just filled with family pictures. No luck."

"That's a shame. Just another dead end."

"You're right. At every turn."

One thing for sure was that Ethelene was not aware that Aunt Lorea had these pictures secretly secured in an obscure place. Interesting.

Late into the evening, our "to-do list" was completed, and she left. I put on sweats, propped my feet up, and relaxed with a glass of wine. A Class 5 hurricane making landfall could not have distracted me. I was totally mesmerized.

There were individual photos as well as photos of the two. All were documented with dates, locations, and narratives. The first one was a snapshot of them on an ocean liner dated 1936. The description read: *On the Promenade Deck of the Queen Mary. Return voyage from Paris in 1936. I met Perry. He is from Pensacola. This picture was taken the night before we arrived in New York. I can't tell you the joy and sorrow I feel in my heart.*

I was particularly amused with one that had been taken of Aunt Lorea at Pensacola Beach. Aunt Lorea had nothing on except a beach towel. The narrative read: *Perry and I at an isolated place at Pensacola Beach. It was just too hot for clothes. There's nothing like skinny dipping in the emerald waters of the gulf. We wrapped ourselves in the towel after our swim and made love at sunset. 1939*

One picture of Perry was taken in Lillian, Alabama, right after WWII. The note on the back read: *We loved our private end-of-the-war celebration. We danced by candlelight under a canopy of brilliant stars. When I tango with Perry, I forget the world exists. A cottage in a remote location in Lillian. 1945*

On a 1949 photo, she wrote the following: *We spent a romantic evening by the pond as we played our favorite French music and enjoyed the soothing breeze. The smell of fresh gardenias and the taste of champagne filled our senses as we basked in the moonlight. The swaying palms around the pool provided a screen of privacy as we savored intimate moments. Pensacola House. 1949*

Multiple photos of them had been taken in Lillian sitting on the bench in the garden, relaxing in the art studio, and looking at sunsets from the bluff.

I sat in silence. My suspicions were correct. He *had* been a major part of her life and for a long time. It was an obvious affair, and confirming it accounted for some things, but raised as many questions as it answered.

What happened to them? They met on the Queen Mary in 1936 and continued to see each other after they returned home. Why didn't they marry? Was he already married, or was he an eligible bachelor who wanted to remain so? And the 1945 photo in Lillian, Alabama of a cottage in a remote location ... Is that what is now Escondido Cottage? Did they part before the car accident, or did the accident abruptly end their romance? Was there even a car accident, or did Ethelene just make that up to end further questioning from me? I felt the ice was gradually melting beneath the tip of the iceberg.

My thoughts returned to Aunt Lorea's strange reaction when I asked about him during one of my later visits to Lillian. Whatever happened was a continued source of a great deal of pain for her which might explain her death.

I placed the photos on the worktable in the art studio in the order in which they had been taken. Once my task was completed, I had a pictorial timeline with brief narratives of their time together that Aunt Lorea had treasured and preserved, locked away in a fireproof box hidden in the chifforobe.

The journals, what about the journals? Could she have written about their time together in more lengthy narratives? I selected a couple that I hadn't looked at earlier. The excerpts dated back to her life in the early thirties before she married a man named Finley Hughes. I never knew much about their marriage as they had divorced before I was born. Reading further revealed recorded memories about time spent with Perry in Pensacola and about her experiences living at a boarding house. Nothing, however, seemed out of the ordinary. After all, they were just journals. When I put them back, I noticed a stack of white papers tied together with twine underneath the journals in the back. What's this?

Another discovery awaited me. It was a manuscript. The title of the first chapter was *Lorea Rose McKinley Hughes*. The first sentence said: *I was born to Henriette and John McKinley and given the name of Lorea Rose.* The first few pages were eloquently written and carried an air of sophistication which characterized her completely. I was sure the contents paralleled her journals, but once again, time would not permit the cover-to-cover read that I desired. Maybe one day.

Unfortunately, the needed documents remained elusive. Even though I discovered all these items containing so many memories, I had nothing that would help me retain the estate. Therefore, I packed everything away in an unmarked box. To get the strong box to fit in a box with the journals and the manuscript, I had to turn it sideways. That's when I discovered another piece of paper secured into a recessed area on the bottom. Detaching it, revealed that it was a note with my name on it. She was speaking to me, and her voice was riveting.

Lori,

I know that one day you will find my pictures, my journals, and my manuscript. When you do, I hope that you can understand and accept what happened and appreciate the beauty of a special friendship and love that few ever experience. It's a wonderful story here. Do with it what you may.

Love,

Aunt Lorea

I buried my face in the note. She intended her message to be her final gift. In her mind, she felt that she had left behind a profound legacy of love and devotion, void of the usual monetary rewards. She desired acceptance of that because she willfully chose to maintain a firm commitment to Perry, treasuring their friendship and love to the end.

Just as I had done in the past few months, I cried in sorrow laced with a soft wrath. With trembling hands, I struggled to securely hold the paper note. Rationally, I knew that she had left behind something of great importance to her even though it was not the documents that I needed. It was a different kind of inheritance. Would I truly ever understand and appreciate that? Emotionally, I still could not justify the loss of Escondido Cottage, and I would always wonder why she didn't leave a will along with her special story. I knew that unsolved mystery would forever haunt me, and I also knew, in my heart, that something was still missing. Where are the hidden answers? Even if a discovery eventually materialized, would it even matter? Reflections about all of this will persist until maybe, it drives me mad.

Memories only survive by those who treasure and preserve them. Never let them die.

Part II

Chapter 5

LOREA ROSE MCKINLEY HUGHES

I was born to Henriette and John McKinley and given the name of Lorea Rose. My parents were immigrants who boldly journeyed from Europe and settled in Alabama. Since mother was French and father was Irish, it was not a likely match; but they were very happy and experienced a productive and fulfilling life together. They owned McKinley Mercantile, a dry goods business in Montgomery, Alabama, and were well-known and respected in their community. Even as children, my two brothers and I were expected to know about the necessary social graces when visitors came to call. Therefore, mother taught us proper etiquette and specific nuances associated with a social life. It was customary in our social circles for parents to encourage friendships for their children with other prominent families to ensure that their sons and/or daughters would marry into the right family.

Mother entertained often, but I was not allowed to participate in evening parties until I was of age. Sneaking halfway down the staircase, on multiple occasions, to watch galas was exciting as I dreamt of the day when I could participate. Once I turned sixteen, it was acceptable to attend. During the holiday season following my sixteenth birthday, I was presented at a Christmas Gala in a hunter green velvet dress adorned with a garnet necklace and matching earrings. It was my coronation.

Unlike other girls my age who were demure and soft-spoken, I embraced a more spirited approach to life. Father understood and conveyed to mother that I was not a likely candidate for learning different patterns of fine china and the secret ingredients for chicken salad recipes that were expected of women who were coming of age.

Since I had grown up with two older brothers, Patrick and Colin, I was heavily influenced by their outward, rowdy demeanor and preferred the fun and excitement associated with outdoor life over the more domesticated, mundane, day-to-day living that characterized the female lifestyle. Nevertheless, based on mother's insistence, I attended a finishing school to study music, art, and language. French was an elective. Symphonies by Bach and Beethoven became quite familiar, as well as the big band sound of swing that saturated the musical environment. The works of Frost and Browning satisfied my literary appetite and motivated me daily in journal writing. The power of the pen greatly influenced me. Art teachers delivered stimulating lectures as they connected art and history. Inspired by the artistic compositions of Degas, Monet, and Renoir, I painted often.

Since I lived at home, mother hovered over my social life which created tension between us. To escape on the weekends, I volunteered at the local library and met friends downtown for coffee and gossip. Subsequently, my life was flat and pulseless. I desperately needed something more stimulating, but I was financially stymied.

Mother regularly hinted that it was time for me to consider marriage, rendering her judgment according to Montgomery standards. My two brothers married shortly after finishing secondary school, and therefore, it was logical for her to begin charting a course for me.

Participation in just the right social circles was pushed to attract just the right man, hopefully resulting in a relationship that would inspire marriage. That was going to be somewhat difficult as social events were less frequent because of the depressed economy. However, being an old maid was taboo and the clock was ticking.

There were many young, eligible bachelors in town, but

mother had her eye on the Hughes family whose son, Finley Marion, was groomed for assuming a position in the family-owned timber, forestry, and tobacco industries. Even though the Depression had taken its toll on many families, the Hughes family remained financially stable, and my father's store had miraculously also survived economically. A union between both families would ensure security for me as well as a prestigious societal position. Therefore, mother skillfully began her work.

She made sure that we sat near the Hughes family in church. Social occasions for the young people in our neighborhood were hosted several times a month in our home. She indulged in charity work and always made sure that Finley and I had contact, working side-by-side for the cause. The plan worked. Finley formally began calling, and we attended a few social events during the holiday season. In addition to the traditional Hughes' party, mother hosted small gatherings just to orchestrate continued opportunities for courtship. At some point in time, if mutually approved by both families, the male was expected to propose marriage in a prompt manner to avoid any connotation of indecency.

Even though Finley had been educated at Marion Military Institute in Alabama, he was not ambitious because he knew that he was destined to carry on the established family businesses. He was handsome, mannerly, and conservative which supported his desire to be one of the pillars of society. He loved quiet evenings spent at home with family and friends and would fare well as a family man.

I was quite fond of him, but I was not sure that we were suited for each other. Being more reserved than my brothers, who set the standard for me regarding characteristics I most desired to live by, Finley spoke of the proper things in life such as the appropriate attire for every occasion, the correct placement of silverware on the table, and how to receive visitors. Even though mother and the finishing school I attended had prepared me well, Finley's regimented upbringing definitively governed his total demeanor, personal beliefs, and social posture.

Nevertheless, mother had married a complete opposite and found fulfillment in the relationship. I had a different spirit than mother and resisted. Oftentimes, complaining of not feeling well, I declined invitations to social gatherings. However, the separation from Finley didn't change my anticipation of a forthcoming proposal from him, and I needed to be prepared as a prompt answer would be expected. Since I was not as self-assured as I thought I should be on my decision, it became necessary to speak with mother. One evening, the right moment arose.

"Mother, I am having second thoughts on whether Finley and I are suited for each other."

"Lorea, I do not understand why you persist in avoiding something that is so important. Why do you have this doubt?"

"I don't know, I'm confused. Father and you have been happily married for many years, even though you are both very different. You found a common purpose and made a wonderful home for all of us. Therefore, I do not question the institution of marriage, only whether I am ready for this big step and whether Finley is right for me. Or more importantly, whether I'm right for him. The social life and the responsibilities that are expected seem very confining and may not be what I want. Is it so unjust for me to have those fears?"

Standing up from my chair, I walked over to my dressing table, sat down on the stool and looked blankly into the mirror. After a brief silence, I continued with questions.

"Mother, I thought I would know when the time was right, but how do you truly know? I feel like I am rushing towards a life that lies in preparation for me, but one for which I might not be as prepared as I should be. Is this kind of life what I really want? What am I to do?"

She gracefully moved to my dressing table and took my hair in her hand.

"Here, my dear. Let me comb your hair. Everything will

be fine, you'll see. Being the intelligent, educated woman that you are, I am not surprised that you have many, many questions within your head. However, one must have faith in making sound decisions like this. One must trust others that have set the example. Rest assured, you will find it in your heart to marry Finley as he will provide for you and respect your desire to be a knowledgeable and forthright woman."

"Maybe you are right, mother, but there is still this uneasiness that I can't explain. Valentine's Day is approaching, and I have an idea that Finley will propose. I must be ready with an answer."

Turning me around, looking directly into my eyes, and placing her hands on my cheeks, she attempted to reassure me once more.

"Yes, you must. That would be the proper thing to do."

"Proper. Yes, of course. I must be proper and observe the rules. I can't forget the rules can I, mother?"

"Now, Lorea. Mind your manners. I will not allow that kind of impudence."

"Forgive me. I am not displeased with your advice, only perplexed with my reluctance. I need more time to think. Do you understand what I'm saying?

"Yes, I suppose I do, but do not take too long, dear. Time is running out," she said as she made her exit, offering me one last reassuring look before closing the door.

In reflective thought, I knew that my decision should not parallel analytical studies, but mother was right. I needed to stop engaging in self-doubt and decide my fate. I eventually reasoned that Finley knew me well as a person and would never marry me expecting something different.Therefore, on February fourteenth, his anticipated proposal was accepted.

The June wedding was economically and tastefully done. Many friends attended bestowing monetary and other practical gifts. A brief honeymoon was planned for us in Asheville, North Carolina at the Grove Park Inn, which was our wedding gift from both families. Upon our return, we settled into married life.

Chapter 6

DOMESTICITY

As expected, Finley went to work for his father, and I engaged in the daily chores associated with the duties of a wife. Life was predictable and dry, and I had more than enough time for reading, writing, and painting. Those means of self-expression fulfilled me. However, Finley preferred that I maintain a very traditional profile now that I was married. Each time he came home from work and found a painting in progress, he discussed the cost of what he considered a *frivolous endeavor* and reminded me of my new life and responsibilities.

One evening, I tried to express my feelings. Surely, reason and logic would prevail, and he would understand. After dinner, while he enjoyed a cup of coffee and smoked his pipe, I appealed and began my negotiation.

"Finley, I need to speak with you about something very important."

"What is it that you would like to discuss, my dear?"

"Well, I know you think that painting is overindulgence on my part, but I want to paint something lovely to place above the fireplace mantel. That drab painting that your Aunt Mary gave us as a wedding present is uninviting. I don't care to look at an old farm scene each night we sit and converse in the living room. Wouldn't a picture with flowers brighten up the room?"

Placing the coffee cup and his pipe on the table beside his chair, he folded his fingers under his chin and laughed as he forwarded his rebuttal to me.

"Lorea, you know that we can't remove the farm painting from the living room. Aunt Mary would be most insulted. After all, she thought it was a wonderful present and graciously gave it to us."

I stood up and walked over to the mantel gazing at the lifeless piece of art.

"Wedding present, indeed. It was probably a wedding present someone gave to her that she stored in the attic for years because it was too horrible to use anywhere in her own house. Now, we are the lucky saps that had to find a suitable place for the atrocity."

I walked to the back of his chair and rubbed his shoulders, continuing my plea.

"Please, Finley. I don't want to hurt Aunt Mary's feelings. I just want to have something more to our liking than that old farm scene. I'll find another place for it, I promise. When we know she is coming, we will move it back to the mantel. She will never know we replaced it. What do you think?"

"My darling, I think that would be a deceitful thing to do. She gave it to us out of love and endearment, and we should honor her sentiments. Besides, you don't have time to paint. You have many household duties that require your full attention each day."

I moved to the footstool in front of his chair, sat down, and took his hands in mine.

"Time? Full attention? I am truly giving all household duties and you my full attention and have ample time remaining for other things. Please consider my feelings on this."

Disengaging his hands from my grip and offering me a condescending stare, he removed his handkerchief from his pocket and began polishing his glasses.

"Why can't you be like the other wives? Being acceptable is important. You should know that."

"Acceptance is important, Finley. That's what I am saying to you. Accept me and what I want to do. I don't want to be like the other wives. You know how passionate I am about the arts. You knew this before we were married. Did you think I would change?"

"Lorea, I thought you would do what was expected."

"What's expected? Since we have been married, I have proven to you that I can run the household with plenty of time left for more aesthetic endeavors. I just don't understand your reluctance to appreciate my talent and my desire."

"As I have said over and over, art represents a frivolous side of life, dear. If you desire something more substantial than your household responsibilities to fulfill your time and your desire for self-expression, why don't you try your hand at needlepoint?"

"Needlepoint? I can't think of anything more boring."

Horrified at his narrowed viewpoint, I stalked into the kitchen, swatted fiercely at a fly on one of the kitchen countertops and stewed. I felt belittled and rejected. How controlling and stiff he was! I wasn't going to let him have the last word and stormed back into the living room.

"Painting is freedom of expression, and there's nothing wrong with that."

"Lorea, we have exhausted this subject. I have nothing further to say. Now, I would like to read my paper. Is there more coffee in the kitchen?"

My French-Irish blood boiled. I could not believe that Finley expected me to take up needlepoint for creative expression! I could readily accept managing the household according to his wishes, but there were other ways to fill my time when there was time to spare. Self-choice was important. What was he afraid of? What was the underlying reason for his stubbornness? My doubts about marrying him resurfaced as I began to question our compatibility.

My father had always indulged mother when she desired hosting social gatherings. That was her choice for self-expression. I guess that was not considered *frivolous* but necessary to maintain a certain status in the community. I resented Finley's narrow-minded position. I was not asking him to open an art studio with nude models or asking him to allow me to paint down at the riverfront each day with the artsy locals. I simply wanted to paint at home in my free time. Finley knew, from the very beginning, that I had a flare for creativity. Even though this did not seem to disturb him when we were courting, he was not willing to accommodate me now. He was too caught up in what was *expected* for me to do, and I felt very controlled and stifled. Therefore, we argued frequently, and I found myself withdrawing from him more and more.

In the months that followed, conversations resulted in heated debates, and I knew this was not fair to either one of us. Subsequently, I became more and more despondent. Something had to give. I was desperate.

One evening, as Finley returned home from work and assumed his ritual of reading the paper in the living room and smoking his pipe, I tried a new approach.

"Finley, I have a proposal for you."

"Not the painting idea, again, Lorea. Please."

"No, I want to talk with you about something much more exciting."

"Well, that's refreshing. Please continue," he said without emotion.

"I would like to propose a trip to Paris. Now, don't say anything right now. Just listen to what I have to say. As you know, my mother's sister and niece, Aunt Irenee and Camille, live close to Paris, and I think we should plan a trip to visit them. Since they were unable to attend our wedding, they have extended an invitation to host us there as a wedding gift. The cost would be somewhat deferred because we would be staying with them. Our only expense ..."

Not letting me finish, he slammed the paper in his lap and thrust a powerful reaction my way.

"Absolutely not! Have you taken leave of your senses? How do you think I could justify such a trip? We are still in a depressed state of economics in case you haven't noticed. Even if I could finance the trip through the businesses, what would everyone think? That would appear most frivolous, indeed! My dear, you need to contain yourself. I consider the matter closed."

"Is frivolous the only word you know to use when you're opposed to something? What if I said that a trip to Paris, right now, might be more important for us and our marriage. Does that sound unreasonable to you?"

"No, absolutely not! Why do you persist with such, let me say instead of frivolous, absurd ideas? First painting and now Paris. And what's wrong with our marriage?"

His roaring laugh could have been heard throughout the neighborhood which infuriated me.

"I don't think my idea about Paris is absurd. I'm thinking about us. We have been painfully distant lately. I know that it would be financially difficult to engage in such a journey. Yes, it's almost unthinkable, but I don't think it is out of the question. I think we would enjoy being with each other and seeing Paris immensely," I stated as I continued to plead my case. "Also, you know, France is known for utilizing modern forestry techniques, and a visit to study that process would be a business opportunity that would justify the trip."

"And precisely what do you know of modern forestry techniques?" He curtly responded.

"Well, I have overheard conversations between your father and you about the new techniques that are emerging in Europe."

Taking off his glasses, he sarcastically countered, "There you go again, concentrating on something that is not appropriate for you."

Fencing with him, I lunged forward with my rebuttal, "According to you, everything is inappropriate for me except what you want me to do."

"Lorea, you need to accept this life you chose and concentrate on proper duties. Now, would it be too much to ask you to fetch me a cup of coffee?"

"Did you say *fetch*? Why don't you just whistle for the neighbor's St. Bernard? I'm going outside to the porch for some fresh air. This room smells like a wet dog."

My efforts to convey the merits of the trip were to no avail. He refused to budge. Plus, he seemed so cold and insensitive, never really acknowledging the growing distance between us.

I knew his viewpoints were as important to him as mine were to me, but he could not discern the differences between creating a canvas and creating a needlepoint. Obviously, neither of us was going to compromise. I knew that I could not keep waking up each morning knowing that I would be sad all day and dreading the evening bickering. Eventually, a new thought emerged.

What if he would agree to send me, just me? Would that be acceptable? Heavens no! What was I thinking. That would be entirely frivolous, probably my most absurd idea yet!

Nevertheless, determination moved me forward. I needed an ally, and I knew exactly to who I should turn to. I solicited mother's help. Surely, through her persuasive means, Finley might at least agree to the solo journey.

As soon as Finley left for work the next morning, I didn't waste any time presenting my bold idea to her.

"Well, mother. What do you think?"

"Lorea, I agree with Finley. It is an absurd thought mainly because ladies just don't travel unaccompanied, and financially, the timing is wrong. What would everyone think?"

"Mother, I'm shocked at you. Women do travel alone. Not everyone is married, you know, and I really don't care about what everyone thinks. Aunt Irenee has extended an invitation for a visit and a trip over would not raise eyebrows in my opinion."

"Well, I guess that's true, but there's still the financial part. If Finley is opposed, how do you propose to finance such a trip?"

Before I could respond, father appeared at the kitchen door. He had soiled his white shirt with coffee and needed a garment change. Eavesdropping on our conversation, he was approaching with inquiry.

"What's this I hear?"

"I was discussing a proposed trip to Paris with mother."

"Good grief! And who might the lucky travelers be?"

"Just one traveler, father. Me. I want to visit our relatives in Paris. I have only seen pictures of mother's sister, Irenee, and my cousin Camille, and I have only exchanged letters. They have offered to host a visit as a wedding gift, and I so want to meet them personally. Don't you think it would be wonderful?"

"I agree that it would, but what about Finley?"

"What about him? Well, he's too busy with the businesses. Convincing him of the advantages of the trip has been to no avail."

"I see."

"I hope you do, father. I need this trip. To be quite honest, Finley and I are arguing quite a bit. I want to paint and he wants me to do needlepoint. You know that's not who I am. If I take this trip, I might be able to satisfy the intense hunger for expression that consumes me, and then return to my Montgomery life. There's a problem though, about the cost of the trip. Even though I would not have the expense of a hotel, I would still need money for transportation over and back and some spending money."

"I gather that Finley won't provide the necessary funds."

"No. He doesn't acknowledge *frivolous* and *absurd* ideas."

"I see. I need to ask you something openly, Lorea. Is your marriage in trouble?"

Without answering, I simply looked down at a book on Paris that was cradled in my lap. He knew.

Several meetings occurred between my parents and me before father intervened on my behalf. I knew he was searching my heart for answers and justification, but I confined my responses to the merits of the trip, and he respected my right to privacy, unless I chose disclosure. As always, logic and sensibility governed his approach to the problem, and he presented a proposal to Finley.

After offering to finance the expenses for the trip and setting a reasonable timeline for the entire excursion, Finley finally agreed. I was sure that part of his submission was in an effort to avoid something that was not discussed but brewing ... divorce.

Relatives in Paris were contacted and within a few weeks, after weather conditions improved over the Atlantic Ocean, I sailed to France.

Chapter 7

PARIS

The Great Depression shattered the American dream, and what was once a land of opportunity had become a land of desperation and poverty. Between the years of 1929 and 1932, family incomes were significantly reduced. Survival was first and foremost not only financially, but emotionally as well. People had to find sustenance in listening to the radio, playing simple games, and reading. Life, as we had known it had changed, and a drab spirit hovered like a never-ending fog years later. Even though our families had not experienced the tremendous loss that many had, sadness and despair consumed everyone.

* * *

Traveling to Europe took multiple days. Even though joy consumed me, periodic feelings of guilt clutched me like a tight-fitting cloche. Was the trip truly frivolous? Had I been totally selfish? Reasoning always brought me back to one thought. If I had refrained, I would have forever succumbed to any sense of independence, and my creativity and spirit would have been frozen along with my feelings towards Finley. Therefore, in my mind, I was justified.

My second-class passage on the RMS Aquitania proved to be interesting as the voyage was known as the "booze cruise" during Prohibition. However, when Prohibition ended, booze cruising remained intact. At night, it was frightening as intoxicated passengers paraded around at all hours knocking on doors and howling with laughter. I was glad that the train ride into Paris was more stable, which calmed my frazzled nerves from the boat.

Giddy with excitement, I disembarked at the main train terminal in the heart of Paris, straining my neck in search of Aunt Irenee and Camille. How would I ever find them in such a molasses-thick crowd of people coming and going in different directions? It was the busiest station I had ever seen.

"Lorea! Over here!"

"Bonjour, Camille! Is it really you? I thought I would never get here. I can't believe I'm finally here."

"You are indeed, and I can't wait to introduce you to Paris. You may never want to leave!" Camille jubilantly exclaimed.

"You may be right. This is like a dream come true," I proclaimed as I turned towards Aunt Irenee who immediately embraced me with a bear hug.

"Welcome, ma petite. We are so happy to see you. We have been counting the days until your arrival. I know that you have much to share with us, but I am sure that you need rest."

"Oh, Aunt Irenee, I can't even think about rest right now. Thank you so much for allowing me to stay with you. You are most gracious. Here, I have a letter from Mother."

Once I saw familiar faces, I knew that my decision to come to Paris had been well worth the physical effort, as well as the emotional journey. A state of almost wildness ensued. Paris, at last!

Aunt Irenee was a replica of mother, more so than in photos. She wore a basic brown jacket and skirt with a simple white blouse. An amber rhinestone brooch was pinned to the lapel. Her dark hair was pulled back in a bun adorned with a beige hat and a deep brown grosgrain ribbon circled the crown. Her shoes were black lace-ups with wide heels providing support for her thick ankles. I was surprised that she spoke English as well as she did. My French, however, was minimal. Only basic expressions characterized my fluency. Camille, well versed in English, would serve as our translator if needed. With continued exuberance, I turned to converse with her.

As anticipated, Camille had a stylish appearance. Her crepe dress was white with black cording accenting the collar and the pockets. The black and white hat, offsetting her dark brown eyes and hair, accentuated an abundance of rouge and lipstick. Her gloved hands embraced a clutch purse. She looked fashionably smart, yet not overdressed.

"Camille, how lovely you look! I wondered what you would be wearing. I want to learn all about Parisian fashion and visit the famous places I've read about."

"And indeed, you shall. I look forward to showing you this wonderful city, but I must tell you, there are places that I don't even know about! One could never learn everything there is to know about Paris, even in a lifetime."

"Yes, I am sure. You will need to be patient with me. Remember, I am from a very small town in Alabama. You can see everything there in a couple of days riding in a slow moving, horse-drawn carriage!"

"Lorea, I am sure you are toying with me about horse-drawn carriages! Come, now. We have much to talk about."

"Yes, we do. Finley sends his regrets by the way."

"We were disappointed to learn that he would not be accompanying you, but with the economy the way it is, we were certain that influenced your decision to come alone. And how are things back home, Lorea?" she inquired as we walked towards the luggage car.

"Actually, life is quite sad for so many families because of the Depression. Finley remained at home to assist with the business as his dad is not in the best of health," I explained, refraining from commenting on the real reason for my visit. Maybe in time, if the right moment presented itself, I would share my innermost thoughts with her.

Luggage was collected, and we proceeded to an automobile that would provide our transportation to Aunt

Irenee's home on the edge of the city. She had borrowed a car from a close friend to expedite this part my journey. She explained to me that before 1933, the tram system was used for passage in and around the city. However, that mode of transportation was discarded to make room for wheeled traffic for which most Parisians were not prepared. Being from a small Southern town, I was not used to moving about in such a largely populated area with such heavy traffic. My indoctrination to big city life had begun.

Aunt Irenee's home echoed the French countryside with soothing colors and comfortable furnishings. A handsome pine cupboard filled with beautiful pottery, a rack of copper pots, and an extensive collection of roosters consumed the kitchen space. Areas conducive to family time and conversation were present in different rooms with an abundance of pillows and wool throws. The furniture was less formal than the Victorian furniture predominant in American homes, and nothing matched. End tables, sofas, and chairs seemingly had been hand-picked and purchased based on the uniqueness of each piece instead of buying an entire matching collection. Bedrooms were cozy and graced with an abundance of fresh flowers in different types of containers. A bowl of fresh water in each room was changed daily for grooming purposes. I was particularly amused that the bathroom was located in an adjacent section of the house accessible through a back door in the kitchen. The relaxed atmosphere was quite different than what I was used to, but I welcomed the uniqueness of it all. I was very content.

"Aunt Irenee, your home is so warm and pleasant. How refreshing!"

"Ma petite, we have looked forward to your visit. As Camille said, you can't see Paris in just a few days or even months. If you don't see everything you wish to see during this visit, another one must be planned. Maybe next time Finley can accompany you."

In the days that followed my arrival, Camille and I talked

incessantly about the Parisian culture, focusing mainly on art, literature, and times past and present in Paris. Hearing about the frequent and grandiose Fancy Dress Balls that ushered in the thirties mesmerized me. Even though the Depression in America affected the world economy, wealthy French people began the decade with these grand galas.

"Camille, I've always heard about French parties. Are they as luxurious as they say?"

"The 1930 summer season was the greatest of all. Women's fashions were as sleek as money could buy, and ballrooms were elaborately decorated defying all sense of the modest pace that most people had to observe. One of the most dazzling soirees was hosted by a dressmaker by the name of Jean Patou. Everything was wrapped, covered, or stuffed with silver," she described as she wrapped a shawl around her shoulders, stood up, and walked as if she were an important guest entering the grand foyer.

"How natural you look, Camille," I said regally as she threw her head back, laughed out loud, and continued to stroll majestically back and forth. "This is fascinating. Tell me more."

"Well, the White Ball would have dazzled you. It was the most beautiful and ethereal of all. Everything was white from the plates and napkins to trees and furniture. Guests wore white plaster masks and wigs coordinated with white attire. It was the most talked about dress ball for a long time."

"Oh my, and this happened each year in spite of the declining world economy? I guess this was something that that French society just would not compromise, no matter what."

"That's right, Lorea. No matter what."

Following a day of rest and relaxation, Aunt Irenee, Camille, and I ventured into the heart of the city. We toured the Latin Quarter where artists hung freshly painted canvases on the grill work outside of apartment buildings. The Moulin Rouge captured my adventurous spirit. Museums took several days to view classic works of art. The Cathedral of Notre

Dame was profound in its architecture and history. Having my picture taken at the Eiffel Tower was electrifying. Dining at Café le Dome, the famous terrace café at 108 Boulevard Montparnasse, and visiting the Place Vendôme, a bazaar of luxury goods in exquisite shops, were experiences never to be forgotten. I could not resist purchasing a new line of perfume by Cody using rose petals, lavender, and jasmine blended with spices such as nutmeg, vanilla, citronelle, and ginger. How could I visit Paris and not buy anything! I was indeed, being so *frivolous*, and I loved it.

Conversations between Camille and I occurred each day over an array of beverage choices. Our favorite was champagne when we could afford the splurge. Most of the time, however, we observed a daily ritual of enjoying coffee at multiple venues along the Champs-Élysée and quaint places in the art district.

The social practice of conversing at sidewalk cafés was engaging, and the sound of Paris, the music and the language, made the experience authentic. My journal brimmed with descriptive entries.

During the first two weeks, we visited as many places in the city and countryside as possible. So much of what I had believed to be true about Paris was confirmed, but a sense of change was apparent. The mood of the new decade for the average citizen of Paris was not that of high fashion and lavish parties. Women could barely afford to look at new fashion much less buy it. Hairdressers, manicurists, seamstresses, perfumers, and dress shops catered to middle-class and working-class women alike. More than half of the young, working people lived in one room or kitchen-bedroom apartments. Most of these had no toilet, lights, heat, or water. The fear of war had brought on a sense of uneasiness and tension as young Parisian men revolted against the proposed compulsory military service.

"I would love to stay forever, Camille. Paris is so exciting, so busy, so full of life even though times are very tense for the French people. Look at this beautiful street, the world-famous Champs-Élysée. How beautiful it is with trees, shops of all descriptions, and people bustling back and forth with the Arc de Triomphe in the background," I paused taking a deep breath, "However, in my wildest dreams I could never have imagined that I would see pamphlets and exercises being publicized to inform citizens about anticipated air attacks and gas warfare. It must be so frightening for you."

"Yes, is very different than the twenties. There is a new, evolving climate here. Things seemed to change drastically when Adolph Hitler became Chancellor of the Reich in 1933. We are faced with so many social problems, and the whole country seems to be in a pacifist state. Patriotism is dead. It died in the trenches on the Marne at Verdun during the Great War. Many people feel that it would be better to be a breathing German than a dead Frenchman. I truly wish that you could have experienced Paris a decade ago."

"Me, too, Camille. I am such a romantic, and Paris still remains the city of love and light to me."

"I am glad you were able to come. I am glad we have had this time together."

In the days following our conversation, Camille's inner sadness became apparent. With the blink of an eye, change was rapidly occurring. Musicians were disappearing from the streets as a new sound engulfed the city. The big band sound rolled in like a thick fog. Soda fountains appeared, and a popular commodity was chewing gum. These, as well as other cultural changes, promptly altered established norms and this was hard for the French people to accept, increasing feelings of melancholy and loss. This emotion wounded my heart, and with an unexpected sense of urgency, I wanted to go home.

Paris had been interesting, some things I expected, others not. The fashion, the emphasis on the arts, and the beauty of the countryside were accurately anticipated. The average Parisian, however, could only appreciate but not afford material things above that which sustained a simple lifestyle. I was astonished the extent that the Depression in America had influenced the Parisian economy and how political unrest provoked a different culture. This I had not anticipated.

Aunt Irenee and Camille had been wonderful hostesses. It was as if they had pre-read my mental list of all the many, varied, and unusual things that I wanted to do and see while in Paris. Their willingness to allow me to visit for more than a couple of weeks, as originally planned, was most gracious. Maybe one day, I could reciprocate.

After booking passage on a newer ship called the RMS Queen Mary, I tearfully bid a fond farewell to Aunt Irenee and Camille. Little did we know that times would continue to change, more drastically than ever imagined.

My pen moved across journal pages automatically recording thoughts about my homecoming reception. Would Finley be happy to see me? Our correspondence was frequent but strained, especially when my visit was extended.

Being in Paris augmented personal desires. I experienced a new world in a culture that embraced artistic expression. Would I be able to resume my expected lifestyle in Montgomery? Had the trip satisfied my desires for creativity or merely stimulated them even more? My new look was far more stylish than when I left. How would that be received? Disturbingly, a sense of resolution for which I had hoped for once I visited Paris was not there. I was more perplexed than ever.

Chapter 8

THE VOYAGE

The RMS Queen Mary was a luxury hotel on water and considered the epitome of travel on ocean liners. A variety of lounges and bars, two chapels, an indoor swimming pool, outdoor tennis court, a hospital, playrooms, and even a travel bureau for passengers provided comfort for all voyagers.

The largest room was the Grand Salon, a first-class dining room spanning three stories in height. It featured a large map of the transatlantic crossing with two tracks symbolizing winter and summer routes. Wood from different regions in Great Britain was used in most public areas and staterooms. Evenings in first-class were grand events as dining and fashion were elegant.

Being a second-class passenger, I would engage in a less formal atmosphere. Nevertheless, for four days, twelve hours, and twenty-four minutes, the opportunity to converse with other voyagers and sail on the Queen Mary would be another experience that I would remember for a lifetime.

Boarding the ship was not nearly as challenging as boarding the RMS Aquitania as Parisian life had acclimated me to elbow-to-elbow crowds. Ladened with a hat box carrying the latest millinery fashion and a cosmetic case, I removed my gloves to secure a better grip on my parcels and pushed through the on-ramp crowd.

"Pardon me, Miss. I believe you dropped one of your gloves."

I turned to see a handsome gentleman impeccably dressed in a charcoal grey suit with tapered sleeves, high pockets, and a wide pointed lapel. A monogrammed handkerchief in his upper pocket of his grey suit revealed the initial F. A crisp, white-collared shirt was offset by a maroon, grey, and white striped tie. He was tall and lanky with an air of sophistication. As he spoke, he tipped his light gray hat revealing a somewhat weathered face, slightly graying hair at the temples, and ocean-blue eyes. Momentarily stunned, I collected my thoughts and began to make polite conversation.

"Thank you, sir, you are most kind. I have tried to carry too much at one time, I'm afraid. Thank you for your help."

"I am glad that I could be of assistance to you. Your accent suggests that you are American?"

"Yes, I am and a long way from home, I must say. I have relatives that live in Paris and was there for a brief visit."

"And where is home, if I may inquire?"

"A small town in Alabama called Montgomery."

"Can't be! We are practically neighbors! Please let me introduce myself. My name is Perry Frederick, and my family and I are from Pensacola, Florida. I am in the forestry and timber industries. I have been in France on business as well as pleasure."

"Did you say timber and forestry? My husband's family is in the same businesses. This is indeed a coincidence. Do you by any chance know the Hughes family from Montgomery?"

"No, I do not believe I have had the pleasure."

"He is from an old Montgomery family that has been in those businesses for ages."

"Did he accompany you to France?"

"No, I regret that he was unable to come on the journey with me. I am traveling alone."

"I see. Maybe I shall have the privilege of meeting him one day. We would have a great deal to discuss about the new reforestation techniques everyone is learning about these days."

He paused for a moment and then said in such a polite and respectful manner, "I hope this invitation is not too presumptuous, Mrs. Hughes, but would you care to join my wife and me for dinner this evening? It would be interesting to continue our conversation."

Why was my heart pounding? He was just asking me to join them for dinner. Trying not to seem overzealous, I proceeded tactfully.

"How very gracious of you. Are you sure that wouldn't be too intrusive on my part?"

"Absolutely not. We enjoy the company of others during our evening meal, especially if it's someone close to home."

"Well, I haven't made any other arrangements for dinner."

"Good. Then we shall expect you for dinner. I have a table reserved in the main dining room for 7:00."

"It would be a pleasure, Mr. Frederick."

"Wonderful. As for now, please pardon my abrupt departure. I must attend to the needs of my wife as she is an invalid, and boarding the ship is not an easy task. She and her personal assistant are already on board and hopefully resting comfortably in our stateroom." With that said, he bowed slightly and was gone.

I felt flushed, and my heart was still pounding. Why? Imagine meeting someone on board the Queen Mary that was not only from the South but in the same businesses as Finley. Surely their paths had crossed at meetings or conventions.

Oh my, what should I wear? My wardrobe was limited to suits and casual clothes except for one basic black evening gown which I brought with me, and a beautiful shawl that I purchased in Paris. Both were quite suitable for dinner. It's just dinner on the ship, not Paris, so why was I so excited?

When I entered the dining room, I felt as if I were attending one of the fancy balls Camille spoke about. If only she could see me now. My long crepe dinner gown was suitable. The garnet necklace that I had worn to the Christmas Gala when I was sixteen looked stunning against the plunging black ruffled neckline and my lily-white skin.

The maître d' escorted me to the Frederick table, and the evening began with champagne. Mr. Frederick's electric personality was obvious as he delightfully and eloquently toasted friends, family, and health, being particularly careful to mention the latter because of Mrs. Frederick's condition.

Confined to a wheelchair made travel extremely difficult, but dinner conversation revealed that Mr. Frederick insisted on bringing her with him on his business trip as opportunities to engage in medicinal waters were available. I was not quite sure of the nature of her wheelchair dependency, but I sensed that her condition was permanent. Even though Mr. Frederick's comments were limited regarding her condition, the attention towards her needs was not. His attentiveness during dinner was heartwarming.

She was not at all what I expected. Conservatively dressed in a simple brown suit with a rose-colored scarf, pearl earrings and a matching necklace, she spoke in a soft and frail voice. Her dark brown hair was styled in a Gibson girl manner which suited her general appearance. She was polite and cordial, which matched Mr. Frederick but lacked in personality, differing greatly from his. Even though an ever-present tone of sadness hovered over them, Mr. Frederick continued to serve as a delightful and amusing host.

After dinner, Mr. Frederick asked me to dance. I hesitated until Mrs. Frederick commented.

"It's quite all right, my dear. Since I am disabled, I enjoy seeing Perry waltz and tango. He is a very skillful dancer."

"Did you say tango?" I looked towards him with amazement. He definitely looked like the type that would waltz beautifully, but the tango? My stunned look elicited an immediate response from him.

"Yes, indeed, Mrs. Hughes. I do tango. You seem surprised."

"Quite surprised, Mr. Frederick."

"Please, everyone calls me Perry."

"Very well, Perry. You do not look like one who dances the tango."

"And what does a fellow look like that dances the tango?"

"I really don't know why I said that. I guess one just creates an image based on appearances, and you look so ..."

"Yes?"

"Well, so businesslike."

"Do you tango, Mrs. Hughes?"

"Good Heavens, no. Well ... actually, though, I did once when I participated in a dance class, but that was a long time ago."

"Well, there is no time like the present to oil a rusty wheel. Shall we?"

"Very well, and since we are on a first name basis, please call me Lorea."

Placing his arms around my waist, we moved towards the dance floor.

"Lorea it shall be. That is an unusual name."

"It is. It means Laurel. My mother is French. It was her sister, Irenee and my cousin, Camille, with whom I visited in Paris."

"Ah, I see. Well, it is a lovely name, just as you are tonight. You look stunning."

Momentarily taken aback by his last remark, I stumbled for words.

"Well ... I. Thank you, Mr. Frederick. I mean Perry."

Twirling me around once before we positioned ourselves for the first steps of the tango, he looked at me seductively. Was he just creating the right aura necessary for such a provocative dance or was the look just for me? The sensuality of the moment stole my breath like a thief in the night. Daringly, I returned his intense gaze.

I have no idea how I was able to dance the tango. As inexperienced as I was, his strong arms piloted our moves with ease. At times, I blushed as our bodies deliberately touched. The passionate look coming from behind his striking eyes pierced my veneer. No one had ever looked at me like that before.

Between the dance and the champagne, my head was still spinning when I returned to my cabin. The evening was electrifying. Nothing that I had done in Paris was comparable. To think that I had crossed the Atlantic, lived in Paris for a several weeks, and was now crossing the Atlantic going home, finding uncontainable excitement on my return passage.

There were several more encounters during the voyage with the debonair Mr. Perry Frederick. Chance meetings occurred on the promenade deck as we endured the crisp, cold wind to savor a bit of needed exercise. Afternoon tea was especially enjoyable for the guests, and Perry and I did not miss the opportunity to visit with each other as well as other passengers.

Both of us were avid readers and would cross paths in the library. I craved his attention and found myself searching for him everywhere. Why? Just because we danced one evening couldn't possibly mean anything. It was just a dance, wasn't it?

"Good morning, Lorea."

"And good morning to you, Perry." I see you have taken advantage of browsing the wonderful collection of books on board."

"Indeed. I have so few opportunities to read when I am at home although I try to read something to Eleanor each night. Any recommendations?"

"Have you read anything written by Katherine Anne Porter? Her stories, set in Texas and Mexico, are admirable works of art. Some say they are equal to that of Hemingway provided they are working in the same genre."

"No, I can't say that I am familiar with her books. Eleanor prefers the classics like *Jane Eyre* and *Tale of Two Cities*, but I am grateful for the recommendation. Sounds like something that Eleanor would enjoy. I will pursue that when we get home. Not to change the subject, Lorea, but I have something that I would like to ask you. I hesitate, but nevertheless I would like to know if you would consider having a cocktail with me tonight. I want to know more about your husband's companies. Eleanor won't be present for dinner as she is completely exhausted from the trip. Her personal sitter, Mrs.

Van Mytre, will be with her for the night. It's the last evening on such a beautiful ship, and I would rather not spend it dining alone. What do you say?"

Catching me totally off guard, I hesitated.

"Well, I do have quite a bit of packing to do, but ..."

"You hesitate. I am sorry if my actions are too forward. Please forgive my impetuousness."

My conscious was telling me that meeting him would violate all sense of integrity. How could I return to Finley, hoping for a promising reunion while being infatuated with another man? But I wanted to be with him. The attraction was there, and it was obvious his feelings harmonized with mine. What should I do? My yearning heart overruled my righteous mind, and I accepted.

"Actually, Perry, I would love to have a cocktail with you. There is so much on my mind, and I would gladly like to divert my thoughts to something of a lighter nature. But nothing formal. Could we make it casual?"

"Casual it will be."

"Wonderful. Let's find a quiet lounge, shall we? I am not in the mood for jazz, but maybe a tango later in the evening?" I teased.

"But of course, your final lesson. It will be a pleasure, Lorea."

"For me, also, Perry."

I met him on the promenade deck, and he escorted me to a secluded, out-of-the-way lounge where we listened to velvety music and drank champagne. Small talk about life in general eventually slipped into more personal information. I learned that Perry was ten years my senior although there did not seem to be a generation gap between us. Our views on life, politically, socially, and economically, were totally harmonious. The only apparent difference between us was children. He had two sons that Eleanor had birthed before her current condition. Not being a parent, I was humored by funny tales of children growing up and the idiosyncrasies governing parenthood.

Perry was interested in my account of my first Parisian experience and knowing more about my life in Montgomery. I found myself engaging in more than just casual conversation about Finley.

"Perry, there's something I want to tell you. I had a motive for my visit to Paris that for some reason I feel compelled to share with you. You see, Finley and I are experiencing some trouble in our marriage. We are struggling to find mutual compatibility. I have not been able to find satisfaction in domestic life even though I went into the marriage knowing full well what was expected of me. I need more than creating needlepoint tapestries and baking apple pies to satisfy me. I want to paint and write, but Finley objects. He desires a more stoic existence for me, one that matches the lifestyle of all society matrons. I went to Paris to see if I could satisfy my artistic nature, but the whole experience only complicated matters more."

He probed further, "... and how is that?"

"I am not sure; I just know that I'm more confused than ever. Did I really think that I could live in Paris for a while and return to Montgomery and assume my usual duties? I didn't think that was an unreasonable expectation before, but I do now. Thinking about all that is going on in the world right now and seeing my cousin Camille in anguish about the plight of her country, I feel very selfish, and I need to return home in order for me to try and regain personal composure and commitment."

"So, what are you going to do?"

"I don't know, exactly. But I am going to make every effort I can to make the marriage work. Finley is a fine man and works hard. He deserves better. I don't know that I was the right match for him, and I had doubts before we married. However, I felt things would work out, but we quarreled often. I had to leave to see if time and space would heal our fractured marriage. Now, I am not sure if that was the right thing to do. So, even though I'm very confused, I am going home to try and salvage what we have. If we cannot find a solution to our mutual needs, divorce is likely."

"And that would be almost unspeakable for your families, right?" he affirmed as he took my hand in his.

"Yes, you're right. You do understand, don't you?"

"Of course, I do. I have a similar situation with Mrs. Frederick, one that is very difficult for me. Personal fulfillment is nearly impossible because of her condition, but I am committed to taking care of her. You see, her disability resulted from an automobile accident for which I was responsible. You and I are burdened but in different ways," he commented as he bowed his head for a few seconds.

"And divorce is unthinkable, right?"

"I could never divorce Mrs. Frederick. I couldn't live with myself if I caused her anymore grief. So, I do what I can to take care of her. She can always count on that. Hey, enough of this gloom, Lorea. You mentioned painting. That's a love of yours?"

"Indeed, it is."

"Well, please tell me more. Who is your favorite artist?"

For the rest of the evening, we confined our conversation to topics of a lighter nature. The only interruption was from a photographer who took our picture at sunset on the promenade deck as we made our way to the lounge. At midnight, we said our farewells and danced a tango down the hall to my cabin. Taking my hand, he kissed it lightly.

"Thank you for some of the best days that I have had in quite some time. The pleasure of your company has been delightful," he gratefully stated.

"And thank you, Perry, for a wonderful return voyage filled with interesting conversations, light-hearted laughter, and teaching me the tango. I'm overwhelmed with pleasure as well."

Offering a brief smile, he whispered, "goodbye." After nodding politely, he slowly walked away looking back several times as I continued standing there in silence, watching his departure until he disappeared.

Docking was early the next morning, and madness

consumed the ship as everyone hurriedly disembarked. A package was delivered to my door right before I left. To my surprise, it was the photo that was taken the night before accompanied by a dozen long stem red roses. How had he managed to get the photo developed so quickly, and where did he get the roses so early in the morning? I desperately wanted to thank him for everything.

My heart raced. I hurriedly gathered my belongings and made my way towards the off-ramp. Methodically, I moved about the ship looking everywhere. Feeling as if I were moving in slow motion, I frantically searched every face in the crowd. Where was he? I kept repeating the words to myself. Not being able to subdue my feeling of urgency, I began wrestling with the guilt invading my thoughts.

Sad and desperate all at the same time brought on a flood of tears as I blindly grabbed a tissue from my purse, causing the photo to tumble to the floor. Picking it up, I stared at it in silence. Would I ever see him again? I felt horribly empty.

Maybe the photo was all I would ever have which now was the most important memento of the entire trip. Little did I know that it would be the most important memento of my entire life.

Chapter 9

MY HOMECOMING

As the train approached Union Station in Montgomery, I blankly stared through the window. We were in a holding pattern on the bluff overlooking the station waiting for the tracks to clear, which seemed to reflect my life at this time ... in a holding pattern waiting for the tracks to clear.

The train station opened in 1898 revealing a handsome structure designed in a Romanesque Revival style. Constructed with brick and limestone, the building features a six hundred foot overhead shed in the back that was heralded as one of only three sheds in the world of its kind. The first originated in France. Beautifully crafted stained glass windows in different hues of purple, rose, and brown added beauty to the design. Located on Water Street, just two blocks from the town square, Union Station serves as the transportation and trade center for all commercial and private residents of the city. My father often spoke of the historical opening. Horse-drawn carriages, adorned with garlands of all types of flowers, paraded prominent residents through downtown which ended in a spectacular gala held at the station.

Once passengers disembarked from an incoming train and new passengers boarded, the relatives bidding farewell to those departing could hear the familiar sound of *all aboard* belted loudly by the conductor, signaling the train's departure. The words emulated a sense of adventure, travel, and discovery. It was my favorite part of visiting the station.

Since my father's store was only two blocks away, he routinely met incoming trains to collect parcels that had been ordered and shipped via rail transportation. When I was a child, I accompanied him to retrieve goods. I knew most of the longtime, employed Red Caps that assisted departing and arriving passengers with their luggage. Placing all personal belongings on huge, U-shaped wooden carts with big iron wheels was a feat. It would take two or three Red Caps to pull the weighty carts across the tracks either to or from the luggage section. A special treat for me was getting hoisted to the top of the mounds of luggage for the ride. I imagined it was much like riding a huge elephant swaying and bumping with each step. I knew that if I ever got to Africa, I would be an expert rider!

Seeing Union Station generated a new sense of anticipation for me as my feelings upon leaving, and now arriving, had been one continuous wild ride vacillating between excitement, sadness, and confusion. I stared blankly at everything and nothing, waiting to see what emotion would surface. Where would I go from here?

A sudden jolt indicated the train was finally moving, which brought me back to the immediate. Slowly, the Atlantic Coastline Train rolled into the station, as the Red Caps began pulling the big carts towards the designated track. Ladies waved hello with their white handkerchiefs while children covered their noses and ears as the train roared past them with steam rising from beneath and brakes loudly screeching.

I searched the crowd for familiar faces. Who would be there? What would Finley have to say? His letters had been bland, void of warmth. I often thought that the trees they cut and harvested in the family timber business for the sawmills were more alive. But what could I expect? He could only write about what he knew and what he did each day, and I knew that script well. Subsequently, a mannerly persona characterized his correspondence with *Thoughtfully Yours* and *Respectfully Yours* offered as salutations, void of any expression of love.

What kind of letters would Perry have written? I had to stop thinking about him. I had to discontinue with comparative thoughts. That was not good under the circumstances. And what was I to do with the picture of us on the Queen Mary? I couldn't bear the thought of destroying it, not yet anyway. It would have to be hidden until I had some resolution to the situation at hand.

I wondered about everyone's initial reaction to my new look. I was sure that my Garbo hairstyle, shorter hemline, and chic clothing would certainly raise a few eyebrows in town. My new attire consisted of a brown wool suit, a stylish belt in dark red leather, a tailored silk cream-colored blouse, spectator shoes in two shades of brown, and coordinating gloves that I bought at the Place Vendôme. As a going away present, Camille presented me with an olive green felt hat that was offset by a pheasant feather tucked inside of red and cream silk bands. Wearing it tilted to one side was considered smart fashion. In addition to the clothes, I indulged in purchasing an exquisite shawl that I wore on the ship during dinner each evening. I also purchased an expensive, large rhinestone bracelet that I acquired from a small antique shop on the outskirts of Paris. The fake stones assembled in three strands were either a deep red, a soft moonstone, or dark amber. I felt stylishly liberated. I wondered if I had emerged from my cocoon with new emotional apparel to match the physical. Would societal expectations stunt any future growth? Acceptance, as opposed to ridicule, would be important.

As I stepped onto the foot platform hurriedly put in place by one of the Red Caps, I once again scanned the oncoming crowd of people rushing forward with excitement to greet friends or family.

"Do you have luggage, ma'am?"

"Oh, Mr. B! It's so good to see you."

"My goodness, Mrs. Hughes. Is that you? I didn't recognize you at all. You sure took me by surprise."

Mr. Burns, known lovingly to all as Mr. B had served as the

head Red Cap at Union Station for many years, never missing a day of work. Always dressed in a pressed black uniform, he performed his duties with a smile. His humor was always contagious as well as his bright smile. He prided himself on having the whitest hair in all of Montgomery as that meant longevity of service.

"It is wonderful to see you, Mr. B. It seems as if I have been gone forever! It is fun to be one of the passengers for a change. I don't suppose that today I will be riding on top of the luggage cart?"

"No Mrs. Hughes, I don't suppose you will. I need to get your luggage now. I see Mr. Hughes heading this way."

"Mr. B you are a good man, and I kindly thank you for your assistance."

As Finley approached, I waved, swallowed hard, and extended my right arm forward to give him a hug. The astonishment on his face was apparent and his response guarded. His all-weather coat, draped over his left arm, restricted use. Both hands tightly gripped the brim of his hat. He released his right hand from the hat and leaned forward in almost a bowing gesture, resisting contact.

"Well, well. Mrs. Hughes, I presume?" he sarcastically commented.

"Yes, Finley? Surprised?"

He was predictably cold, creating a thorny exchange between us. Refraining from any type of extended exclamatory or declarative statement, his response was indifferent.

"Not at all. Do you need help with your luggage?"

"That won't be necessary. I saw Mr. B a few moments ago, and he will be here with it promptly. I joked with him about riding on the big carts. Goodness, how time changes things! Are mother and father here?"

"Yes, they are inside. Your Mother thought that the wind coming from the river might set off her arthritis."

"Oh, yes. I forgot. Well, how are you, Finley? It's so good to see you after being gone for such a long time. I've missed you and I'm glad to be home."

"Yes, it's good that you're home. The holidays are just around the corner."

Was that all he was going to say? He's glad that I am home for the holidays? I guess so. He'll want me to start baking pies, for sure.

"And the businesses? I hope things are going well."

"Yes, everything is stable which is certainly generous for all of us since the Depression."

We turned and walked towards the large doors that opened up into the lobby of the train station. Still, putting forth an effort to engage him in conversation, I continued.

"I would agree. Finley, I had no idea how the Depression affected other countries. I will have to tell you all about Paris, but of course, I guess you know that being in business and all. I did have an opportunity to meet someone on board the Queen Mary that knew all about the reforestation techniques that are being studied in France by American industries. Remember? I mentioned this to you before I left?"

"Yes, I do remember. I remember that you tried that approach to justify my accompanying you to Paris. I also remember expressing to you that this was certainly not anything that warranted your attention. I must say that I am a bit surprised, not only with this new look that you have brought home from Paris but with your newly acquired knowledge."

"Well, then. What do you think about my new look?"

"I knew that you would bring something of Paris home with you. I am more curious about your continued comments about the forestry business, though. How would you know of such things other than what you have overheard dad and me conversing about?"

"As I mentioned, Finley, I met someone from the South aboard the ship on the return voyage, and we talked a great deal on the subject. Oh Finley, there's mother. She's waving. I must hurry. She's so excited." I was glad that somebody was.

"Lorea! Lorea! You're home at last!" She loudly proclaimed as we embraced each other.

"Yes, it seems as if I have been away forever. How are you?"

"We're doing fine, and how well you look."

"Thank you, mother," but I knew that didn't necessarily mean approval of my Parisian flare.

"Father, it's wonderful to see you, too."

Without commenting, he took out a handkerchief and wiped his eyes. Mother was still chatting incessantly.

"Can I borrow your handkerchief, father? I am a bit tearful, too."

Emotionally, I was wildly spinning. At one point, I almost felt faint. Finley had been standing aside as I savored the reunion with my parents. He must have noticed that I placed my hand over my eyes for several moments and quickly came to my side.

"Are you all right, Lorea? You look rather pale in spite of your rosy cheeks."

At last, a warm response from him only to verbally scald it in the end. Luckily, Mr. B was approaching which prevented me from making a hasty, inappropriate remark.

"Here's your luggage. Was this all you had, Mrs. Hughes?"

"Yes, Mr. B, and thank you again, for your help."

Finley echoed my words and generously tipped Mr. B as we proceeded towards the front of the station where the automobiles were parked. Mother had planned a welcome home dinner for me which temporarily subdued the awkwardness that characterized my reunion with Finley.

It was a much larger gathering than mother had shared with me. It was an event which I was sure would be in the society columns the following day. It was mother at her best, entertaining friends and relatives. She had prepared a feast. Moving about the different rooms in the house where guests were engaged in conversation, I could sense that all eyes were focused on me. Voices lowered as I approached. Noticeably, they drew their lace handkerchiefs to their mouths to drown out the nature of their conversation. I couldn't resist the opportunity to engage them in verbal play.

"Well, ladies. Who would like to ask the first question? I

know that you are just dying to hear about Paris. Mrs. Carter, you look like you have a burning question."

"Well, I heard that the latest fashions in Paris have women showing their knees. That's sinful. Is it really true?"

"Yes, especially if you see the Can-Can being performed. You can see more than knees, you know!"

Gasping in horror, she asked, "Did you get to see that, Lorea?"

"You know Mrs. Carter; you can see anything you want in Paris. It just depends on where you are and what you want to do."

The next question came from Myrtle McGraw.

"You know they say that Paris is full of *ladies of the night* who hang out in brothels."

"Well, Mrs. McGraw, do tell. With whom have you been talking? My contacts in Paris didn't mention such things."

I turned towards another acquaintance in the group who was smiling wickedly. I couldn't wait to hear her question.

"Lorea, are the men there as romantic as they are portrayed to be? I hear they're merely rogues looking for ... " she paused.

"Looking for what, Mrs. Howard? With all due respect, do you think I would have any first-hand knowledge of that? Remember, I stayed with mother's sister. Rogues are everywhere, not just in Paris. It is truly a romantic place, though, but romance is where you find it whether in Paris or Montgomery. Wouldn't you agree?"

Her white handkerchief over her mouth prevented a response. Ironically, I found that sometimes ending with a question deterred further interrogation. However, it didn't deter the whispers that consumed each room.

What were these people thinking? Their distorted inquiries solicited *dirt*. I was not amused. Every conversation had a courtroom essence with questions, opinions, and judgments rendered at every turn. I was stifled but not surprised. Eventually, the courtroom drama had to unfold I just didn't know that it would be my first night back home. The verdict was inevitable. Montgomery society did not approve, and society ruled. Verbal lubrication, good or bad, characterized the evening. Nothing had changed nor ever would in a small, Southern town.

I found myself missing relaxed conversations with Aunt Irenee and Camille discussing interesting topics on literature and art. I found myself thinking about the quiet evenings on the ship, especially the last evening with Perry. Deep in thought, I failed to hear Finley speaking to me.

"Lorea, you seem to be far, far away, perhaps still in Paris?"

"Perhaps. I do apologize, and you are right. I am lost in thought. Apparently, I am more exhausted than I realized. I will thank mother and father for the wonderful homecoming dinner and politely offer an excuse for our early departure to the remaining guests. I would like to go to our house. I really need to rest."

The house was cold, but not nearly as cold as I felt inside. I prepared coffee while Finley brought in my luggage. My homecoming had been a disappointment. I wanted to run back to the train station and reverse my journey. I wanted to be back on the Queen Mary with Perry. I had to stop thinking about him, though. I just had to. I wish I had never mentioned to Finley about meeting someone from the South. What was I thinking?

Finley lit a fire and we conversed briefly. He had very little to say other than politely soliciting comments about Camille and Aunt Irenee. We spent most of the first hour drinking coffee. His final inquiry was more than I wanted to share at the moment.

"Lorea, please tell me about your voyage across the Atlantic. You have hardly mentioned it."

"Let's talk tomorrow, shall we? I must unpack a few things before bedtime."

"But it is not every day that one crosses the Atlantic on the Queen Mary. I am curious. You mentioned meeting someone from the South that knew about reforestation."

"Yes, I did, but I'm just too tired to talk about that now. Can it wait?"

"Wait? That's all I've been doing since you left, is wait. I want to hear about the Queen Mary and your time on board. It had to be memorable. It was expensive enough.

Laughing to myself, I stood up, walked over to him, and patted his shoulder.

"Not tonight, Finley. Tomorrow we will talk. And yes, it was expensive as well as memorable. Would it be better to say frivolous? Good night, dear."

Chapter 10

GOOD LUCK PENNIES

I had no idea what time of the day it was when I awoke, but the smell of freshly brewed coffee invaded my senses. I slipped on my flannel robe and cotton slippers, and shuffled towards the kitchen to greet Mary, a housekeeper employed by the Hughes family for years.

She was known for her gentle, soft-spoken spirit and caring nature. She prided herself in maintaining a neat, well-groomed appearance, choosing plain, black dresses with white lace collars as her personal style. Her hair was graying at the temples which accentuated her strong cheekbones and warm brown eyes. It would take Mary hours to shop at the market as friends from every corner of the city would stop and desire conversation. She had horse-trader shrewdness and could bargain with the best about ongoing rates for produce.

"Good morning, Mary."

"Welcome home, Mrs. Hughes. Did you sleep well?" She inquired as she served coffee.

"Yes, I did sleep soundly. In fact, I could have slept more. However, I need to unpack and get on with the day. I did not see Mr. Hughes when I awoke. Did he go into town?"

"Mr. Hughes asked me to convey to you that he had a couple of things at the company that needed his attention. He wanted you to sleep as long as possible. He said he should be back after lunch."

"Very well. In the meantime, while I'm enjoying my coffee, you can catch me up on current local news."

"Not too much to tell, Mrs. Hughes. Although, Mrs. Abbott down the street, fell down the front steps at her house and hit her head. Broke her leg too, poor lady. I've been taking meals to her since she can't stand up to cook. Ora Burton's husband died suddenly. He's had trouble with his health since the Depression, you know. Not sure what she's going to do now. Remember young William Bentley? Joined the Army without telling anyone beforehand. His mother is still upset about that. She cries every time someone asks about him. Things just keep on changing."

"It does seem that way, Mary. Speaking of change. I am going into town later this morning. Do we need anything from the market?"

"No, I don't believe we do. Mr. Hughes asked me to go to the market yesterday to buy flour, eggs, sugar, and vegetables. I'm cooking some good Southern fried chicken tonight because I figured that entree was probably not on menus in Paris. Plus, Mr. Hughes thought you might want to bake a cake. He said that he was sure that you would want to get right back in your usual routine."

"How thoughtful of you, and how predictable of Mr. Hughes."

"Yes, Mrs. Hughes. He said that you would be settling down."

"Yes, of course. The coffee is so tasty, tempting me to enjoy another cup, but I need to hurry off as soon as possible to catch the trolley. I'm eager to visit my father at the store. If Mr. Hughes arrives before I return, please tell him that I will be home around mid-afternoon. Oh, and would you please do me a huge favor? I would love a big glass of iced tea with lemons for dinner, if possible."

"We have tea but no lemons. Not sure you can get them right now."

"Don't worry, Mary. I'll stop by the market coming home. Hopefully, I can find a big one to use in the tea but also to use in that cake that I am supposed to bake."

The cool, autumn breeze made the trolley ride a brisk one. The foliage was beautiful but would quickly lose its color before Thanksgiving and Christmas gatherings. Fall seemed later this year, though. Maybe seeing different landscapes had created new eyes for me and changed my perspective.

Nevertheless, the activity on the neighborhood streets were the same, with cars passing the trolley and couples strolling peacefully down the sidewalks dodging children playing everywhere.

Today was an important day for trading and shopping as Saturdays yielded the most income for local merchants. McKinley Mercantile would be buzzing with customers. I knew that only a brief visit with father was possible, and we would not have time to put a penny on the tracks at Union Station, a ritual we had observed for years. According to local lore, if pennies are found on the track after the train departs, good luck is imminent for those placing the pennies.

As I strolled down Dexter Avenue, the main street in town, one would have thought I was appearing in the nude. Intentionally, I chose to wear my homecoming outfit for my returning debut, but Montgomery residents did not deviate from the acceptable dress code. I laughed at the thought of trying to find good fashion in town, at least what I wanted to wear, even though clothing modeled by mannequins in shop windows appeared more stylish than I remembered.

I periodically stopped to greet familiar faces and make brief comments about Paris when asked. Even though mother had welcomed me home with a grand party, the guest list was limited to close friends and relatives.

Mae Williford, an acquaintance from the girls' finishing school that I attended, greeted me outside of a millinery shop as I amused myself with the window displays.

"My goodness, Lorea McKinley, I mean Hughes! When did you get home?"

"Why Mae Williford, it's been forever! I arrived yesterday."

"Shopping already, I see. Just like in Paris."

"Most certainly. It is surely a way of life there. There is

always something new and exciting to see and do."

"Indeed. It must be hard to come back home after such an exciting trip. Life in Montgomery might be so dull now. Pardon my failure to inquire, but how's Finley? Is he well?"

"Finley is fine. The businesses are fine. Everything is simply fine, Mae."

"I'm so glad to hear that, dear. The Depression surely took its toll, but things are improving. Would you agree? The economy is recovering as well as other things?"

"Let's hope so. Now, I really must get moving. I want to stop by my father's store. Take care, Mae. It was interesting visiting with you, as always."

With lightning speed, I shifted my attention. I certainly did not want her following me to probe for more information. I had detected suggestive remarks like dull ... recovery ... Finley's well-being. She was baiting me, for sure.

I darted in and out of clusters of shoppers who were engaged in small talk since their last trip to town the Saturday before. I refrained from eye contact with anyone to avoid any further verbal exchange, even though I knew the atmosphere in the store would be a hub of activity, rich with dialogue.

Indeed, it was, and even more so than usual. I was relieved to see customers fully engrossed in what they were doing. The crisp air, improving economy, and new merchandise had created more traffic. Once inside, father welcomed me with a nod as he pushed a fifteen-foot lean-to ladder down an aisle that would enable him to retrieve goods from the top shelf in the store. I acknowledged his greeting with a wave and managed to squeeze between customers, making my way to the old wooden counter where the cash register was located, and where goods were displayed.

Originally, the store served as a storage depot for cotton during the War Between the States. When Union troops seized it, it became their supply headquarters since it was strategically close to the Alabama River below the bluffs at the train station. When the war ended in 1865, it sat silently still, recovering from the economic devastation that was rampant in the South. However, since the river front in Montgomery was a perfect location for distributing goods from a central location within the state, the area around the store eventually became the center of train and river traffic.

From the turn of the century until the Great War, the store again served as storage, housing goods ready for shipment up and down the river. When the war began, it served as an overflow depot for soldiers going overseas. After that, it became a mercantile store that father managed and later purchased.

By 1936, supplies for the local farmers consumed McKinley Mercantile as outlying areas were mostly agricultural. However, it eventually evolved into a hardware business while also maintaining mercantile status by carrying seeds for planting, yards of cloth, canned goods, and kitchen supplies. Father stocked a glass container with rock candy at eyeball level in a cabinet for smaller customers. Selling for only a penny, he knew how to allure the children into the store!

Mr. Johnson, father's store assistant, smiled briefly while offering change to a waiting customer.

"Welcome back, Lorea."

"Thank you, Mr. Johnson. It is so good to be home. Can I help?"

"I am sure that your father would be most appreciative if you could lend a hand. This has been the busiest day in quite a while. He's over there on the ladder."

"Yes, I spotted him when I arrived. I will chat with him in a little while when things settle down."

I removed my hat and suit jacket and put on a store apron to begin assisting with the steady flow of customers. I greeted familiar faces and made the acquaintance of unfamiliar ones. Mary was right. Things were changing.

Not noticing the time until mid-afternoon, I knew a phone call was necessary to share my whereabouts and delayed arrival time. My tardy return would not be acceptable, though, as I was not following my usual routine. Dessert for dinner might have to be rock candy instead of the expected cake.

At the end of the day, when the sound of shoe heels on the pine floors subsided, father closed the big oak doors at the front of the store.

"Lorea, I am sure that you had not imagined working in the store on your first day home from Paris!"

"Nothing could have given me greater pleasure, father. I do not know how Mr. Johnson and you could have fully managed the endless stream of customers that shopped today. Before we go home, I have a request. Do you have a penny? I would like to put one on the tracks."

"You bet, I have more than just one! This has been one profitable day."

The train terminal was a hub of energy. Farmers were everywhere waiting for rail and riverboat deliveries. Passengers crammed into the station as trains arrived and departed. Since late fall marked the onset of the holiday season, traffic would increase and would not peak until after December.

"Father, it's looks as if Union Station is having another grand opening!"

"It sure does."

The sound of the train whistle on the bluffs overlooking the station diverted our attention as we knew the holding pattern was over, and our pennies needed placing. As we raced to Track Four, I began our conversation, eager to hear his thoughts.

"It is so good to see you, father. I am sorry that I was not able to visit with you last night."

"Your mother's party was especially important. You have been away for a lengthy period, and your mother has had to put inquisitive minds, or would it be more appropriate to say nosey neighbors, at ease. Now that you are home, you can fend for yourself."

"After last night, that's a given. One would hope that personal matters would remain personal, but we do live in a small town, don't we? So, did I meet with everyone's approval?"

"Approval?" He asked, looking at me curiously.

Strategically, we placed the pennies and assumed a watchful position on the outside passenger benches.

"What matters, Lorea, is what is important to you. Your mother and I desperately wanted to live in America. Immigrating to a new country was frightening for us, but we let our hearts guide us. It was not the smartest thing to do at the time, but it worked out. My father used to say that nothing was more important than family and land. We found both, and our hearts are still happy. Is yours?"

I sensed that no reply was necessary as he turned his head towards the train tracks. His purpose was to provoke thought, which he did. Was my life what I wanted it to be? Was I content? Only I could answer those questions.

I kissed his cheek as he smiled and offered me his handkerchief to wipe away my tears. His thoughts and words, not necessarily eloquent in nature, had strangely produced a temporary peace for me. We sat there in silence until we heard the familiar call *all aboard* as the conductor prepared everyone for departure. It was time to collect the pennies.

Chapter 11

DUTY CALLS

During most seasons, people in Montgomery spend Sunday afternoons swaying in porch swings and rocking in oversized rockers, standard accessories for each home. Seasonal refreshments are customary. For the noon meal on Sundays, pot roast is a staple and one of Mary's specialties.

The Sunday after my homecoming mother and father joined us at noon to enjoy a delicious meal prepared by Mary. I knew this luxury would end shortly.

"Mary, that was one fine meal, except for the absence of dessert," Finley stated at the end of the meal.

"Thank you, Mr. Hughes." Mary promptly looked my way.

"It's ok, Mary. Begging everyone's understanding, I regret not being able to muster up the energy to prepare a special dessert for today. I was dreadfully tired last night. Next Sunday, I promise to serve something special that is nice and non-traditional."

Sensing the tension, mother quickly commented. "I agree with Mr. Hughes, Mary. That was a delicious meal. I have heard about your expertise. Your reputation is quite well founded," she respectfully commented.

Mary offered a gracious smile and began clearing the table.

"I will assist Mary before joining everyone on the porch. It is time for me to get back into a routine as Mr. Hughes has so aptly expressed."

"Yes darling, I am pleased to see your eagerness to return to normal as Mary will be leaving this afternoon. It was so gracious of mother to temporarily share her service while you were gone," Finley pointed out.

"Of course, Finley. I predicted her immediate departure."

After Mary and I washed, dried, and stored away the china and silver, we spread a sheet over the leftover food on the dining room table. With the cooler weather, everything would be fine until early evening when Finley and I would consume leftovers. When cleanup was completed, I joined the Sunday gathering on the porch for light conversation.

Eventually, mother, father, and Mary departed, leaving Finley and I rocking quietly. The only audible sounds came from occasional passersby waving and shouting cordial greetings. After a while, I broke the silence. Strangely enough, Finley did not initiate a conversation about Paris or the return voyage. I invited it under my terms.

"Finley, speaking of dessert, I am now familiar with wonderful French dessert recipes. I do believe that you would enjoy them. What do you think?"

"My dearest. French desserts are certainly not any better than our fine, traditional ones here. I do not see the necessity."

"Why Finley! That sounds so stuffy. Trying new things is exciting."

"Haven't you had enough of trying new things? Your time in Paris should have certainly satisfied that."

"Well, truthfully, it did not. The joy of sampling new food choices fascinated me. And speaking of new things, I was thinking about occasionally working in father's store. The business is growing, and I would be a tremendous help. I certainly enjoyed spending time there yesterday. My goodness! We could barely keep up with ..."

"Lorea, Lorea! One minute you are talking about creating French desserts and the next minute you are suggesting working in your father's store. That is quite impossible. Simply out of the question."

I stopped rocking, leaned forward, folded my hands in

my lap, and stared intensely at him. His controlled temper tantrum continued.

"Forgive me if this sounds less than exciting, but you must resume your customary household responsibilities. Besides, we must be thinking of having children. Expectations for that are forthcoming."

"Expectations! Always expectations! Finley, you knew that I had a creative flare when you married me. You were willing to accept that then. The intense domestication that our society and you impose are stifling, much more than I ever realized. I feel smothered, and my resentment for that has intensified."

"I regret that it has, but you were aware of what life entails as a married lady. Intense domestication? You accepted that when we exchanged vows. Quite simply, Lorea, it is a matter of obligation of duty."

Rage was upon me. I stood up and walked towards the front door. I was not going to listen to this anymore but wanted to have the last jab.

"I see. Obligations. Duties. The promise to obey, right?"

"Yes, that sums it up nicely. You did promise to obey as declared in the marriage vows. Now, for the evening snack I would be delighted with a roast beef sandwich."

"That sounds delicious, Finley. And while you are in the kitchen making one, please make one for me, too." I snapped as I slammed the door so hard that I was surprised the glass windowpane survived.

For the weeks that followed, every interaction between the two of us was confrontational and disrespectful. Unable to sort through our differences and come to any terms of agreement on anything, it was evident that we seriously differed on multiple issues. Every discussion that ensued resulted in non-productive, heated arguments or total silence. How did we miss this mismatch before we married?

Somehow, we were going to have to sustain our hostility at family gatherings during the holidays. We would have to make appearances at every scheduled function and appear to be the happily married couple that both families, as well as society, expected. I would endure, especially during the holidays.

This was mother's favorite time of the year with families and friends coming together to celebrate their ties and traditions. I would not impose personal agonies during such a spirited time. Yet, how could I conceal my depression? How could both of us shroud our lack of affection? We might as well have been two strangers meeting at a party with nothing in common since proximity and conversations were avoided.

It was going to be obvious to those familiar with us that something was wrong, but I would persevere. Afterwards, maybe if we both conceded on certain issues, then we might realize a compromise that would save our marriage. If not, an undesirable path forward was surely imminent.

Mother planned a grand New Year's Eve party, and guests cheerfully ushered in the new year. Finley's parents attended along with a host of other close acquaintances that were regulars at mother's parties. Questions were still shoveled towards me like a railroad worker shoveling coal into the belly of a steam engine.

I wore the long black crepe gown that I had worn with Perry the last night on the ship. It was painfully reminiscent, preventing me from concentrating on the event at hand. I revisited the sunset evening where we talked together and danced the tango, and wondered what he was doing for New Year's Eve. I wished that I could talk with him and solicit his advice.

"Lorea, you were certainly quiet this evening." Finley commented as we drove home in silence.

"I guess I was just not in the mood for a party."

"You, not in the mood for a party? Since when?"

"Let's not argue, please. Tell me about conversations with people you visited with tonight. What is new that I might have missed?"

"Conversations, my dear, centered around you and your trip. You are quite the talk of the town, the *belle of the ball.*

I grew weary of the same conversations throughout the night. You need to put Paris behind you and focus on me for a change."

"I have no desire to be the center of attention, Finley. I am also growing weary of duplicated conversations at each gathering. And yes, we have sensitive issues to address. I genuinely want you to be happy, and I know you need certain things in your life to satisfy that. However, I need certain things, also. You need a predictable routine, and I am not against that at all, but please allow me to provide that for you within my own style. I promise that I will not neglect my responsibilities."

"Style? You mean baking non-traditional desserts, painting silly sunflowers, and working in your father's store. Right?"

"Well, yes, but not daily, just occasionally. I do not see anything wrong with those choices every now and then."

"Once again, I do. Life at the Hughes's household needs to reflect the expected way of life and what your duties are, accordingly. You do not seem to understand that."

"The only thing that I understand at this point is that you are not willing to appease me in any way. Please try to think about it from my perspective. I beg you. I am not asking for much, just for you to accommodate me in occasional personal choices for what I need for fulfillment."

"And what about me and who I need to be as a husband and a businessman?"

"Finley, that is precisely what I am already doing. Marketing occurs on a daily basis, your favorite meals are efficiently planned and prepared every day, the house is cleaned multiple times during the week, the laundry is finished in a timely manner, and all other household concerns are fully addressed. Plus, I am active in local civic groups supporting community endeavors."

"Well, those duties and responsibilities should be more than enough to occupy you."

"Yes. That is true, but I have found that time for other activities is possible. I am very efficient, you know."

"Lorea, I doubt you can maintain all duties and responsibilities and accomplish anything else."

"I see. Let's talk about it again when it is not so late, and our heads are clear. My thoughts are clouded, possibly from muscadine wine."

"Your clouded thoughts have nothing to do with the wine," he snapped.

I refrained from commenting.

* * *

January was very cold, and we experienced drab and lifeless days that never seemed to end. Dinner evenings around the fireplace were void of activity. Finley held firm thinking that I would succumb to his demands out of frustration, and I engaged in the same mode. However, weeks passed, void of movement on the issues, and I remained hopeful that elapsed time would eventually lead to dual acceptance, and we could progress forward, supporting both of our mutual needs.

However, the alienation between us continued, preventing intimacy or solutions to our differences. Hours spent with mother passed the time which was exactly what I was doing, passing time. We baked often, confining our cooking to the traditional. Finley was content and commented frequently to his pleasure. His mood was always agreeable if I restricted my activities to the expected, but I was the only one compromising.

When spring arrived, I desired life, just like new budding foliage pushing forward. In early April, Finley traveled to Pensacola to attend a scheduled business meeting. For a full week I was not bound to my usual duties, although spring cleaning was upon me. Freshness was needed in all rooms, especially in the back bedroom which remained lifeless throughout the year.

An intense urge engulfed rational thought. Why not transform the unused back bedroom into a studio for reading, writing, and painting? Since Finley never ventured into that vacant space, it could serve as a perfect source of personal inspiration. Keeping the room concealed behind a closed door would prevent discovery eliciting another argument between us. In time, I could cleverly demonstrate efficiency while attending to multiple tasks. To keep him distracted, I would keep an apple pie or a red velvet cake visible in the kitchen. It was an invigorating plan. Therefore, with spirit, I began the makeover.

New sheer curtains draped in a swag fashion over the existing rods allowed light to penetrate the somber room from two side windows. A fresh coat of cream-colored paint blended nicely with the natural sunlight, allowing suitable lighting for painting, and my easel and paints emerged from dormancy.

Twin beds were rerouted to a long wall. New off-white, chenille bedspreads with fluffy, gold velvet pillow rolls serving as headboards. I discarded an old wool, moth-eaten rug from the middle of the room and replaced it with small rugs in shades of brown, yellow, cream, and peach, placed beside each bed.

I relocated a writing table to a back window with a view of a graceful weeping willow tree and moved an unused armchair next to a small fireplace. A quilt with bright floral designs in square patterns that I found in a trunk in mother's attic served as a makeshift slipcover.

A pole lamp from the living room was repositioned to the emerging new workspace. Amber-colored fringe was sewn around the bottom of the brown shade, and the soft light from the lamp provided additional warmth to the atmosphere.

Between the smell of oil paints and turpentine that filled the room, I had to open the windows. The spring breeze was refreshing, but the familiar smell that permeates an art studio was even more stimulating. This was the self-expression I truly needed as I worked tirelessly, filling up a canvas with sunflowers in a Van Gogh style. The piece was perfect for replacing the stagnant farm scene over the living room mantel. Aunt Mary's gift would find a retirement home somewhere else less prominent, despite Finley's objection.

He would most certainly have to agree when I featured the colorful painting over the mantel.

"Hello, is anyone home?"

Oh my, it's Finley. He is back earlier than expected. I was glad that I had finished refurbishing, although I had not mentally prepared for war. Courageously, I greet him, nervously rubbing my hand on my smock.

"Finley. You are back early."

"Yes, I am. Where were you?"

"I was in the back bedroom."

"What are you doing in there?"

So much for my undercover work! Caught off guard, I courageously decided to invite him in for a look.

"What do you think?"

"What is this? What have you done?"

"I thought this room could use an uplift. I made it into a studio-like bedroom. Isn't it wonderful? As you can see, I have already started writing in my journal and painting sunflowers."

"So, I see. And whatever possessed you to do this? I do not recall giving you permission, my dear."

"Permission? I am not a child, Finley, and I did not realize I had to have your permission. I know I should have consulted with you, but the time seemed right while I was undertaking spring cleaning. Someone needed to give this room purpose, and I decided to do just that. You will see, having this space available for painting and writing will not infringe on my time to take care of household chores."

"And might I ask, where did you get the money to do this?"

"Well, I have been very economical in planning meals the last few months, and I certainly have not spent any money on clothes. With the savings ..."

He turned away abruptly to leave the room, throwing his hands in the air, barking orders, "Take it all back, immediately."

"Take it all back? But Finley, as I explained to you, these few things were not that costly. I found good bargains and used household items that we already had."

"We are not spending the money for something so frivolous, and I thought this room would eventually serve as a nursery? If you want to refurbish it, do it with that in mind. Now, I am hungry. Since you claim to be able to totally fulfill your household responsibilities, I am sure you have something prepared, right?"

"Well, since you are home earlier than expected, I do not have anything cooking in the oven, but I do have fresh chicken salad in the refrigerator," I said with a sneer.

"That would be fine, along with a piece of cake or pie. I am sure you have those ready. I will enjoy it in the dining room," he replied with a toneless voice.

Tension invaded my entire body. How could he be so cold, so controlling? Struggling with disbelief and irritation, I removed my smock and slammed it to the floor. I felt like a savage beast gearing up for a fight against a predator. I wanted to pound his chest, scream loudly, and call him a despicable name, but his armor would buffer my aggression, and his resilience would endure. However, giving in was not an option. Wrath engulfed me as I prepared a chicken sandwich served with ice cream for a noon snack.

Somehow, I had to make it through to the evening meal. Maybe if I gave him time to absorb everything, he would reconsider. He just needed a good dose of kindness, even though a hearty dose of castor oil was my preference. Nevertheless, I served dinner at the usual time with a standard menu of meatloaf, potato salad, peas, and of course, dessert.

Silence prevailed, but it strategically provided time to plan my next move.

"Finley, I missed you while you were gone. The house was so empty. How was your trip, darling?"

"It was quite rewarding. I met business owners and enjoyed conversations over dinner."

Small talk ensued about encountering business constituents, and he smiled during the conversation, something that was foreign to his face.

"Well, Finley, it sounds like a wonderful trip. I can certainly appreciate that, and I am sure that you learned a great deal."

"Indeed, I did, especially from this one gentleman, Perry Frederick."

The sudden sound of his name coming from Finley stunned me.

"Perry Frederick?" I commented weakly.

"Yes. Quite a fellow. He is in the timber and forestry business in Pensacola and has been involved in learning about new reforestation techniques in France. He made a presentation on the technique. Now that I mention it, I recall a conversation we had when you first arrived home. Didn't you say something about meeting someone from the South on the voyage that was familiar with reforestation?"

"Well, yes. Yes, I did mention that."

I quickly diverted his attention away from his direct inquiry.

"Finley, how is the apple pie? Mother and I made it yesterday."

"It is delicious, Lorea. You see, good desserts do not have to be French to be delectable. Now what were we talking about? Oh yes, the presentation I heard. There was a cocktail party and dinner one evening, but I never had an opportunity to directly converse with Mr. Frederick. The crowd was quite large, and everyone tried to solicit his comments to delve more into his expertise. People smothered him with attention. The next time that I am in Pensacola, I would like the opportunity to meet him and discuss reforestation."

I held on tightly to maintain my composure. Please do not ask if he was the person I met on the Queen Mary. Please do not make that connection. I struggled to maintain a neutral expression. If Finley asked, I would not lie, but I did not want to share the fact that I had met Perry. I was not ashamed of anything that had occurred between us, but it was the only thing that provided a sense of happiness for me. I did not want contamination from Finley. I was glad that I had not accompanied him to Pensacola as originally planned. How awkward it would have been if together we had suddenly encountered Perry.

Finley's mood eventually mellowed. Taking advantage of the moment, I promptly served him another piece of apple pie. Placing it on the table by his coffee, I offered him a *pie a la mode* smile as I envisioned smashing it in his face. I hated the mental games playing in my head.

For the remainder of the evening, we sat blandly in the living room. Finley read the paper, smoked a cigar, and retired to bed. I did not join him. Instead, I sat on the sofa engaging in reflective thoughts.

I knew that I would never see Perry again to thank him for the wonderful week on board the ship, and never be able to thank him for awakening my spirit. However, if Finley journeyed to Pensacola again for a meeting, I could go with him and hope for an opportunity to speak to Perry. A casual conversation with him might subdue further thoughts about him.

After my internal musings, I decided that the idea of having a personal conversation with Perry was out of the question. It would be entirely inappropriate. Time spent together on the Queen Mary was just a diversion for a man that needed a little spark in his life, and that was all it meant. Maybe I was a romantic soul looking for something that really does not exist in real life. Therefore, I would continue to try and find oxygen in the marriage even though Finley was depleting it.

Sunlight peeping in the window awakened me at dawn. Multiple thoughts about the situation with Finley temporarily returned, but I knew the morning routine must begin no matter what, and I dutifully prepared breakfast.

As usual, we ate in silence while Finley read the morning paper. Afterwards, he gathered his coat and hat and proceeded to leave for work. He turned and spoke briefly.

"That was a delicious breakfast. When you return the goods that you purchased for the back bedroom, please come by the office. We could have lunch together downtown."

"That would be nice, Finley. We could eat at the lovely

Riverfront Restaurant."

"Lorea, I was not suggesting a place that expensive. I would like to have a sandwich and coffee at Carl's Café by the market. If that is not suitable, I'll see you for dinner. A baked ham with all the trimmings would be a good choice, along with dessert. Think you can do that?"

He sarcastically smiled and left without lingering for my response. My heart was heavy.

I had no intention of returning the purchased items. Instead, a visit with my parents was urgent to prepare them for the possibility that I might leave Finley. Knowing their thoughts would be significant, as divorce would be scandalous. I telephoned immediately after Finley departed and requested a visit to confer with them on something of significant importance. By noon, we sat down for our discussion.

"Mother. Father. It is extremely hard for me to reveal concerns that I have about my marriage. Please try to understand what I am about to tell you." I took a deep breath and began my discourse.

"Finley and I are not doing well in our marriage."

"Why is that?" mother questioned.

"Basically, he is very rigid and uncompromising in his expectations of my role as his wife. I want more freedom to engage in writing and occasionally painting. Finley opposes those choices and prefers me to confine any extra time to sewing, knitting, or needlepoint to conform with what other wives do. It is stifling."

I see. Have you been negligent in fulfilling your responsibilities in any way?" Mother was quick to ask.

"I have not."

"Then what seems to be the problem?" Father probed.

"As I said, Finley has a narrow view of the way married life should be, and mine is broader. We quarrel often and barely speak. We have been unsuccessful in solving issues surrounding family life. I do not think it is fair for either of us to continue being so miserable. Therefore, I am considering a divorce or separation if we cannot resolve our differences."

"Lorea! What are you talking about? What will people think?" Mother screamed.

"Mother, I do not care about what people will think! I am extremely unhappy and angry, and so is Finley. We just cannot continue like this."

"Does Finley know how you feel? Have you spoken with him about this?" Mother asked firmly.

"Oh yes, indeed. He is fully aware that things are not going well. However, he will not alter his opinions on any issue at all. And no, I have not confronted him directly with the idea of a divorce or separation. However, I can honestly say that I know that he would defy the idea, but I have made up my mind that change is needed. Neither of us should have to tolerate living with each other under the current circumstances."

"You're right, Lorea. He would not approve. I am sure of that," mother stated adamantly.

"That is just one problem! Finley always must approve of everything. In his mind, I must be obedient and uphold established societal norms. He refuses to accept any personal desires or actions contrary to that. It is almost forbidden. I wish we could work things out, but Finley continues to suppress anything that is not his idea and objects to anything that deviates from the norm. I simply cannot live like this, and he shouldn't have to either. I have thought about what I might do if we cannot come to a reasonable agreement."

"Lorea, please consider what this would mean. I think if you try, you and Finley might be able to find a solution. You must think of yourselves, of course, but others as well. Talk with him and explain your feelings. Make him understand the seriousness of your state of mind so that he might be willing to compromise. Please come to your senses, Lorea," Mother pleaded.

"I have tried, Mother, but he is firm on what he expects, and did you just asked me to *come to my senses*?"

Father quickly intervened, "You mentioned that you have thought about what you might do if separation or divorce become an option."

"If I leave, I have decided to move to Pensacola."

"Pensacola!" Mother exclaimed. Why would you move there? We have no family connections there."

"I know. That is exactly why I would move there, to avoid judgment and snobbery. I did meet someone on the train coming home who was returning to Pensacola to work at the Naval Air Station. She shared with me that jobs are plentiful there. I am not worried. I will find something, but I might need a little money from father and you in the beginning. As soon as I find a job, I will pay back the loan. I will need your support if I decide to leave."

Mother began to pace back and forth across the living room rug, wringing her hands periodically and swabbing her face with her handkerchief as she struggled to maintain her composure.

"Although your father and I knew that Finley and you were having a little difficulty adjusting to married life, this comes as quite a surprise to both of us. Right, John?"

"No, Henriette, it does not. I have been concerned about their marriage for a long time now."

"You didn't mention it," Mother countered.

"Indeed not. It was not our affair. It was something that Finley and Lorea had to work out. I know that you will agree with me that it is important for them to find happiness just as we did."

"Yes, but ..."

"But what, Henriette? They can make their own decisions. Now, let it be."

"Very well. Since I am outnumbered on this issue, I will say no more. I retire this conversation to your father and you," Mother stated sourly as she left the room.

Finally, I had shared my predicament and now it was time to move forward. Even though Father understood that divorce or separation would be horrible for the family, he was willing to endure the scandal for my happiness, if necessary. Knowing that I had his support was comforting.

However, on the way home, my mother's *come to my senses*

statement jerked back and forth in my head like a confused yo-yo. I thought about Paris. My time away had not mended the fractured marriage, only alienating both of us further. I was beginning to question the real issue causing Finley's resentment and firm stance on personal independence for me. It is hard to believe that the trip or the desire to paint occasionally would be the root of the problem. Was it unreasonable to choose my own activities for personal fulfilment? Had I not shown him that I could efficiently sustain my responsibilities and still engage in creative endeavors? Resolution to these questions remained elusive.

I thought about the voyage on the Queen Mary. Did the brief time with Perry influence my actions to the point that I am now considering separation or divorce? It would be highly presumptuous of me to even think that Perry might be having sentimental feelings about me. After all, I witnessed firsthand his love and devotion to his wife. So, this may be the one time that I agree with Finley and the use of the word 'absurd.' It was absurd to think Perry would want a different lifestyle other than the one he was currently living.

However, the idea of separation or divorce did strengthen as the day progressed. When Finley arrived home from work, determination governed my actions. I would make one last attempt at salvaging our marriage before surrendering to an alternative solution. Even though his morning departure was sour with sarcasm, I greeted him with a warm, friendly smile and the requested menu.

After dinner, I approached him. Comfortably positioned in his easy chair and sipping on a cup of freshly brewed coffee, I pulled a footstool up beside him.

"Finley, I have something of a serious nature that I would like to speak with you about."

"Of a serious nature? Let me guess. You were unable to return the purchases, and you are expecting me to change my mind. I noticed that you returned nothing. Am I right?" He arrogantly questioned.

Instead of retaliating with a combustible response, I

calmly replied.

"Finley, I will gladly return the few items that I purchased for refurbishing the back room, but if I do, can we discuss *my* expectations for living together in an amenable way to avoid the strenuous situation that we are experiencing. I think with a little compromise, we can work things out to our satisfaction. What do you think?"

"I think this childlike behavior of yours is a subtle temper tantrum because I asked you to take back the goods you purchased."

"Temper tantrum? You really think that is what this is, don't you?" I replied in disgust.

There was no response, and I just looked at him. I was hoping that he would surely realize the seriousness of the situation and be amenable to a serious discussion, but he failed to hear me, once again. Picking up the evening paper on the coffee table, he began reading, ignoring me entirely. I stared back and pursued.

"Finley, I am trying to talk to you. Do you really think that this is merely a temper tantrum?" I questioned in disbelief.

Still void of emotion or comments back to me, he sat upright in his chair reading the newspaper, never moving, never changing expressions. In frustration, I grabbed the newspaper away from him and slammed it on the footstool.

"Will you listen to me? I beg you, Finley. Talk with me."

He sat motionless, with elbows propped on the arms of the chair and his fingers folded beneath his chin. His stern eyes and posture were in perfect unison.

"Finley, please say something."

"There is nothing to say that I have not already said, Lorea. Haven't I made myself quite clear? There is nothing left to discuss."

"You have. But I disagree. There is much to discuss! We can talk with our minister and our families. I have already spoken to my parents, and with everyone's help, we can seek a reasonable resolution. If we separate or divorce, the scandal will be awful."

"Did you just say separate or divorce? Goodness! What absurd and frivolous ideas you continue to have. Rest assured, I have absolutely no intention of talking to our minister or our families. How embarrassing that would be for me! I am angry that you even mentioned this to your parents without consulting with me."

"I have tried to consult with you, Finley, but you are deaf to my cries for understanding."

Ignoring my statement, he maintained a stern deliberation. "I am a man of respectable statue in this town, and I will not even consider sharing things of a personal nature with anyone. I am the head of the household, and I have made my expectations quite clear. If you are unable to perform your wifely duties and maintain this household in an acceptable manner, then maybe we made an unwise decision to marry. However, we will just have to do the best we can to maintain dignity and position, and you can dismiss any idea of divorce or separation."

"Is that all you are concerned about, Finley? Position and dignity? You really do not care about personal happiness for either of us, do you? That is why I will not dismiss the thoughts of divorce or separation. I simply cannot go on like this. I am begging for us to make one last attempt. Are you sure that we have done everything possible to salvage our marriage?"

"Positive. We made a commitment, right or wrong, and we must prevail. No separation. No divorce."

"Very well, then. Be sure to convey that to our families which will clarify what I am about to do," I said as I stood up and moved away from the living room area.

"Clarify what?"

I turned my body towards him, heaving a deep sigh in his direction.

"I would like for you to clarify to them that you absolutely refused to try and work out things between us, thus preventing resolution. That is unacceptable."

"Work things out between us? Lorea, how many times

have I said that all you must do is perform your wifely duties, and everything will simply be fine."

"Perform? Like a trained seal, right? Same old routine. Nothing new, nothing exciting. Finley, I am unhappy, and so are you. Our marriage is stagnant, and you realize that too but are unable to admit it. Therefore, I have no choice other than to leave so both of us can move on with our lives."

Pausing briefly, he looked at me with a smirk on his face.

"Leaving me? Just like your trip to Paris, right? My, how absurd the idea is."

"Finley, absurd is your behavior and lack of compassion. I am leaving, but this time, I am not coming back. You are impossible to live with because you are so rigid, cold, and unsympathetic," I practically screamed as I snatched the newspaper and used it to slap him in the face. Even though his face was red with embarrassment, he froze.

"Finley. I am so sorry. That was uncalled for. This is exactly what we do not need. Do you understand?" I asked in desperation.

"As a matter of fact, I do. You have made it very clear that you disapprove of my expectations about marriage, no matter how much I work and provide for us," he firmly stated as he paused for a moment with a contemplative look in his eye. "Your refusal to accept your full duties as my wife has caused continuous problems, and we argue often. We live in the same house, but not together. So, I think we both now realize that we aren't going to find compatibility and have reached the conclusion that we need to do something about it. And with that said, I do have something to ask."

"And what is that?"

"When can I expect you to pack up and leave this house?"

At that moment, I knew my decision was justified, but I had one last shot to fire in retaliation.

"You can expect my departure as soon as I gather my belongings and dispose of Aunt Mary's eyesore painting just like you have our marriage."

Chapter 12

A NEW LIFE

The experience of divorcing Finley was devastating to both sides of the family, yet I knew that it was the right thing to do. He would eventually marry someone who would satisfy his preferences for the deeply rooted, domesticated style of living that he expected. It was something I genuinely wanted for him.

Temporarily relocating to a distant relative's home south of Montgomery until the divorce was finalized impeded instantaneous change. Personal contentment for me would transpire slowly even though my life was a void of agonizing conversations and a dampened lifestyle. When divorce papers were finally signed, father accompanied me to Pensacola, verbally revisiting mother's curiosity about my selection of this town to rebuild my life. Since I was not sure of my own motives, I respectfully reminded him of his trust in me, and reassured him that I would be fine.

I found a clerk's position at Rutherford's, an exclusive dress shop on Reus Street in downtown Pensacola. The income was barely adequate for simple living, but I did not care. I proudly wore my newly found sense of liberation, and that sustained me even though my internal thoughts needed repair from the despondency caused by a shredded marriage. I deserved ample time and space for reweaving my life.

I also found lodging in a boarding house close to town. Occasionally, one of the girls in the boarding house would borrow an automobile from a friend or relative that led to marvelous day trips to art galleries, museums, and historical landmarks. Swimming at Pensacola Beach was a favorite event when weather permitted. Domesticated life, Montgomery style, had truly vanished.

Thoughts of visiting Perry were threadbare as no hint of a relationship had been suggested to me during our voyage. It would be improper of me to think otherwise. However, just knowing that he was in proximity somehow bestowed a false sense of comfort that I deemed necessary for my mending. In time, depending on my personal situation, I would determine if I needed to thread the needle and reach out to him.

During the next few months, I wrote home often and traveled back by train for special occasions when I could. However, intrusive probing about my personal life from family and friends was the focus of each visit, and I began abbreviating my time there, retreating to Pensacola for refuge. No one in Pensacola inquired about my personal life as I had introduced myself as Mrs. Lorea Hughes and shared that my husband and I were no longer together. I asked for privacy regarding that, and my wishes have been respected.

The owner of the dress shop, Fred Rutherford, a middle-aged family man with five children, was a good employer. Smartly dressed, he took pride in wearing silk ties and matching pocket handkerchiefs as his clothing signatures. His jovial personality created the perfect reception for his customers, which contributed to the success of the dress shop.

Because I had worked in father's store, Mr. Rutherford valued my assessment of new merchandise and often solicited my ideas for improving the ambiance in the shop. Customers especially enjoyed browsing through fashion magazines while we created viewing racks displaying the latest apparel. Oftentimes, prominent women purchased ten to twelve outfits at a time, especially if they were going abroad or planning their wardrobe for special local events. I enjoyed *dressing them for the dance*, envisioning attending each soiree myself.

Becoming familiar with their personal style of dress amplified sales, and business continued to boom. Therefore, as a bonus, Mr. Rutherford made me the Assistant Manager, which simply meant adding bookkeeping to my job and a slight wage increase. Meticulously reviewing each account, I noticed one in the name of Eleanor Frederick. Although I had not seen her in the store, the account confirmed patronage. Was someone else buying clothing for her who was anonymous to me?

The new pay increase in my new position enabled me to move into a simply furnished apartment a few blocks from the shop. However, I continued to eat at the boarding house to save money, affording me a little extra cash for inexpensive purchases that brightened my new residence. Finally, I had a place of my own, and finally, a place to paint! I celebrated the thought, especially remembering how I relocated Aunt Mary's musty, atrocious farm scene with pigs, chickens, and goats to a prime spot in the trash can of the kitchen before I left Montgomery.

My first composition in Pensacola reflected my own style with bold colors depicting a refreshing array of flowers nestled in a ceramic vase. Surprisingly, a robust sense of retaliation flooded my frame of mind. So, when the oils dried on this first piece of art, I hung it over the apartment mantle as revenge and celebrated with a French dessert and champagne!

My days were industrious as Rutherford's continued to experience good fortune. However, talk of war in Europe echoed throughout customer traffic in local establishments. Tension was pervasive but failed to halt parties and large galas for the wealthy, for which Rutherford's accommodated all apparel needs through a sophisticated line of clothing. Accessories such as gloves, shoes, and jewelry became an important sideline for the shop, and sales continued to escalate. Mr. Rutherford predicted a forthcoming banner year.

Eventually, bookkeeping and ordering consumed a great deal of my time, reducing valuable contact with regular customers. I relished rainy days as patrons suspended shopping which meant that I could work on the books and purchase orders without feeling tugged in two directions. However, one stormy afternoon, Mr. Rutherford came into the office in the back of the store and asked me to see to the needs of a customer.

"Lorea, I need your help with something. There is a customer that I would prefer you to see. Do you mind?"

"Of course not. Right away. Any requests that I should know? Clients usually refrain from venturing out in this type of weather."

"You're right, but you will understand when you see her."

I quickly surmised that a socialite was taking advantage of an empty shop on a stormy day to enjoy exclusive attention. They could be quite persnickety, which would baffle Mr. Rutherford and cause his brow to perspire. I quickly parted the curtains that separated the office from the main part of the dress shop and proceeded towards the front. Standing by the cash register was a tall, stately woman dressed in black. Drenched from the heavy rainfall, she retrieved a floral handkerchief from her handbag and wiped her face and neck. Annoyed, she sighed and looked my way with a tilted head as I greeted her. Her face looked familiar. Had she been in the store before?

"May I help you madam?"

"Yes, you may. First, where might I hang my wet coat and hat?" she asked in an abrupt manner, with one hand on her hip.

"There is a rack right here for such occasions. I am more than happy to take care of these for you." I politely offered. "Now. Where were we? How can I be of assistance to you on this lovely day?" I joked trying to lighten up the atmosphere with a bit of humor which did not saturate her like the rain had done.

"My name is Gertrude Van Mytre, and I am the personal

assistant for Mrs. Eleanor Frederick. She is waiting over there. We would like to purchase quite a few items."

Of course, she was familiar. We had indeed met. The personal assistant for Mrs. Frederick. How could I have forgotten? I looked towards the front window of the store and saw Mrs. Frederick facing the street in her wheelchair. Startled and apprehensive at the same time, my heart experienced an uneven rhythm. Was Perry with her, too? Had he escorted her in?

Not until I realized that he was not in the shop did my motionless body move in her direction and my heart steadied to a reasonable beat. She looked the same as she did on the ship, conservatively dressed in a suit with a pearl necklace and matching earrings. They were the same ones she had worn the evening we dined. Taking off her gloves and placing them under the handle of her purse, she looked my way, expressionless.

"Mrs. Frederick? I am Lorea Hughes. Welcome back to Rutherford's."

She did not immediately respond but slowly raised her hand and greeted me in the same soft-spoken, guarded manner similar to our first meeting.

"Thank you. What did you say your name was?"

"Lorea Hughes."

"Have we met? You look familiar."

"Yes, we have. Even though I have not made your acquaintance in the shop since I have been with Rutherford's, we met on the Queen Mary some time ago. Mr. Frederick graciously invited me to join your dinner party on the first evening on board the ship. I appreciated the invitation as I was traveling alone."

"Yes, of course. I do recall the occasion. I am pleased to make your acquaintance again. You are obviously employed here and must live here as well."

"Yes, to both of those."

"I see. How interesting. I am sure that Mr. Rutherford enjoys having such a lovely clerk caring for his customers. It has been a while since my last store visit, and Mrs. Van Mytre has quite a lengthy list."

"Very well, Mrs. Frederick. I am confident that Rutherford's can accommodate your needs. Shall we proceed?"

Mr. Rutherford made coffee and for over an hour I presented dresses, shoes, hats, jewelry, and gloves. Mr. Rutherford wanted me to take the lead, but periodically engaged in cordial encounters with them to promote customer satisfaction. Even though there had been little or no conversation between the two ladies, they eventually offered me a list of items they wanted to purchase with sizes and colors specified.

"I am sure you will enjoy these dresses and accessories during the holidays, Mrs. Frederick. You have made beautiful selections. Would you like them delivered?" I politely inquired.

"No. Mrs. Van Mytre will take them now," was her emphatic reply.

The boxes and bags needed for packing were in the back of the store, and Mr. Rutherford and I hurriedly placed everything in appropriate containers as we were sure Mrs. Frederick's endurance was waning. However, as the only customer in the shop, she received immediate attention thus shortening the duration of her outing. Anticipating an empty store because of the weather, her visit was a strategic and smart move on her part. Being handicapped and willing to endure bad weather said a great deal about her true strength.

I gathered as many of the parcels as I could carry and sat them on the wooden case by the cash register where Mrs. Frederick and Mrs. Van Mytre were patiently waiting. Mr. Rutherford followed me with the remainder of the packages.

"There, Mrs. Frederick. Your purchases are ready, and we just need you to direct us to your automobile."

Before anyone could respond, the bell over the front door rang signaling someone entering the shop. Everyone turned to look.

He was as handsome and debonair as ever. My heart began

beating wildly, again. I felt certain that any moment I would faint. Swallowing heavily, I looked down and away, slightly turning my head to prevent full visibility of my face. He walked towards Mr. Rutherford and extended his hand for the traditional handshake. How was I going to manage this? Was I ready to accept disappointment or elation, depending on Perry's reaction to seeing me again? Would he even remember me?

"Mr. Rutherford, it is a pleasure to see you again," Perry said with a slight bow.

"Likewise, Mr. Frederick. And it was a pleasure, as always, to serve Mrs. Frederick. Your timing is good as purchases are complete and to Mrs. Frederick's satisfaction."

Perry immediately responded by walking over to her and placing his hand gently on her shoulder.

"Wonderful! I was afraid that my delay at the bank would hinder my promptness. Are you ready to go, my dear?"

"Yes, Perry, but you need to settle the account."

"Well, of course," he stated in a business-like manner as he turned back towards Mr. Rutherford.

I took a deep breath and decided to look up as I realized that it was going to be impossible for me to avoid contact as introductions were most likely forthcoming.

Our eyes met. Immediately, a fixed gaze appeared on his face. He was obviously stunned. Likewise, I stood frozen like I was standing chest deep in icy water. I tried to signal my facial muscles to muster up a smile, but the emotion of the moment denied mobility of any kind. Silence prevailed. Something needed to move the moment. Luckily, within seconds, Mrs. Frederick broke the sound barrier.

"Perry, do you remember Mrs. Hughes? She was on the Queen Mary with us when we came back from France."

"Why of course I remember. Lorea Hughes. How could I forget the lady that thought that the tango did not fit my image?"

His humor melted the ice-covered shield around me as we both laughed. He stepped towards me and took both of my hands and squeezed them tightly between both of his. His simple touch was warm and inviting. Feeling like everyone was reading my mind, I pulled my hands away and began straightening my hair and adjusting the scarf around my neck. Words eventually came.

"I do apologize for misjudging you, but you really didn't look like the tango type," I replied with lighthearted laughter. "It was a lovely evening which I enjoyed very much."

"It was a splendid occasion, indeed, Mrs. Hughes! I am so delighted to see you once again but surprised to see you working here at Rutherford's."

I simply stated, "It is a wonderful dress shop. I was lucky enough to find permanent employment here once I moved away from Montgomery."

With that comment, Perry nodded twice, tightened his lips together, and nervously shook off the raindrops on his hat which he had failed to do when he entered the store. His actions conveyed to me that he remembered our conversation the last night on the ship when I mentioned divorce if things did not change when I returned home. I knew he understood my message.

"Perry, please invite Mrs. Hughes to our holiday celebration to usher in the new year. I do appreciate all her time and help today. I am sure everyone will dance the tango at midnight, and I am sure you remember what a good partner she was for you."

"Wonderful idea, Eleanor. What do you say, Mrs. Hughes?"

"I haven't danced since we did on the Queen Mary."

"That makes two of us, and more reason why we should give it another go."

"Well, I certainly do appreciate the invitation, but I will be out of town as I am traveling back to Montgomery for a brief holiday visit. Plus, my hours are quite extensive at the shop, and I really do not have time to attend dinner parties."

Why were these words coming out of my mouth? It was a perfect opportunity to legitimately see Perry again. The laughter might have melted the blanket of frost around me, but my feet remained cold. Why? What was I thinking? Even though I thought that contact with Perry would not be proper, my hesitation was unexpected and baffling. Perry interrupted my thoughts.

"Nonsense! I am sure you will not be working the evening of New Year's Eve, Mrs. Hughes, which should ensure your availability to join us. It is a wonderful event with people, food, dancing, and ample champagne. If you are in Pensacola, I insist that you come."

Looking at Mr. Rutherford, Perry directed his next comment to him, continuing in his endeavor to persuade acceptance.

"Mr. Rutherford, please instruct Mrs. Hughes that her attendance is necessary to evaluate each gown's popularity as I believe that most of the seasonal apparel will have been purchased in your shop. Wouldn't that be like working and her services in the shop would not be necessary for that evening?"

"You are right, Mr. Frederick. It's a good business strategy as I am sure that many of the gowns we have sold right here at Rutherford's will debut at your gala. Shop hours would not be necessary that evening."

"Good, we have a deal then. Are you in agreement, Mrs. Hughes?" Perry persisted, and I offered my final comment.

"Very well. I will attend. I certainly cannot refuse a good business opportunity for Rutherford's."

"Wonderful!" Perry exclaimed. "Eleanor and I will add you to the guest list. I look forward to seeing you at the party. Until then ..."

With that, he bowed and smiled. A look of pleasure radiated from his eyes as he stared into mine. I got *his* message.

I had never known anyone quite like him. He was captivating, polite, and full of life. I was delighted to be able to be in his company again at the gala. What was I going to wear? I needed to look stunning.

Chapter 13

NEW YEAR'S EVE

It had taken Mr. Rutherford and I about a week to process the December sales, requiring many late nights at the store. He was superstitious about opening the first workday of the new year without closing out the old one. It was along the same line of thinking about eating black-eyed peas on New Year's Day to ensure financial gains for the coming year. However, I did not mind as he graciously afforded me the opportunity to select an evening gown and coat from the latest arrivals.

"It will be good advertisement!" He boasted for days trying to justify the extravagance of the expenditure.

I was euphoric as the only gown I owned debuted when Finley and I married and was not suitable for this occasion. Because of limited financial means that characterized most everyone's economic state in the thirties, my wardrobe mirrored a simple lifestyle. Only bare necessities were affordable, but I gladly accepted it. My new life was my new apparel, and I wore it well.

However, selecting the evening wear needed to attend the Frederick's party was important. It had to be appropriate for the occasion, and I knew what I wanted, something classy and bold. When the last December shipment came in, my gown appeared.

The black lace sleeveless design with a V-shaped, plunging neckline and a bare back, emphasized natural curves. Just below the hips, the fabric flared into billowy folds around my ankles. Small rhinestone beads enhanced the entire dress and matched the single-stone earrings and necklace that I also selected from the shop. A forest green, knee-length velvet coat hung loosely from my shoulders. My black-sequined evening bag and a pair of black satin ankle straps from past holiday seasons coordinated nicely with the newer items. A small amount of the delicate rose, lavender, and jasmine French perfume that I purchased in Paris added a delicate touch. It was daring and seductive, perfect for the tango. I was blissful.

Spending another evening with Perry and feeling his arms around me would be enchanting. At midnight, the fairy tale would end. But right now, Cinderella was going to the ball, and I was ready for my carriage.

The doorbell signaled the time for my departure. Opening the door, I was astonished to see Perry as an earlier message indicated that the family chauffeur, Mr. Stevens, would provide my transportation. I was overjoyed to see a charming prince, instead.

He looked magnificent in a tuxedo accented with white gloves and a black top hat. His masculine-scented leather and citrus cologne lured me towards him while his electrifying eyes were enticing. My cheeks glowed with excitement.

"Good evening, Lorea," he rumbled, bowing slightly and removing his hat. "You look surprised."

"Totally. I was expecting Mr. Stevens."

"I know, but I had some last minute things to take care of in town, and it seemed appropriate that I should offer you a ride, as you are my special guest this evening, aren't you?"

"I guess I am! And I must say, this is an extraordinary occasion for me. Thank you for this kind invitation."

"My pleasure. And might I compliment you on how stunning you look tonight? Simply ravishing. I hope I can concentrate on the tango when it is time," he said as he took my hand and twirled me around.

I felt gratified. Receiving compliments for being stunning as well as ravishing was precisely what I had hoped he would say. Excellent choice of words, Perry!

"Thank you. It has been a long time since I felt this alive."

"Lorea, I have thought about you often since we met. I have wondered what had happened to you. I cannot believe that you are here in Pensacola. If my suspicions are correct, you are here alone."

"Yes, Perry. I am divorced, if that is what you are wondering. The situation Finley and I were in became unbearable, and while painful and arduous, we went our separate ways."

"I am terribly sorry to hear that. I am sure it was."

"Yes, it was. The entire ordeal was hard on everyone, but I have a new life, and I am doing well. I have not shared my current marital status with anyone. I want that to remain a private matter. So, I am still using Mrs. Lorea Hughes as my official name."

"I am glad to hear that, and of course, your marital status will remain private if that is what you want. If you don't mind my asking, I would like to know what brought you to Pensacola?"

I turned and walked away. Caught off guard, I was not prepared with a suitable comment. Responding to my hesitation, he walked over to me, placing his hands directly on my shoulders, turning me around.

"Lorea, I should not have pried into your private life. Please forgive me," he pleaded as he tapped my nose with his fingers. I acquiesced with a modest smile.

"Now, please allow me to present you with this corsage. I could not resist its splendor. I hope it meets with your approval."

"The orchid is exquisite! I was not expecting ..."

"Yes, I know. I love the element of surprise," he said with conviction.

"Yes. It seems so, Mr. Frederick. Now, here. Help me pin it on? It is so delicate."

The soft white color with yellow and magenta markings in the center looked gorgeous on my gown. Lightly touching my cheek with his hand, our eyes met in an affectionate stare. Even though I could not respond to his inquiry about why I came to Pensacola, I felt like he knew exactly what was on my mind but was too much of a gentleman to pursue the conversation when I resisted.

What was I doing even thinking about all of this? Feelings of guilt began lurking beneath my primrose façade. I just could not allow further indulgence. Yet, at the same time, I craved the pleasure of his company, and I was not going to let feelings of remorse spoil the evening. I turned to pick up my evening bag and suggested that we leave for the party.

The Frederick house was only a short ride from town, and within a few minutes, we were walking up the front steps leading into a stately, two-story house of stone, marble, and granite. Perry shared that it had been in the Frederick family for decades.

Ornate iron and leaded glass doors opened into a large foyer with black and white marble floors. An enormous mahogany table with a massive floral arrangement of poinsettias and all types of greenery served as the entrance hall centerpiece. Garlands and fresh flowers adorned the iron balusters on the grand staircase.

Handing my coat to a household assistant, Perry escorted me into the living room. Candles in the windows and lights on a large Christmas tree provided subdued lighting, creating a soft, festive mood. Mrs. Frederick was sitting in her wheelchair by the fire with her hands folded in her lap holding a lace handkerchief. Wearing a simple maroon velvet gown with a black lace shawl and a corsage composed of white roses and small cherry-colored berries tied together with white satin ribbons, she extended her hand and motioned for me to take a seat on the tapestry sofa by her side. Her sincere greeting corresponded with the warmth of the room.

"How nice to see you again, Mrs. Hughes. Please make yourself comfortable. Would you like a refreshment?"

"Yes, I would! The seasonal aroma of cinnamon and apple cider is invigorating."

"It is. One always knows the holiday season has arrived when the aroma of cinnamon and apple cider fill the air.

Perry will have to assist you. I am unable to do so as I am not feeling well this evening. I do apologize."

"An apology is not necessary, Mrs. Frederick. Sometimes, holidays are strenuous. I totally understand."

The dining room was scrumptiously prepared for the party. Cooks moving back and forth created traffic jams, especially in the butler's pantry connecting the dining room to the kitchen. The entire area was a hub of activity. Final preparations of hors d'oeuvres, meats of all types, vegetable dishes, and desserts were underway. No one noticed when Perry and I entered the room. Assuming his hosting duties, he promptly poured me a glass of hot apple cider and cordially extended an invitation to tour the ground floor.

The back portion of the house consisted of a handsome mahogany-paneled library, a conservatory with a glass dome, and a large, open area where a small orchestra primed their instruments. Exquisite Victorian lamps, window candles, and tree lights created cozy ambiance in all areas. Garland adorned mantelpieces and doorways. Crystal cut-glass vases on every table overflowed with fresh flowers, and stone planters housed large palm trees. Sets of doors opened onto wide, elevated concrete porches bordered with lavish iron grill work. The magnificent view featured groomed gardens with shimmering light from lanterns and oil lamps competing with the moon. The entire estate emulated traditional elegance. Prior experiences in life could not match this experience, which added another dimension to Perry's persona.

Melodic sounds from the orchestra filled the room as guests arrived. With Mrs. Frederick by his side, Perry formed a receiving line, remaining longer than customary as guests arrived fashionably late. I thought it was insensitive because of her confinement to the wheelchair, but I guess that was accepted protocol in Pensacola high society.

Perry did not seem to mind, but by 9:30, Mrs. Frederick looked even more frail and weary. I wondered how she could continue as the hostess until after midnight. Shortly after that thought, she whispered something to Perry, and he nodded towards Mrs. Van Mytre who was standing close by. Both ladies disappeared into the elevator located beneath the grand staircase.

For hours, people mingled, enjoyed a variety of beverages, and danced to popular tunes. Guests with and without escorts generated opportunities for conversation which freed me from depending on Perry's attention.

The last names of most attendees were familiar, as I recognized customers from Rutherford's and other prominent families from the newspaper society columns. I was sure that my appearance in an expensive evening gown suggested affluent means, and I was doubly sure that it would take them the rest of the evening to figure out exactly who I was and with whom I attended. My secrecy remained a priority, though.

Had it only been a couple of years since I escaped a similar society in Montgomery? The wealth was not comparable, but the social rules for play matched, and I knew the game well. Questioning my intent once more, I contemplated the situation. Did the attraction for Perry resonate from the last evening on our voyage, or were my feelings swelling because of his charm and zest for life? All I knew right now was that I needed to be with him, even if one tango was all that was possible. As if he overheard my thoughts, he appeared by my side with a glass of champagne. I blushed for an instant imagining that he had read my mind.

"It is time for celebration, Lorea. Shall we usher in the new year?"

"Indeed Perry," raising my glass to signal agreement.

Toasts continued as guests enjoyed bubbly champagne and frolicsome laughter. I beamed.

"You seem quite amused."

There he goes again, reading my thoughts.

"I was just thinking that this is the best New Year's Eve celebration ever."

"Well, I am glad that the occasion is a source of enjoyment

for you. Spirited merriment certainly fills the air. People love to toast, which is precisely what I would like to do again. But this time, let's toast to something very special."

With that said, he intensely gazed into my eyes.

"Lorea, to voyages. May there be more," he stated as he lifted his glass to meet mine.

"Voyages?" I questioned him before I sipped.

"Yes, indeed! At sea or on land," he responded, teasing me with an affectionate smile.

"Perry, I am not sure what you are tempting me with? I don't know what I should say."

"Well, let me ask you this. Did you enjoy visiting together on the Queen Mary?"

"Certainly. The time was unforgettable. I have thought about it many times and wished for ..." I trailed off on a whisper.

"Wished for what, Lorea?" He whispered back.

"I don't know if I can answer that right now, but I will say that I like excitement in my life, and I had a wonderful time in your company on the voyage home."

"Me, too. So, I'm going to make that a yes answer." He boldly stated while lifting his glass. "Until we voyage again," he proposed as we clicked our glasses together. "Now, shall we dance?"

We circled the dance floor to an unfamiliar waltz instead of the tango. The strength of his arms enabled me to move gracefully. I wondered if there would even be a tango. This was a conservative move on his part as his conduct as a prominent citizen would be scrutinized. Eyebrows needed to remain level.

I did not know whether my head was spinning from the champagne or from the aura of being in his arms. His cologne hypnotically entangled me, as well as his breath on my cheek. This moment did not need to end.

After several dances, Perry spoke to the orchestra leader. Turning back towards me with a seductive look on his face, I knew the dance. I quickly surmised that the moves associated with the tango were socially acceptable as one's demeanor is dictated by the nature of the dance. Subsequently, we refrained from modesty as our bodies moved together in a slow, deliberate motion. His hungry eyes matched the look of passion radiating from mine. A burning sensation in my neck spread to my entire body. The moment was sexy, as we magnetized into one solitary figure. Beneath his heavy breathing, he sweetly growled, "My heart is dancing."

I barely heard the cheers and applause from onlookers toasting the performance of the last dance for the evening. Shortly afterwards, people began leaving. The household staff assisted them with their coats and hats, and Perry escorted me to the foyer where Mr. Stevens was waiting. I extended my hand, palm down, to Perry to begin my courteous exit, but he interrupted.

"Mr. Stevens, it will not be necessary for you to drive Mrs. Hughes back to her residence. Mrs. Frederick is not feeling well, and the doctor has been notified. I need to pick up medicine for her even at this late hour. Mrs. Hughes's home is on the way. I will make sure that she arrives safely."

"But Perry, if Mrs. Frederick needs medicine, you must deal with that immediately," I countered.

"I shall, but it will only take a brief moment to escort you home."

A hurried departure and speedy return to my apartment deterred any type of intimate interaction. However, once he parked the car outside of my apartment, a soft moment allowed us to privately conclude the night.

"I hope you've enjoyed the evening as much as I have, Lorea."

"You know that I have, Perry. Truthfully, it is another evening with you that I shall never forget. Being your special guest meant a great deal to me. Now, you must go. Mrs. Frederick has medical needs that need attending."

"Not before I see you to the door," was his chivalrous response.

"Very well, but you need to hurry."

Assuming a fast pace with him towards the apartment caused me to drop my door key on the front steps. Rushing to retrieve it, I fell forward. Perry grabbed me, breaking my fall as his arms clung to my body.

"For goodness sakes! I am so sorry. I guess it is champagne, or the dance, or something working on my sense of balance. How clumsy of me."

Holding me tightly, he waited for me to stabilize my footing. When I did, he continued to hold me, eventually placing his fingers under my chin and lifted my face.

"Perry, please, I must go inside."

I tried to turn away, but he continued to embrace me.

I knew that I should not let what the moment was producing happen, but the sensualness of it overruled. The softness and sweetness of the kiss was not like anything that I had ever experienced. However, I quickly pulled away, lowering my head shamefully.

"Perry, you need to go. This should not have happened. You must get back home. I insist."

"I know I do, but I promise that I will not let distance come between us again. Do you hear me? I think we both know what we are feeling. Don't you?"

"I am afraid so."

Patting my shoulders gently, he turned and walked away. I wondered when we would see each other again. Looking back at me before entering the car, his deep voice affirmed his intentions.

"Until we voyage again."

Chapter 14

A DIFFERENT DANCE

Mid-morning light awakened me on New Years' Day. It streamed through the bedroom window, pulled back the covers, and drew me out of bed. The lace at the bottom of my nylon nightgown played hide and seek with my ankles, teasing them with random wisps of cold air.

My bare feet on the cold floor protested the chill as I headed for the kitchen to make coffee. Within minutes, I was back in bed, smelling the morning wake up call. Lingering a while longer under the warmth of my flannel bedspread, I folded my hands behind my head and pondered my evening with Perry. It had been perfect in every way, but the romantic interlude was unsettling. There was an obvious attraction between us, but was it just the idea of romance that provoked the intimacy, or was there a deeper meaning? Even if the latter were true, how could we continue with such behavior? What could we hope to gain? He was married, with children, to a woman that was physically disabled. His obligations, his prominence, and my current marital status would prove unforgiving to society if a relationship between us occurred.

Even though I heard his last comment to me, another voyage was not possible. We could only sustain a platonic friendship. That was it. I had to hold firm. Therefore, maintaining an emotional distance during any future encounters in the shop with either Mrs. Frederick or Perry was essential. Nothing could be detected between us to protect his family. Also, I had my job to think about. Losing it might mean moving back to Montgomery, which I could not endure. At least that is what my sense of morality and rational thoughts dictated, but I knew what was really in my heart. I wanted to see him again.

Enough thinking. It was time to join my friends at the boarding house for New Year's Day lunch.

A fun-filled celebration with black-eyed peas, turnip greens, potato salad, cornbread, and sweet potato pie lured in everyone. It was a traditional Southern meal that everyone observed on that day, especially the black-eyed peas. The amount eaten was directly correlated with luck and prosperity for the next year. Therefore, a large bowl filled with peas and scallion onions would serve as the staple for the meal and double as the centerpiece for the table.

When I arrived, Betty, a long-standing tenant, greeted me.

"Lorea! How wonderful to see you. You certainly look fabulous, today. You are glowing."

"My, what a nice compliment, Betty. Thank you, and how wonderful you look. Is that a new suit?"

"Sure is. Like it?"

"Yes, I do. The rich shade of chocolate is striking with your honey-colored hair. Where did you buy it?"

"In a shop back home. It was my Christmas present to myself."

"Well, it is very stylish. I wish we had one or two in Rutherford's."

And how is business?"

"Mr. Rutherford has an enormous smile on his face extending from ear to ear. Does that satisfactorily answer your question?"

"You are too funny, Lorea. Now, come on back to the kitchen. Erma has finished cooking, and help is needed with serving."

The eating area was spacious enough to accommodate twenty-four people around a long, harvest table that, at one time, had been used by nuns in a monastery. The well-preserved pine planks were slick with furniture oil, enriching the deep amber color of the aged wood. Bright yellow walls and colorful botanical prints reflected boarding house friendliness. Most residents were young, single females, and gossip was rampant.

Betty was the longest running tenant and often volunteered to assist Erma, the main cook, in serving food and assisting with cleanup. Employed at the Pensacola Naval Air Station, Betty worked odd hours doing odd jobs. She was present at most meals and talked about becoming a welder since the work hours were more stable and the pay was better. Her stories about life at the Naval Air Station were quite entertaining, and she gushed when she mentioned handsome young pilots. I thought her main objective for working there was to snag a young naval officer with matrimony. I could not imagine her as a welder, although her tenacity made it believable.

Like a tiding of magpies, everyone chatted noisily about their jobs, visiting families during the holidays, and the latest news from Europe. My thoughts drifted to Perry. How was he spending New Year's Day? What sort of meal graced the Frederick table? How was Mrs. Frederick feeling? Did the medicine help? Were family activities planned, or did the Fredericks engage in a day of rest and relaxation after the big party? Was Perry thinking about me and the night before? Would he accompany Mrs. Frederick on her next visit to the dress shop?

"Did you hear that, Lorea?"

"Sorry. Hear what?"

"My goodness! We're talking about Hitler and the possibility of war, and you seem to be in a fog."

I collected my thoughts and commented to the group sitting around the table drinking coffee and eating dessert, "That does seem to be on everyone's mind for sure. I have been thinking about my aunt and cousin who live in Paris."

"Have you heard from them lately?"

"Yes, I did in early December. They sent me a beautiful, leather-bound journal as a Christmas present. They know how I love to write, and knew it would be the perfect gift, but

I haven't heard from them since then. Maybe I'll write a letter tonight after I finish a journal entry."

"You certainly lead a boring life, Lorea. I can't imagine spending New Year's Day evening writing in a journal. Where is your sense of adventure? Some of us are going to the pier tonight to see fireworks. You are welcome to join us. Surely that would add an element of excitement to your journal entry."

"Thanks for the invitation, Betty, but I think I'll take a rain check. I am feeling a little tired after last night."

"Last night? What happened last night? You didn't tell us anything about last night. Did you attend a party or something?"

"Yes, as a matter of fact, I did. You see, I don't lead such a boring life after all."

"Apparently not. Well, do tell," Betty begged as she pushed the conversation forward.

"I really don't have that much to tell other than one of the clients at the dress shop and her husband invited me to join them at their house for a New Year's Eve party."

"Was it one of the wealthy families, Lorea? You did refer to her as a *client*."

"Yes, I would say that they are a prominent family in Pensacola."

"Well, tell me. I am dying to know. What was it like? I have always heard about society parties! Who was the family? What about the food and the decorations? What did you wear?"

"My goodness, Betty, you do go on! One question at a time, please. Why don't we go into the living room to finish our coffee?"

I needed a little more privacy as I did not want to share with the entire population at the boarding house what I considered private information about me or my personal life. Everyone was so busy talking and getting extra helpings of dessert, they did not notice our departure.

"First of all, there's not really a whole lot to share."

"What do you mean nothing to share? You attend a New Year's Eve party at the home of one of Pensacola's prominent families and you say there is nothing to tell. Why are you being so secretive? Am I going to have to read the society columns to find out about the party?" she asked while belting out a sarcastic laugh.

"I am not being secretive," I fired back.

"Yes, you are. It's like you are hiding something. You are always so quiet about anything personal. Are you seeing someone special?"

"No, I'm not, and why would I be hiding anything? It was simply an invitation to a dinner and dance party from a patron."

"Did Mr. Rutherford receive an invitation?" she probed.

Of course, but he asked me to represent the shop. What does that have to do with anything anyway?"

"Nothing, I guess. But I would have thought that he would have been the one to go instead. He is the owner."

"I am the Assistant Manager, you know. I accepted, and he declined. You know, you are really making more of this than you should. I simply accepted a party invitation for dinner from this couple that I met on the Queen Mary when I came home from Paris. I had not seen them since the voyage until Mrs. Frederick came into the dress shop right before New Year's Eve."

"Mrs. Frederick! Eleanor Frederick? Do you mean *the Fredericks*? Let me get this straight. You were invited to a New Year's Eve party at the Frederick's, and you didn't say anything about it?" she questioned. "You've got to be joking me."

"Betty, I didn't know that an announcement was required prior to attendance. It all happened very quickly, and there is not a whole lot to say."

"Not a whole lot to say! Get me an invitation to a society party, and I'll have plenty to talk about."

"Yes. I am sure you would."

"Is this what you are going to write about in your journal

tonight?"

"Partly, but I have other things to record, too."

"Well, Lorea. I would say that your first entry for the new year should be a whopper. I know now why you declined my invitation to go to the fireworks display tonight. That couldn't top the celebration at Frederick's in a journal entry. Hey, how well do you know them, anyway?"

"As I said, I met them on the Queen Mary during my return trip from Paris and occasionally dined with them during voyage. Just recently, we became reacquainted when Mrs. Frederick visited the shop. Mr. Frederick was with her. That's when I received the invitation. That's it."

"I am very surprised that Mrs. Frederick invited you to dinner on the voyage. She is not a social butterfly as her condition puts a damper on things. I don't know what her exact condition is, but people say that she really doesn't care for social gatherings and only indulges because of Mr. Frederick. He is quite handsome, you know, and very much a party man. Did you know that he often takes her to Europe for the thermal baths?"

"No, I would not know things like that, Betty. Remember, I am barely an acquaintance, and I try not to pry into the personal lives of others. I try to maintain appropriate selections in the shop for all social seasons as customers do come in the shop to purchase new apparel. I am only interested from that standpoint.'

"Being prepared is one thing, Lorea, but attending a grand party is another. Obviously, she likes you."

"I hope that she does. It's good for business."

"How many Rutherford's customers were there at the party? Any new and interesting people in attendance?" she relentlessly pursued.

"I am not privileged to the guest lists for local parties, but yes, I saw familiar as well as unfamiliar faces. I enjoyed talking with a variety of people during the evening. Hopefully, Rutherford's will get some new business."

"Being the astute businessperson that you are, I am sure

Rutherford's will be a hub of activity in the days to come, especially those curiosity seekers wanting to find out more about the lovely Lorea."

"I think you should be working for the newspaper instead of the Naval Air Station. And speaking of curiosity seekers and the news, since this sensational party ushered in the new year, the society column in the morning paper will have a full account of the entire evening highlighting the food, decorations, guests, and an abundance of other juicy information. You need to get a *hot off the press* copy before anyone else at the boarding house does. You would not want to be the last one to know, would you?"

"Lorea, be nice. I am just interested, that's all. You still haven't said anything about what you wore. Surely you aren't going to avoid commenting on that!"

"Okay, but once again, there is not much to tell. Mr. Rutherford loaned me a gown and a velvet coat from the store. Good advertising, you see. Both were quite simple."

"I doubt that. I know you, and you would have wanted to look elegant. I am sure you were the belle of the ball. Was a photographer there?"

"Betty, the first newspaper delivery at the downtown newsstand is at 4:00 in the morning!"

Growing tired of the interrogation process, I extended a new year's greeting to everyone and complimented Erma on the meal. Exhaustion from her endless questioning consumed me. The brisk walk home was a well-deserved escape from Betty's intense interest in the whole thing.

Awaiting me at my door was a fresh bouquet of red roses. They were from Perry with a brief note:

> My heart dances.
> Perry

He had been thinking of me just as I had him. I closed my eyes, embraced the gorgeous bouquet, and swayed back and forth. I was glad that I was alone in my apartment with my thoughts. I wanted to relive everything. I wanted to feel the strength of his arms around me and the contour of his body as we danced together again. I wanted to feel his warm breath on my cheek. I wanted to again experience the visual passion when our eyes met at the end of the tango. My heart was also dancing.

I could not wait to write in my journal. Now, it was time to dance with the pen.

Chapter 15

POINT OF NO RETURN

Pensacola society relished newspaper accounts of their galas. Mr. Rutherford dutifully read the society columns to keep track of upcoming events that would influence customer traffic. With him flanking me on one side and Betty on the other, a steady stream of information flowed my way. Therefore, when Betty came by the shop a couple of days after our New Year's Day celebration at the boarding house, she was quick to share new gossip.

"Did you know that the Fredericks are vacationing in the Florida Keys for an extended period? It was in the newspaper."

I bounced a comment back to her, using my best poker face, "No, but I am envious. You know the weather is beautiful there, much better than Pensacola at this time of the year."

With the shrewdness only seen with seasoned gamblers, she continued playing her hand, but I was wise to the game.

"According to the gossip column, they are going to be there for an extended period. Guess Mrs. Frederick will have his undivided attention. It is my understanding that an outstanding health facility is located there. How about that?"

"If that is factual, then how wonderful for her, but I know nothing about their personal life."

"Well, I just thought you might since she is one of Rutherford's best clients."

"Speaking of clients, Betty, what do you think of the new scarves that I ordered for the shop? Are they too bold?"

"Maybe for Mrs. Frederick," Betty snorted.

In a strange way, I was glad the Fredericks were gone as their absence would reduce my anxiety about the possibility of awkward moments in the shop. However, I could not help but wonder about the purpose of the trip. Was it a ritual trip each year because of her health? I would have thought he would have mentioned it somehow before he left. Maybe that was his intent when he brought the flowers, or were they delivered by a florist? The answers really did not matter right now. Eventually, I might learn the nature of the visit, but in the meantime, what mattered was having time and distance between us to smother the embers.

During the next few weeks, I concentrated on my work, spending long hours looking through clothing catalogs, selecting fashionable clothes for the collection at Rutherford's. I was exhausted. Therefore, when Mr. Rutherford offered me a couple of days off, I seized the opportunity with gusto. Before the day ended, I purchased a train ticket and headed for Montgomery. It was a timely proposal for a much-needed vacation.

"Lorea, the news from Paris is not good," Mother shared. "Any minute, I am expecting to hear from Irenee. I have an idea she will be wanting to come to the United States. It is so unsafe in Europe."

"That is what I am hearing, too. There is genuine reason to be concerned. I am sure they are unhappy and frightened."

"Speaking of happiness. Did you know that Finley remarried?"

"No, I did not. That was quick."

"Indeed, it was. Nevertheless, he married a matronly-type young girl that he met in church. Her family is well-known for their conservative beliefs, which is a perfect match for him."

"Well, I truly hope he will be happy, Mother. Honestly."

"Oh, I think he will. The new Mrs. Hughes has settled quickly into the stoic life that Finley seems to relish, and rumor has it that children are expected soon."

"Wonderful. I am truly glad to hear that. They can put that back bedroom to acceptable and expected use." I could not resist the sarcastic comment.

As usual, Father and I ritually placed pennies on the train tracks. He was more inquisitive about my new life than Mother, but I confined conversations to the shop and boarding house friends. When I failed to add depth, inquiries continued. I reassured him that I had found the right place for me, and when the right person came along that I would jump at the chance of settling my heart. That appeased him.

The time at home was priceless. I left with a sense of resolution that I had not anticipated. Finley had made a new life for himself, thus alleviating the feelings of guilt that I carried since the divorce. Mother and Father had finally accepted my new life. I had come alive, enjoying independence and freedom. I was totally content.

I returned to the shop, rested and eager to unpack the arrivals from New York. Since Valentine's Day was approaching, I bought several stylish hats, very much like the ones featured in a French magazine published by Auclair called Marie Claire. I did not know if Pensacola society would go for the tall toque style, but it was worth a try. The hats were black and adorned with a variety of roses, violets, feathers, and rich netting, perfect for Valentine's Day.

Added to the racks were dresses in a variety of colors made of wool crepe fashioned in a smart, tailored look with predominant shoulder padding at the bodice and pleats at the skirt. It was my guess that the older women might not embrace the dresses as much as the hats since the dresses accentuated a younger figure. However, the hats would be acceptable to all, adding a more modern look even to basic attire.

It did not take long for the latest word to travel amongst social circles about new fashion at Rutherford's. Most were curiosity shoppers, spending the day in town for lack of something better to do during lifeless, winter days. However, members of the Pensacola Ladies' Club were more serious shoppers, and on several occasions, I was asked to model the hats and dresses before they considered purchasing.

Constantly redressing the mannequins for a variety of customers to promote sales became a ritual. Mr. Rutherford and I laughed at the looks on peering faces as they passed by the shop window, sometimes viewing the nude mannequins during clothing changes. Gasps and giggles could be heard from inside. What would they think about the shops around the Moulin Rouge? I howled at the thought.

The New York buying splurge was daring and expensive. The economy was improving, but most people could not afford anything other than simple wear. Therefore, when a host of patrons flooded Rutherford's the weekend before Valentine's Day wanting to buy our expensive, one-of-a kind dresses and hats, we gladly extended shop hours.

Mr. Rutherford and I knew that customers would only make purchases when society bestowed blessings, and that would require a daring patron's approval. Only members of the card-playing, tea-drinking Pensacola Ladies' Club had that power. Once endorsed, the buying frenzy would begin. The fashion domino game was amusing to watch.

Dullness set in after the Valentine's Day rush. As usual, Mr. Rutherford brought in the morning papers, plump with information about luncheons and parties. I predicted a forthcoming visit from Betty as she would try to coax me into telling her exactly what was purchased and by whom. No sooner did that thought occur than the bell on the shop's door rang.

"Mr. Rutherford, I am sure it is Betty. I've been expecting her. Tell her to join me in the back. I don't want to stop unpacking this new merchandise."

Mr. Rutherford parted the curtain that gave privacy to the back of the shop and headed towards the front. Within a few minutes, he returned with a curious look on his face.

"Mrs. Hughes, you have someone wanting to see you."

"Oh? Who is it?"

"It's Mr. Frederick."

"Mr. Frederick? Is here?" I gasped, startled.

"Yes. He is waiting at the counter and specifically asked to see you."

"Did he say what he wanted?"

"No, he just simply asked if you were in the shop and were available to see him."

"Well, I am quite busy unpacking these boxes, and I am a frightful mess."

"He's expecting you to wait on him, and he is an important customer, you know."

"Very well. Give me a couple of minutes to freshen up. Please ask him to wait for a moment if you will."

"Please hurry, Lorea."

I was trembling all over, barely able to untie my apron. This was unexpected. I thought he would be gone for a long while. Isn't that what an extended period meant? Now he shows up at the store. What should I say? What was he going to say?

I needed to regain my composure and act normally. How could I, though? Everything was not normal. This is exactly what I did not want, especially here in the shop under Mr. Rutherford's nose. I could not prolong the wait. If Perry left the shop impatiently, then Mr. Rutherford would be upset. I took a deep breath, smiled, and parted the curtain.

"Why, Mr. Frederick. How nice to see you. I hope that Mrs. Frederick and you received my thank you note."

"We did. It was forwarded to us in Key West. We have been there since the first of the year. We appreciated your thoughtful note, and we look forward to hosting another party soon. This time Mr. Rutherford, you and your wife must also attend."

"My apologies Mr. Frederick, I don't attend parties. The shop consumes my time. Plus, my wife is quite shy at big gatherings and confines her social time to doing church work and spending time with the family. I appreciate your kind invitation, but I am sure that Mrs. Hughes will be more than happy to attend on behalf of Rutherford's."

The curt response puzzled me. I wondered if Mr. Rutherford

offended Perry by suggesting me instead.

"Very well, then. Mrs. Hughes, let me take this opportunity to announce that we will be having a spring party. The gardens will be in full bloom, and Eleanor enjoys being outside during that time. Can I include your name on the guest register?"

"Well, as the Assistant Manager, I guess I am the next in line," I answered hesitantly.

"Good! Now, onto business," directing his conversation to both of us. "The real reason for my visit to the shop is to purchase one of the hats that Eleanor is talking about. Letters from home are filled with news regarding stylish new millinery that some of her acquaintances have bought at Rutherford's. You know how women do rave about new hats! I'm in town for a business meeting and I promised her that I would purchase one. She was unable to accompany me as she is undergoing some special health treatments and could not withstand the long journey. She is confident that Mrs. Hughes will be able to select just the right one."

"Oh dear, Mr. Frederick. All the hats sold in one weekend. I only purchased eight because I didn't know if our clientele would buy them. I am so sorry."

"Please. No apologies are necessary. Even though Eleanor will be disappointed, I am delighted to hear that business is good. Will you be ordering again, though?"

"Yes, indeed! I submitted a reorder yesterday."

"Wonderful. When they come in, please put one aside for Mrs. Frederick. Now, since it is noon, I would like to know if Mr. Rutherford and you would join me for lunch at Delamonte's?"

Mr. Rutherford, once again, briskly declined. "I appreciate your generous offer, but I am eating lunch at home with my wife. She will be expecting me shortly, but I am sure Mrs. Hughes would enjoy lunch at Delamonte's."

"Then I shouldn't detain you. Please give Mrs. Rutherford my warmest regards."

Turning to me, he extended a personal invitation.

"Mrs. Hughes, how about it? Will you join me for lunch?"

"No! I can't! Not today! Please, forgive me, that was so abrupt. I don't mean to sound unappreciative. Delamonte's sounds mouthwatering, but if Mr. Rutherford is leaving for lunch, I must stay here as customers are coming in that have appointments. Another time?"

Mr. Rutherford offered me a curious look. He knew that we did not have appointments that day. The moment was awkward, and I squirmed. Putting on his coat and hat, Perry smiled and nodded.

"Very well. Another time it is. Now, I must be on my way." His words and manner were formal and crisp.

Bowing slightly, he began his exit. Mr. Rutherford followed, properly opening the front door. Looking back at both of us, Perry tipped his hat saying, "Have a pleasant afternoon and evening," and was gone.

What have I done? I must be crazy! I had the endorsement of Mr. Rutherford to eat with Perry. Why did I not take advantage of the situation? Within an instant, I turned down an opportunity to visit legitimately and privately. Should I run after him? He couldn't be far. Then, what would that look like to Mr. Rutherford? This is an impossible situation.

My fortitude was building, and I was proud of myself for that, but I knew that it was not really what I wanted to do. I wanted to see him. Fighting temptation caused irritation and confusion to consume me for the rest of the afternoon. By closing time, those emotions changed to heartache and misery.

A winter rainstorm moved in by the end of the day. With only a raincoat and a flimsy umbrella, I walked home aimlessly as wind gusts tore at my clothing. I was numb from the encounter with Perry as well as from the cold. I needed to sit down and sob. All he wanted to do was to have lunch, and I behaved foolishly. I was sure that Perry thought the same, but I did exactly what I needed to do. I had to maintain a respectable distance between us. Respectability. Respectability. Always respectability. Sounds just like

Finley. Had my sense of independence and freedom already disappeared?

With tears blinding my vision, I removed my gloves and fumbled for my keys. The blowing rain prevented me from noticing the figure of a man standing under the awning in front of my apartment door. Not until I dropped my gloves on the front steps and heard a voice did I realize that someone was there.

"Pardon me, madam, I believe you have dropped your gloves. Seems like this is how we met."

"Perry! You are here." I choked on the words as a deluge of fresh tears saturated my cheek.

"I'm such a fool. I didn't want you to go, but I didn't know what else to do. We shouldn't be together, but it was terrible of me to have rejected you like that. I feel awful. I do want to see you, and the tone in your voice when you left scared me. I thought you were gone for good. I'm so sorry for how I spoke."

"There is no need for an apology, Lorea. I should be the one asking forgiveness. It was thoughtless of me to have caught you off guard as I did. I wanted to see you, too, but I was afraid to come to your apartment as I would not have a reason for being here. The only way was to come by the store to inquire about a hat and to extend an invitation to a spring party, which I only made up just to have an excuse to see you."

I leaned on his chest with my head down and my hands gripping his lapel, crying uncontrollably.

"It doesn't matter. Just hold me. I need to feel your arms around me."

"We need to get out of this storm. Let's go into your apartment where it is dry as well as private."

Once inside, he took me in his arms and held me tightly. After a moment, I pulled back and caressed his chin with my nose. I wanted him to kiss me, but his velvety voice diverted my thoughts.

"Lorea, you're soaked from head to toe and shivering. You

must get out of your wet clothes. I see a fireplace and fresh wood. I will make a fire while you change. Is there anything else I can do?"

"Get the fire going, and I'll be right back."

Quickly grabbing a towel from the hook on the back of the bathroom door, I removed my clothing, dabbed my arms and legs, and wrapped my nylon robe around me. I was anxious to get back to him, but the image in the mirror on the back of the door stalled me. Water dripping from my hair saturated my nylon robe, revealing the contour of my body. It was sensual. I had never felt such a desire.

As I entered the room, Perry stood up. His captivating eyes were intense. His hard stare stole my breath, as he spoke seductively.

"You are beautiful, and I think you're tempting me. I don't know if I can resist."

I reached for him, unbuttoning his shirt, caressing the silken hair on his chest.

"I promised myself that this absolutely would not happen, Perry. It's not right, but I want you, and I have longed for this moment."

"Me, too, Lorea ... since the Queen Mary."

* * *

The cold, crisp air slipped between our bodies as we wrapped ourselves in the folds of a blanket on the bed. The air was delicious, emulating warm flavors of chestnut against the golden-red firelight. Our innermost desires were consummated that night and sealed the bond between us. Consumed with intense love and affection, we were far beyond any point of return.

Chapter 16

RUTHERFORD'S

Perry left Pensacola early the next morning to rejoin Mrs. Frederick in Key West. I expected a shameful sense of remorse and guilt, but to my surprise, contentment surfaced.

Eager to begin the week, I quickly dressed and opened the shop earlier than usual. I wanted to get the morning tasks completed before Mr. Rutherford arrived. I had fresh ideas for the window display and was ready with a plan. Promptly at 8:00 a.m., he entered the shop.

"Good morning. My goodness, you are here early. What's on the agenda today?"

"The sunshine has energized me after the frightful storm last evening, and I wanted to get here early this morning to redress the mannequins in the window before we opened. You know, our female customers would frown on nudity. Truth be known, though, bare forms probably enliven them in some way."

He cleared his throat before his comment.

"Now, Mrs. Hughes ..."

"I know. That was a risqué comment, but I could not resist. What a scandal it would be if a society matron saw someone from the ladies' club stopping to stare at a nude mannequin!"

I could tell by the look on his face that I needed to change the subject.

"Speaking of enjoying the view, I have something I would like to discuss with you. Do you have a minute?"

"What's on your mind?"

"First, I have freshly brewed coffee. Nothing like talking business over a good cup of coffee, and I also have fresh pastry from Edgar's Bakery. I bought your favorite, cinnamon apple crisp. What do you think of the shop's window?"

"Looks okay with the new merchandise."

"Just, okay?"

"Yes, I think the display will lure in a few customers."

"A few customers? What if we could double or even triple our sales?"

"I think you have a proposal for me. Am I right?"

"Yes, I do. Let's give Rutherford's a new look."

"Tell me what is on your mind."

"First of all, the wooden platform in the shop's window needs a fresh coat of paint. Something bright and cheerful. Sheer fabric suspended from the ceiling, tied back on both sides of the window, would add a touch of elegance. A comfortable chair upholstered in a floral print would look inviting with soft light provided by a floor lamp. Positioning a mannequin in the chair reading a fashion magazine would look charming. New apparel would be both simple and sophisticated. A window sign would have the following message: *Smart Fashion for Smart Ladies.* What do you think so far?"

"Keep talking."

"Well, the shop would continue to carry an upscale line of day and evening wear but would feature a wider variety of all types of very affordable apparel and accessories. Appealing to a larger audience would significantly increase our clientele by simply adjusting the mood and adding a wider range of clothing selections. Just think about it."

Allowing time for him to absorb the entire plan, I moved over to a nearby rack of clothes, rearranging the merchandise. Eventually, he rendered his verdict.

"You may be right. Your ideas fared well in February as interest and sales increased. Plus, you do have experience with this sort of thing since your father is a retailer. How much do you think all of this will cost?"

"I can certainly check on the pricing for the window. However, it should not cost that much. We already have the mannequins, and the boarding house has a comfortable armchair in the attic that just needs recovering. There is even an old pole lamp that just needs a new shade. I am positive the manager would be willing to bargain with me to earn extra cash for the kitchen. You know, Mr. Rutherford, every woman dreams of feeling stylish even if they know that their life is quite simple. The power of appeal increases customers and sales. If you like my suggestions, I will begin inquiries today."

"You have put a lot of thought into this, and I like your ideas. However, we need to be mindful of expenditures and profit. What about the new line of clothing that you mentioned? Would we still be ordering from our regular suppliers?"

"We would still order exclusive clothing and accessories as usual, but as mentioned, we would supplement with a less expensive line for the average woman. I have already found sources for those purchases."

"I could have guessed as much. I sense a buying trip to New York, right?"

"No. I was thinking about Atlanta. We must think about the current economy and what customers want and need, old and new. With all this talk of war, people tend to move towards being more economical, even the wealthy. If we buy exclusively for our more affluent customers, business may suffer. Besides, if we buy from Atlanta, shipping costs would be lower, too."

"Mrs. Hughes, you have a wonderful sense for business opportunities."

"Likewise, Mr. Rutherford."

Within the month, I successfully transformed the physical appearance of the shop. Finding multiple bargains afforded me the luxury of adding fresh plants to the window display. Everything had been completed except for adding the broader clothing line.

Now, being savoir-faire with Rutherford's was not all that was on my mind. I remembered that Perry had mentioned going to Atlanta on business. After confirming my trip, I communicated with him to share my upcoming shopping excursion. However, mail was delivered to a local post office in Key West which meant that he might not receive my letter in time. I anxiously waited for a reply. Only days before my departure, I received a telegram:

> *Atlanta sounds wonderful. Will meet you at the train station. My heart is dancing.*
> *Perry*

As expected, the train station in Atlanta was a hub of activity. I hurriedly grabbed my belongings and disembarked, looking anxiously into the swarm of passengers for him. Dashing in and out of crowds of people who were busy greeting incoming passengers or bidding farewell to departing ones, I frantically heard a familiar voice.

"Lorea, over here!"

"Perry! I thought the train would never get here! I did not see you and was beginning to think that something had happened."

"Well, we are both finally here, so let's get going. Where to?"

During the next few days, we frequented nice shops near the hotel, concentrating on buying an array of new merchandise, especially a hat for Mrs. Frederick. Perry shared his concern for her health stating that she was extremely depressed. He was desperately trying to find help for her but to no avail. His concern was heart-warming.

Trying not to dwell on sadder things, we strolled in a nearby park each day with a warm beverage from Saxton's, a favorite amongst residents. Evenings were romantic viewing beautiful sunsets, enjoying quiet dinners with champagne, and listening to soft music for lovers. We were finally together again, and we embraced the moments and each other.

Chapter 17

A NEW LOCATION

My plan had worked. Business accelerated. Waiting customers greeted us each day eager to be the first to buy the latest fashions for parties and vacations. Expressing their approval about Rutherford's fresh look, new apparel, and reasonable prices, they engaged in a buying frenzy. We were overjoyed, even though we soon realized that we could not accommodate the vast amount of merchandise and the increase in traffic in our current space.

Unbeknownst to me, Mr. Rutherford was negotiating with a realty company about buying another store. Once he confirmed the transaction, he surprised me with a visit to the new site.

"What's this?"

"Our new store. Rutherford's now has a prime spot on the main street of town. What do you think?"

"Well, Mr. Rutherford, it's grand! But what about the cost?" I questioned with concern.

"Do not worry about that. You just concentrate on bringing in even more customers by continuing with our current business strategy. Make Atlanta shop owners envious. Think you can do that?"

"You bet! With a continued approach to marketing basic style as well as sophisticated chic at reasonable prices, we will have a steady stream of customers. Profits will continue to be good."

"Any ideas on getting the place ready? Then again, I don't know why I even asked that question," he joked.

"I always have ideas. You know that. First, women want the freedom to browse, so spaciousness is important. We have that here. Plus, they like chairs to relax in while chatting. We could easily add two more without being extravagant. Secondly, jewelry and hats need to be readily accessible. Additional glass cabinets and shelves will accomplish that. Small mirrors placed on top of the glass cases are necessary for quick and easy viewing. Dress racks and floor length mirrors should be placed near the accessories with a couple of dressing rooms close by. A large mirror with a platform for modeling clothing is necessary. It should not be in the center of the store but strategically placed in an area of prominence. What do you think, so far?"

"I'm still listening and wondering if you ever sleep."

"I love a man that listens! And yes, good sleep is a reward for hard work as well as knowing contentment. Now, black and gold awnings should be placed over the front door and store windows. Real greenery in the windows suggests beauty and freshness. Refinish the dull floors and accessorize them with distinct rugs. The walls should be clean and crisp but not white. Color through exciting apparel and accessories will enhance the ambience and stimulate the buying mood. How about it?"

"Mrs. Hughes, before you came, I was barely paying the bills, and now because of your creative ideas and business sense, look at where we are."

"Mr. Rutherford, you will never know how much that means to me. When do you anticipate opening?"

"We need to meet with painters and carpenters, order shelves and display cases, decorate the showcase windows, order the awnings and mirrors, and find rugs and furniture. We need an immediate plan of action to determine deadlines, and you are good at that."

"Well, maybe you could oversee hiring the painters and carpenters and ordering the cabinets and shelves, and I will deal with the rest. Let's get moving."

Extra working hours were necessary to maintain the

current shop while supervising the upcoming one. Days and weeks flew by. When Perry was in town, he visited as often as he could, and we enjoyed summer breezes sitting outside in the garden behind the apartment duplex. No one disturbed us nor questioned his identity. I was grateful for each moment that we spent together as work consumed most of our time.

When the new shop opened, Mr. Rutherford and I were not surprised with the steady stream of customers, but we could barely keep up with the demands of running the shop. That prompted him to hire a bookkeeper to help manage.

Mrs. Frederick began shopping more and was cordial yet distant, which characterized her demeanor. I remembered how sickly she looked at the New Year's Eve party. Sadly, nothing seemed different or improved, and she still suffered from the depression that Perry had mentioned. She often commented that shopping excursions brightened her day.

At the end of the month, Mr. Rutherford agreed to my request for some time off. I knew that Perry would be in town, and we needed time together to soothe the exhaustion from long working hours. An outing at the beach and a quiet dinner were planned. When we arrived at Pensacola Beach, he drove to a small, isolated cottage at the end of a remote beach road.

"Like it?"

"Yes. How quaint. Who owns it?"

"An older couple from North Carolina. The rental column in the newspaper indicated that it was for rent for an indefinite period."

"I see. And ..."

"And it is ours when we want to use it. Shall we go inside?"

"My. You are full of surprises, Mr. Frederick."

The simple furnishings created a quiet and cozy atmosphere. A sofa and two overstuffed chairs and an abundance of textured throw pillows in various shapes, colors, and prints provided lounging comfort. Shell collections, baskets, and throw rugs added to the quaintness.

A set of doors opened onto a small patio. Captain's chairs invited visitors to sit and enjoy the gulf breeze. Glass wind chimes tap danced in the wind. It was perfect for weekend getaways.

In no time, we changed into our swimwear and made our way through the thick, white sand to the pounding surf which was in no way louder than my heart.

"Lorea, have you ever gone swimming in the nude?"

"Well, of course not!"

"Well, no time like the present. Don't be shy. It's just the two of us with the sand dunes, seagulls, and sea oats.

"Perry, you are not really suggesting ...?"

"You will love it and will never want to buy another bathing suit again. Not to wear with me, anyway. Here, I brought a camera to take pictures."

"Now I know you are joking! Pictures in the nude, indeed!"

"Ahh. What a society matron you have become," he roared with laughter. "Heavens no! Don't you know that I am just having light-hearted fun with you? The only way we could have nude pictures would be to develop them ourselves, and that is not possible. However, as a memento, I think I will take a picture of you with nothing on but a beach towel. What do you think about that?"

"You're such a tease," I giggled back.

"Yes, and you love it whether you readily admit it or not! Now, it is time to dance with the waves. Shall we?"

Within seconds, we were running towards the water squealing with delight. The water was cool and refreshing. A large wave caught us off guard causing us to plunge downward as our feet sank in the sand. Pulling ourselves back to the water's edge, we collapsed on our backs allowing the oncoming retiring wave to swirl around us, eventually sucking on our bodies towards the gulf as the current pulled the frothy water back. Perry kissed my face as I caressed his shoulders. The moment was invigorating and sensual. At sunset, we savored a moment of love between us in the secluded mounds of the sand dunes. All was right in the world.

Chapter 18

WAR

Mr. Rutherford and I had opened the new shop in a whirlwind of energy, but the winds of war were stronger. Europeans, as well as Americans, were frightened. Daily news in the papers and on the radio broadcasted disturbing news. Mother received a telegram from Aunt Irenee and Camille announcing a trip to the United States, escaping what they considered dire events evolving in Europe. When passage over was confirmed, communication about the exact arrival date would be communicated.

Established routines were kept to maintain normalcy. Regular customers and new curiosity seekers frequented our new location, sharing the latest news from Europe instead of talking about new apparel. As usual, though, advanced planning for seasonal galas had begun, but a more somber tone characterized the mood of these events as news from abroad consumed conversations.

Soda fountains around the city were popular gathering places before and after work as people ordered coffee and pie and discussed possible dark days ahead. Time had not removed the memory of the Great War and the Great Depression from the minds of all citizens. Therefore, when I received a phone call from mother urging me in to come home for a visit, I was not surprised. Within a week, I left Pensacola.

Before leaving, Perry and I met briefly, and solemn conversation consumed our limited time. His oldest son was serving with the Navy and was training on a battleship. His youngest son had not yet decided about military commitment but had expressed a desire to join the Army Air Corp as soon as possible. Perry was worried and restless.

Before we parted company at the train station, he kissed me softly and said, "With everything that is happening, I do not know how long it will be before we see each other again and under what circumstances. Do what you must do for your family. I'll be thinking about you every day and waiting for your return. My heart dances with that thought."

"I'll be back soon. Everything will be ok, though. You'll see."

As the train stopped on the bluffs outside of Montgomery, waiting for the signal to continue onward, I remembered the last time I was sitting on the train in this exact place when I returned from Paris. My life was in a holding pattern, my future uncertain. Now, I am once again in that same pattern. However, the uncertainty of life was far greater now than before. So much was at stake, not just my future but the future of people threatened by the possibility of war. The pause in my life was quite insignificant at this point. Yet, I knew that I had dealt with one major crisis in my life, and I would survive this one, too.

Father was waiting for me as the train pulled in on Track Two. I was grateful for an inside track as harsh storm weather had set in for the day. It was not a good day for pennies.

"We are so glad that you are home, Lorea. You look so happy."

"Thank you. I am afraid that is only a surface appearance. Cheerful would not describe my mood today with all this talk about possible war."

"Yes, I know. A nervous tone is noticeable everywhere, for sure."

"I know, Father. What will become of all of this?"

"I wish I had answers. Only time will tell. Changing the subject, Lorea, I do have a surprise waiting for you at home."

"I hope it is a good one."

"You will just have to wait and see, but I think you will be pleased."

"Seems like all I do these days is wait for another moment in my life. Oh, please forgive me, Father. That sounded so selfish. Tell me, how is the store? What's the latest around town?"

During the ride home, he shared local news and talked a great deal about the mercantile business. Routines, acquaintances, and gossip remained the same. I wasn't surprised. Nothing really changes in a small town.

"Father, is that Aunt Irenee sitting with mother on the front porch?"

"Yes, it is! Aunt Irenee and Camille arrived much earlier than expected. That is why your mother called wanting you to come home without telling you why. She wanted this to be a grand surprise."

As we pulled into the driveway, Aunt Irenee spotted our approaching car and was already coming down the front steps waving her handkerchief to greet me, calling madly for Camille. Laughter and tears erupted.

"What a surprise! We were not expecting you for weeks because of the difficulty in obtaining passage. How heartwarming it is to see both of you again. You look wonderful even though things are not great abroad."

Camille confirmed my comment since Aunt Irenee was crying and beyond words.

"It was hard to leave home. I have no idea how long we will be here, but your mother has graciously offered us as much time as we need."

"Of course, she would. You are family, and your safety is extremely important to us."

For hours, we sat and conversed about everything from politics to fashion. The news they shared from abroad was alarming. Parisians did not want war, and the fear of another major conflict continued to surface. Diverting their thinking to something more pleasant was needed.

"Camille, since your mother and you might be here for a while, would you like to join me in Pensacola? It would be more enjoyable than staying in Montgomery, for sure. What do you think?"

"That is a splendid idea. Do you have room for me?"

"I have a small apartment, but I can make room. Plus, how timely would it be to take you to the dress shop. Mr. Rutherford and I would appreciate your appraisal of our clothing lines and what we have done with the new place."

Long into the evening hours, Camille and I made plans for her visit and found time to look at fashion magazines that she brought with her from Paris. With the rumble of war, designers were adjusting the mood of their collections to a more military look. This meant squared shoulders coupled with low heels emulating a style that was more functional. Casual attire was simpler with trousers and sweaters. I knew it was just a matter of time before this look appeared in the United States. Camille knew fashion and was a viable source of information.

She was astonished at the simplicity of life in Montgomery. Established rituals governed daily life from milk deliveries on Monday and Friday to front porch swinging on Sunday afternoons. Her fluency in English, coupled with a French accent, created interest from all with whom she came in contact. We visited McKinley Mercantile daily which presented a social venue for her to chat with the locals. She was quite the talk of the town, especially for bloodhounds like Mae Williford. Never had Mae visited the mercantile store so much until the word spread that a gorgeous relative of the McKinley's from France now frequented the store. Camille and I laughed about the unnecessary items she bought just to have firsthand gossip.

During the week, the trolley provided transportation into town, and we toured as much of the historic city as possible. However, the history of Montgomery could not compare with that of France. Nevertheless, Camille expressed interest in everything, particularly the store, Union Station, Capitol

Hill, and the old watering hole at Court Square. She delighted in southern food, especially dishes that were unfamiliar like cornbread, tomato pie, and turnip greens.

My time off went by quickly, and it was time to return to work. Plus, I was anxious to see Perry. With Camille joining me, visits with him would be scarce, but I knew that he would understand my invitation because of the circumstances. On Sunday, the train steamed into the station, and I began familiarizing Camille with Pensacola which differed significantly from Montgomery.

Even though the sugar white beaches and the crystal emerald waters were beautiful, and the unique architecture in the downtown area charmed her, she was not delighted with the humidity. The nylon and crepe garments she brought with her were not compatible with the intense heat, and she quickly became acquainted with cotton clothing and paper folding fans. Style was not essential as survival became her primary concern, especially learning the art of preparing iced lemon tea which added needed comfort to combat the heat. Unlike Paris, outside dining was only possible after sunset.

Camille mesmerized Mr. Rutherford. Even though I often bought magazines highlighting the latest fashions abroad, nothing was as authentic as her presence. He immediately asked for her appraisal of the shop's merchandise as well as the new décor and insisted on buying her lunch to continue their conversation. I declined the invitation to dine with them as I hoped for a private opportunity to go through my mail, knowing there would be a letter from Perry. Posting an immediate response back to him, I conveyed what had transpired in Montgomery and that Camille was with me. Our new contact point had to be Rutherford's instead of the apartment.

Perry eventually appeared at the shop. Not to be obvious with his visit, he bought a lace handkerchief for Mrs. Frederick. Only when Mr. Rutherford began showing Camille the latest arrival of new hats were Perry and I able to talk privately. Eventually, curiosity prompted introductions.

"Mr. Frederick, I would like to introduce you to my cousin, Camille Beaulieu, from France. Camille, this is Perry Frederick whose wife, Eleanor, is one of our loyal customers."

"It is indeed a pleasure to make your acquaintance, Mademoiselle Beaulieu. And might I inquire as to what brings you to the United States?"

"Thank you. I am pleased to make your acquaintance, as well. We are visiting Lorea's parents in Montgomery. Our mothers are sisters. However, our visit is not entirely social. We are concerned about the latest developments taking place abroad. We do not feel that currently it is a safe place to be."

"I agree. The news from Europe is disturbing. I am sure that you are gravely concerned, as are most Americans."

"Yes. There is so much unrest in our country right now."

"How long will you be visiting?"

"Mother would like to remain here for a while until we know more about the circumstances of what is happening back home."

"I understand. All of us would like to know more. Mademoiselle Beaulieu, might I compliment you on your eloquent English."

"Thank you. Having American relatives prompted me at an early age to learn the language. I am afraid, though, that my accent is heavy."

"I would think, charming, Mademoiselle."

"You are most kind, sir, and please call me Camille."

"Very well. My pleasure, and please indulge me by accepting an invitation to an early summer party that Mrs. Frederick and I are hosting. Lorea has already accepted. Might I take the liberty in also saying that there are many fine young men that will be attending, and I am sure that they would delight in making your acquaintance. It is not every day that one meets someone from France in Pensacola."

"Camille, Mr. Frederick and his wife are known for their parties. I have not had the pleasure of attending one, thus far. Lorea represented the shop in my place at the last gala.

It would certainly be an event that you would not want to miss."

"Thank you kindly, Mr. Rutherford. Our festive occasions are nothing compared to the French galas. Nevertheless, I promise that you will enjoy the party, even though this summer's event will not be entirely joyful for the Frederick family. Our youngest son has enlisted in the Army Air Corp and will be leaving immediately for training, and our oldest son is now on active duty at Pearl Harbor in Hawaii."

Stunned by the news, I looked away to conceal my emotion. Obviously, the decision was a recent surprise for the Fredericks, and he was only able to share it with me at this moment. I felt painfully sick inside for him. Coupled with having an invalid wife to care for, he now had to deal with both sons serving in the military in unsettling times. I wanted to hold him and reassure him that everything would be fine. Our eyes locked into a sympathetic stare. Momentarily, there was silence until Perry spoke up.

"I look forward to all of you being a part of our celebration. Eleanor sends her best regards."

With that, he left. Mr. Rutherford removed his handkerchief from his pocket and tearfully commented.

"How terribly troublesome for the Fredericks! Both sons now enlisted in the service. Let's hope that these fine young men ..."

"Don't say any more." I immediately interrupted. "I think difficult times are ahead."

The next day, Perry phoned and was desperate to see me. We agreed on a brief visit to the beach house location. I knew that I had to make it possible, but that meant I had to find entertainment for Camille. Who could I call? Betty! Of course, Betty. She would love to be involved. It might even make the society column which she would love even more.

Once I contacted her, she placed herself in the middle of things. In no time, she introduced Camille to a multitude of friends, and plans for dining and dating unfolded. Camille was blissful. On Sunday, Betty planned a visit to the Naval Air

Station in Pensacola to visit the young officers with whom she was acquainted. She would be the center of attention, especially with an enchanting French mademoiselle at her side. Camille's time away gave me the time with Perry that he requested. I was beside myself with anxiety.

Picking me up at a discreet location downtown, we drove mostly in silence to the beach house, reading each other's thoughts as we were so adept in doing. Once there, we silently embraced. Words were not necessary. We just held each other tightly as the tears came. What had always been a place for joy and passion now took on a different mood, overshadowed with sadness. As we walked together in unison on the beach, he spoke softly. "Lorea. I need you more than ever. My heart is heavy, and it is only you that can make it dance. Whatever happens, please ..."

"Say no more. This is our dance, and it is my turn to take the lead. Let's enjoy the beautiful sunset and this moment together. Shall we?"

* * *

The society columns were full of pre-gala news, reporting as much advanced information as could be obtained. Once the celebrations were over, newspapers articles would highlight the events and sales would skyrocket.

Camille's escort for the occasion was an ensign from the Naval Air Station. Both were eye-catching in their chosen attire for the evening, a vibrant red dress for her and the handsomeness of a white uniform for him. She had insisted on an escort for me, but I tactfully bowed out by convincing Mr. Rutherford to accompany me. Mrs. Frederick made a brief appearance during dinner but excused herself afterwards. Her forlorn expression reflected the mood everyone inwardly felt but disguised outwardly.

Under the circumstances, Perry and I chose not to dance. Shortly after the final toast, Mr. Rutherford and I expressed our gratitude to Perry for the invitation and departed. The next day, the society column artfully captured the Frederick gala, but with a respectfully somber tone as an uneasy tension characterized the mood.

Within weeks, Hitler invaded Poland, and the world braced for what seemed like an inevitable war. Therefore, it came as no surprise when Camille and Aunt Irenee decided not to return to France. Camille found employment in Pensacola that helped reduce the cost of their extended visit. Perry and I visited when we could, holding onto our occasional, precious time together as we went about our daily routines hoping for a resolution to the crisis in Europe.

Chapter 19

THE WAR YEARS

After Poland was invaded, England officially declared war on Germany in September 1939. Europe braced for more. Paris fell in June 1940, and an armistice agreement was signed between France and Germany, signaling France's surrender. In September 1940, German planes appeared over London, beginning the Blitz. The Second Great War had begun, and fear and shock consumed people everywhere.

Eddie's Grill, the local, downtown coffee shop where Camille worked, served as the gathering place for everyone wanting news from overseas. The dire situation in Europe and gossip from the boarding house dominated evening conversations for months after the war began. I missed being able to see Perry more than at the shop, and because of the caution we had to exercise about time together at the beach house, outings were few and far between.

Tired of thinking about the disturbing war news and not interested in boarding house gossip, I began making excuses for not joining in nightly activities there, creating distance between Camille and me. Even though she occasionally visited with me at the apartment, her visits were sporadic and rare. I was not surprised when she announced a change in her living accommodations.

"Lorea, would you be upset with me if I permanently moved to the boarding house? I do not want to seem ungrateful for your willingness to let me live with you for such a long time, but my hours at the café are demanding, and I'm in and out at odd times. So, I really need my own space. Besides, I mostly live at the boarding house now anyway."

"You do not have to justify anything to me, Camille. I certainly understand," trying to refrain from squealing with glee.

I was eager to share the news with Perry. Since Camille had joined me in Pensacola, our struggle to stay connected was complicated. For him to be able to visit the apartment again was a delicious thought! We would have to celebrate with a special meal, and of course, champagne if it was available. I immediately sent a letter to him.

Days went by without a response. There was no message at the dress shop and the society columns were void of news. I was concerned. What was going on? This was not like Perry at all. I discreetly began inquiries through all established sources.

"Mr. Rutherford, I have an idea. Since business has slowed down, what about posting an advertisement about a sale in the shop's window? Maybe that might pick things up a bit. What do you think?"

"Anything is worth a try. Are you suggesting that we place everything in the store on sale?"

"Heavens, no! Just a few items from the inventory that we know ladies like to buy, especially if they are marked down."

"Yes, I guess we could do that. I doubt we will profit very much, but the sale might provide a little lift to everyone's spirit. It's worth a try."

"Good. Then I'll see to that right away. Just out of curiosity, Mr. Rutherford, we have not heard from several regular customers for a while like Mrs. Hamilton, Mrs. Nix, Mrs. Sullivan, and Mrs. Frederick. I wonder why? I hope there's nothing more going on besides the war in Europe."

"I'm sure that is part of it. As you have mentioned, people try to be more careful with spending during times like this. Plus, we know that some of our regular customers take fall trips at this time of the year. I heard from Mrs. Rutherford that the Hamiltons and the Nixes are in the Tennessee mountains. Mrs. Sullivan is visiting her sister in San Francisco, and the Fredericks usually go to Key West. However, someone said that they received sad news about their youngest son."

"What? What news?"

"Mrs. Rutherford told me this morning that she heard at church that he was either injured or even killed in an air crash while training with the Air Corp. I don't believe that anything has been confirmed, though. I am sure we will know soon. Bad news travels fast, you know."

Perry was so proud of his gallant sons. Both had excelled in school and were prime candidates for military service. Subsequently, both sons enlisted after graduation, even though the youngest son's decision was not as immediate because of his concern for Mrs. Frederick's health. After serving, both were slated to take over the family business. If this tragedy happened, it would be devastating. I had to find out. At lunch, I raced towards the coffee shop. News traveled fast there.

"Camille, I just heard something terrible about the youngest Frederick son. Mr. Rutherford just told me that he may have been injured or died in a plane crash. Have you heard anything?"

"No, I have not heard anybody talking about that, but I will ask around. Lorea, you seem so distraught. Is anything wrong?"

"I was just thinking about the Fredericks. How horrible for them if this is true. Mrs. Frederick has not been in the shop at all lately. I was just concerned."

"Well, think about it this way, no news is good news. It might just be a rumor. You know how people exaggerate things they hear and transform any information into something else, especially in times like this."

"Let's hope so. I just pray that it is not true."

I never wanted to see Perry more than now. At the end of the day, I closed the shop and headed home, declining an invitation to join Camille and Betty at the movies. I was too worried and anxious to get home to check the mail. Surely, something from Perry had arrived. As I approached my apartment, something had arrived. Perry's car parked in front of the apartment duplex. When he saw me coming, he got out, and just stood there. I slowly walked towards him and looked into his swollen eyes. The unverified news was no longer just speculation.

"Oh, Perry. No."

"I'm afraid so. We just received confirmation. His plane stalled and crashed during a training maneuver. I don't have all the details, but we know that his body was severely burned, and he didn't make it. Why, Lorea? Why? So young, just beginning his life. He was coming home after the service to work in the business. I can barely speak, but my sorrow is nothing compared to Eleanor's. This tragic news has hurled her into a deeper depression, and she now has around-the-clock care. She is so lifeless, and I fear for her life. Can I just talk for a while?"

"Of course. For as long as you need."

"Things are so bleak now, especially after scheduling a private memorial service for him. Eleanor cannot handle anything more, and I need to be strong for her even though I'm not in the best frame of mind. I am not sure how much free time I'm going to have after the service. I cannot leave Eleanor for any length of time except to briefly deal with the company's business. It may be a while before we can see each other under the circumstances. I hope you understand."

"Of course. You need to be with her so that she can feel your love and support during this horrible time. That is all that you need to think about right now. Now go and know that I will be praying daily for you and your family."

* * *

Weeks passed by. Contact with Perry was minimal, occurring mainly through occasional letters and stops by Rutherford's to buy something for Mrs. Frederick. I always kept something special for him to purchase.

I cherished his visits as I knew it was his way of offering me some of his time while he mourned. Little did we know that even more dark days were forthcoming. On December 7, 1941, Pearl Harbor was attacked, and Perry's oldest son perished on the U.S.S. Arizona. This was the breaking point. With the loss of their last son, staying in the Pensacola house was impossible. Before leaving for Key West, Perry and I met at the pier to say goodbye.

"Lorea, you know I must leave. The grief is so much more than either Eleanor or I can endure. Once again, I am seriously concerned about her well-being, and I have got to take care of her. I hope you will understand. We are leaving tomorrow, and I don't know when I'll be back."

"Perry, I am not expecting anything from you. Your obligation is to your wife. Both of you are emotionally burdened, and leaving town might help ease the sorrow a little. Her condition is certainly something that you must totally attend to right now."

"I know. I am fearful that she might even die."

"Then you must care for her now more than ever, and you must stop thinking about me. That is not fair to anyone. In fact, under the circumstances, we should not see each other or correspond anymore."

"But Lorea, the thought of being without you is unbearable. I don't know if I can endure that on top of everything else."

"Yes, you can, and you must. Both of you have unbearable pain that starts with the accident that disabled her that you blame yourself for. It's time for healing to start. I will not complicate things and neither should you. You are a caring and thoughtful man, and you know what you must do, and I know what I must do. I mean it. You need to be beside her and do whatever is necessary and not look back. Neither of us can. This is what must be done."

My words and the look on his face felt like getting stung multiple times by a swarm of bees. Loss of breath was immediate, yet I knew that oxygen would come back by releasing him from any obligation to me. The sting was toxic, but we were alive. Their sons were not.

I kissed him tenderly and walked away. He had become such an integral part of my life, but I had to let go. My personal needs were nothing compared to theirs. I would find a new life, just like I did when I left Montgomery. However, I clung to the thought that one day, somehow, his heart would dance again.

* * *

Much of the world was at war. Factories that suffered from the Great Depression were now back in business. Nearly all manufacturing had been converted to the war effort. With the naval station at Pensacola, the town and surrounding areas became hubs of activity. Nearby Mobile, Alabama, was the fastest growing war town, and jobs were shifting as people gravitated towards new employment opportunities. Schools were learning to build airplane accessories, and women were working in jobs that had once been exclusive to males. Everyone was focused on the war effort, saving everything from bobby pins to tinfoil, and buying war bonds to help with the expense of war.

Camille and I were no exception. Quitting our jobs, we made the decision to move to Mobile in early 1942. It was our way of contributing to what all Americans felt they needed to do, and leaving town meant firm and deliberate separation from Perry.

Camille found a job at Brookley Field folding parachutes, and I worked at the dry docks inspecting screws and other equipment used in ship building. We were not the only ones working long, hard hours. An incredible number of women were employed as young men enlisted in the service by the thousands. Later we would know that the number increased into the millions. And sadly, by the end of 1942, thirty-five thousand Americans had died, with more to come.

A year and a half after moving to Mobile, my life without

Perry was more painful than I expected, and elapsed time had not healed me as I had hoped it would. What was really causing my pain? Did I subconsciously resent the attention Mrs. Frederick was getting from him even though I fully supported any effort of his to help her? Were bitter feelings resurfacing from my Montgomery life of always having to do things that I didn't want to do? Was I romanticizing companionship and deep love thinking that he couldn't possibly stay away, but he had done so, seemingly easily? Whatever the case, I had too much time to think, and irrational thoughts occurred often. One thing I did know was that I was mourning the loss of him, vacillating between acute sadness and profound loneliness.

Camille and I put in overtime when a push for extra supplies occurred. During my time off, I diverted my thoughts listening to Bing Crosby and Frank Sinatra croon soothing melodies. Movies served as another diversion, even though news reels offered frightening frontline views of the war. Good or bad, Americans wanted the news even though we knew that nothing was worse than the front row seat occupied by our soldiers.

One Friday morning, Camille went back to Pensacola to visit friends in the boarding house. I chose to remain in Mobile, expecting another quiet weekend. Shortly after her departure, a knock on the door interrupted the stillness in the apartment, and a messenger delivered a telegram. It was from Perry. I was in shock. How did he find me? The message informed me that he would be in Mobile for the weekend. Bittersweet feelings consumed me causing me to toss the telegram on top of the kitchen table. I wanted to hear from him, but now that I had, it was almost cruel after all this time. Was anger now another emotion to juggle? If I waited to see him, would I regret it? I did not want him to perceive my anger, but he would. He knew me too well. Therefore, I had to get out of town. A quick phone call to friends in Fairhope, Alabama, confirmed their availability for the weekend, and I packed and left at once.

The note I left behind informed him that I had gone away and could not see him. I painfully asked him not to try to contact me anymore because I was emotionally weak and knew that if I saw him, I would not be able to hold up. However, my refusal only served to fuel my anger towards our situation. I sobbed in despair.

I returned to Mobile early Monday morning and found a note from him in the apartment mailbox.

> *My Darling Lorea,*
>
> *You have sent me away, again, and broken my heart which used to dance. I want you to know that being apart has not helped me during this bleak and lonely time. Remembering the times when our friendship sustained me through some tough days. Had it not been for the memories...*
>
> *So, that is what brought me here. I will not give up. I will try again· I need to see you, and I know that you want to see me. Am I right?*
>
> *I love you,*
>
> *Perry*

Yes, he was right. I desperately wanted to see him. The emotional deprivation had been terrible. I was weary from loneliness and heartache. I was tired of sad heartbreaking news from abroad. I was exhausted from hard work and intense worry. Therefore, refusing to see him was not going to happen again. I would make it very clear that we needed to be with each other even if it was just to enjoy a cup of coffee.

Each weekend, I had hopes that he would be standing at my apartment door, reliving a repeat performance like the one we experienced during the rainstorm in Pensacola that day that brought our secret desires into the open. Surely, he would rescue me again. However, he did not come.

* * *

Weeks slipped by, and I heard nothing. Had he decided that he didn't want to subject himself to another refusal after all? But he did say that he was not going to give up, and I knew he wouldn't. There would be one more attempt, but when? Perry, please let me hear from you played over and over in my head like the arm of a record player stuck on a certain spot on the record.

Waiting to hear from someone you long for is agony. I could not eat nor concentrate at work. Then, as if Perry had heard my silent cries, a telegram arrived. Trembling hands and a waterfall of tears delayed reading. Clutching the paper, I grabbed a tissue and blotted my eyes, leaning my back on the rim of the sink to brace myself in case the message was not favorable. Fearful of a change in heart from him to avoid another rejection, I continued to refrain from reading it. Only after several deep breaths did I muster up the courage.

> Dear Lorea:
>
> I will be in Mobile again this Friday. If you are hurting as badly as I am then meet me at the train station at 5:30 p.m. If you choose to come, I have planned a wonderful weekend voyage for us. If you decide not to join me, I will honor your decision and promise not to bother you ever again. You know you are the only one that can make my heart dance.
>
> Perry

Sheer bliss consumed me. Of course, I would be there. I had desperately tried to do the right thing, which had only added more misery to our lives. His message conveyed that he wanted no more separations, but the choice was mine. Being apart was not the answer. Somehow, we had to make it work.

I paced the floor through the bustling crowd in the train station waiting for the 5:30 p.m. arrivals, wondering why he wanted to meet here? Visually hunting through the faces of the incoming and departing passengers, I strained for that one familiar face. Anxiously, I made my way back to the waiting room, bumping into bodies of scurrying people as I pushed forward. Stopping to adjust my jacket, I saw him coming towards me with a huge smile on his face. Briefly, we just stood there looking at each other without words.

"Mrs. Hughes, are you ready for a voyage?"

"Yes, Mr. Frederick, I am."

He walked over to me and held both of my hands.

"Lorea, I can't even begin to tell you what is in my heart."

"I tried to do the right thing, Perry."

"We both did, but it is not meant for us to be apart. Our friendship is deep, and it only intensifies the love between us. I do not know if this desire to be together again is a wise decision, but I cannot be without you in my life."

"I am here, Perry. That should say everything that I am feeling."

After a long, quiet embrace, Perry broke the silence. "Come. I have a place I want to show you. It is not the Ritz, though."

"Perry, I have absolutely no idea what you are talking about, like I care if where we are going is the Ritz. As long as we are together, it does not matter where we go," I affirmed as he led the way pointing to his car. I was thrilled that we had the luxury of private transportation.

In no time, we were in a small, quiet place called Lillian, Alabama, overlooking Perdido Bay. Perry had to park the car just beyond a grove of pine trees as the old sandy road leading to the waterfront was pitted with deep holes. Almost hanging off the side of the bluff was a rustic-looking little cottage with a screened porch on the front. The interior had an earthy hunting lodge atmosphere. The furnishings were plain and simple. Once inside, we made a fire and lit candles, creating a cozy, peaceful environment. For the weekend, we would be far away from the stresses of war.

"Well, what do you think, my love?"

"I think it's perfect, but how on earth did you find it?"

"I am in the forestry business, remember and familiar with land in and around Pensacola. I met the owner years ago when I was surveying this area. I did not know if it was still intact after so many years, but my inquiries proved otherwise. It is ours for the weekend. However, I took the liberty of buying groceries beforehand so we would have plenty to eat and drink. I hope everything meets your approval."

"You don't hear me complaining, do you?"

The crisp fall air added to the coziness of the cottage as we nestled around the fire and drank champagne. Our conversations were void of discussion about the war. Nothing but pleasure prevailed, and the mood was lithe and supple. We cherished this opportunity to be together again, having great conversations and enjoying laughter again in our lives.

Perry kissed me sweetly and held me close. The silkiness of the moment was breathtaking. His touch had never been so soft, and his seductive foreplay made my head spin. Feeling his touch again was electric as his hands gently caressed me. Satisfying suppressed desires, we enjoyed the pleasure of each other.

* * *

Our lives had been so sad since the war began. During our time at the cottage, he shared his thoughts about Mrs. Frederick and her present state of mind. He also talked a great deal about his personal feelings and how he was dealing with the loss of both sons. One good thing was that his business was booming as the government was buying tons of rosin to make explosives. He anticipated that Mrs. Frederick and he would be moving back to Pensacola within the next few months. A spirit of tentatively renewed happiness was upon us.

I had no idea how long it would be before I would see him again after we returned to Mobile. I was quick to capture memories from Lillian in my journal as I would need to relive them when life seemed empty and lonely. Journal entries reflected my thoughts about our reunion. Even though Mrs. Frederick had his name, his protective care, his devotion, and his sons, I had his heart and true companionship, and I was content.

As the old saying goes, things often get worse before they get better. This was so with the Second Great War. At one point in time, fifty million men had been drafted, and thousands were dying each day. However, during the summer of 1944, things changed. Because of the success of the Normandy invasion, most of Europe was liberated. Victory over Japan Day ended the conflict in the Pacific. Therefore, by September 1945, the Second Great War was over. The world rejoiced in massive celebrations. Everyone had longed for the days when life could return to normal, and it had finally come.

Perry and I had a joyous postwar celebration at the Lillian cottage. That was the only secluded place that was available to us. We pretended the front porch was a balcony overlooking Paris, perfect for dancing by candlelight, drinking champagne, and making love under starlight which we did well into the night.

Eventually, Camille and Aunt Irenee returned to Paris, the Fredericks returned to Pensacola, and I returned to the dress shop. It was time to rekindle my life post-war.

Chapter 20

POST-WAR SURPRISES

Optimism and energy engulfed Pensacola. Forgotten dreams and simple pleasures were reawakened, replacing the rationed, restrictive life that everyone had experienced. It was good to be home.

Food and gasoline were not the only commodities rationed during the war. Silk, used widely in the garment industry prior to the war effort, was needed to make parachutes, thus changing the fashion scene. Clothing became plain and conservative as well as long-lasting and durable. Women improvised by using flour sacks, old curtains, and similar textiles for fabric choices and altered men's suits to accommodate the feminine figure. Even the very wealthy tempered their buying as some considered self-indulgence disrespectful during the crisis. Hats, however, were not seen as an overindulgence, and women splurged with seasonal purchases to wear with basic outfits. Scarves, bandanas, and barrettes were popular selections for tying back and adorning hair.

Miraculously, Rutherford's survived shortages during the war years. The bookkeeper resigned to take a job at the Naval Air Station, relieving Mr. Rutherford of the expense of paying a salary. I had saved a little money and graciously offered to work for free until we could get the shop up and fully running again.

Restocking the store was challenging since merchandise from clothing manufacturers was scant. Simple and domestic items reflected the times. However, the garment industry quickly ignited with an explosion of unrestricted fashion.

Soft blouses resurfaced under fitted jackets that emphasized the waistline. Previously rationed nylon was now being used to make huge petticoats adding flare to mid-calf, full skirts. This latest look required more fabric, and Dior's extravagant use was bold and shocking. Another emerging fashion statement was that of the swing coat styled by Jacques Fath. The unique shape and fullness of the coat worked with the newly fashioned, fuller skirts, ideal for the postwar high pregnancy rate. Everyone was buying something, and fashion returned with a new fervor!

Assuming bookkeeping duties, I learned that several loan installments helped to support the shop during the war years. After my discovery, curiosity prompted an inquiry.

"Mr. Rutherford, I noticed several loans on the books during the last couple of years."

"Yes, I am sure you did. I thought many times that I was going to have to close, but because of the loans and not having a salary to pay to anyone but me, I am still in business. Are the books accurate?"

"I think they are, but I didn't see any payments to pay back those loans."

"No, you wouldn't have. I don't have to pay them back right now because the loans didn't come from the bank. They were personal loans from a client, and as far as paying them back, we have a plan for doing that."

"I do not understand. Who is the client?"

"I'm sure you don't, but I'm not really supposed to say anything yet. I was going to tell you when the time was right, but not now. Until I can disclose the details, you must keep this secret, or I fear that it will spoil everything."

"Spoil what?"

"Now, Mrs. Hughes. There you go again asking questions that I'm not supposed to answer."

"Okay. It is your store. I am just an employee, and I will respect your wishes and trust your judgment. But I do need to ask an important question. Are you going to be able to put me on the payroll?"

"Yes, of course. That's part of the plan" he moaned while removing his coat revealing quite a bit of perspiration on his light blue shirt. "You have been a loyal employee, even coming back here after the war and working without pay. I was not going to say anything, but I feel obligated to tell you something. So, here goes. If everything works out, I am going to sell the shop."

"Sell the shop! Why? Why would you do that?"

"Now don't go getting alarmed, Mrs. Hughes. I assure you that you will have a job. In fact, you will be the manager. That is part of the deal."

"I'm part of a deal, and you cannot say anything?"

"Please try to understand, Mrs. Hughes. The client wanted it to be a surprise."

"Well, I'm surprised, all right, but I'm a little concerned, not necessarily about my job now that you have addressed that, but I'm worried about this decision of yours to sell."

"Keeping Rutherford's open during the war years was difficult, and I am tired of the retail business. I want to retire, and I have had a very reasonable offer that I simply cannot refuse."

"But you don't need to retire. Things are going to get better. Business is increasing once again, and we are going to make huge profits. You'll see. We will be back to normal in no time."

Before he answered, he took a seat in one of the chairs and leaned forward, propping his elbows on his knees, and breathing a heavy sigh.

"Yes, exactly. That is my whole point. Things are looking good again, and that simply means long hours and limited time off. My wife and I just want to enjoy a few things before we get too old. Maybe we could spend more time visiting relatives that we haven't seen for years because I am always working. Maybe we could even afford to buy a new house big enough for our family. Maybe we could even buy a new car. We have never had a new one, you know. I would like to take a nice trip with my family to some exciting place. Imagine doing that and in a new car."

"But can't you do that and work, too?"

"No, I can't, and I don't even want to think about trying. I would like to do something less worrisome than running a dress shop. So, the time has come for me to make a change and my mind is made up."

"Well, I hope that your decision is the right one for you. I do wish you well, of course, but I'm selfishly sad because it just won't be the same here without you. Please know that I am grateful for the opportunities you have given me. My experiences at Rutherford's have proven to be valuable for me."

"That's kind of you to say, Mrs. Hughes, and I must say that I've learned a lot from you, too."

"We have been a good team, for sure. That is why I don't want you to retire just yet, but I sense your decision is final. All this is so sentimental with all that has happened, but I don't want to dwell on that. I'm too upset, right now, so I'm changing the subject a little. I have another question. Now don't roll your eyes. I just want to know if you can tell me anything at all about the new owner?"

"There you go again, asking questions that I shouldn't answer."

"I believe that you can trust me, Mr. Rutherford."

"I know I can, but I've already told you more than I should." Taking a handkerchief from his coat pocket, he wiped his brow, looking distressed. "A little more information won't hurt, I guess, but you must promise discretion in the matter."

"Of course. I promise. Who is it? My curiosity has almost broken my skin out in hives."

"Very well. I don't want that to happen. Now you promise, right?"

"Yes.Yes.Yes. Now who is it?"

"Mr. Perry Frederick," he proudly announced.

"Perry Frederick? Perry Frederick will be buying the shop?" I shrieked feeling like someone had launched me from a cannon with no landing zone in sight.

"Yes, he was the one that gave me the loans and offered to buy the shop after the war when things returned to normal. It was a gentleman's agreement, and I know that he will make good on his proposal. He was firm in his desire to buy the shop as well as his desire for the offer to remain private. We talk often, and I have reassured him that I haven't said a thing. Please, Mrs. Hughes. You must not say a word."

"My, my, Mr. Rutherford. I am just short of being completely stunned. In fact, I *am* stunned beyond words, I assure you."

Bouncing to his feet and clapping his hands together, he exclaimed, "Good! Being beyond words is exactly what I want you to be, Mrs. Hughes."

With that said, I turned and walked towards the front door contemplating the deal. Why that Perry! What is he up to now? Even as well as I know him, he continues to be full of surprises. How am I ever going to pretend to be unaware of his secret? That devil.

Private time with each other had become more complicated as the apartment that I rented was a busy complex unlike the simple duplex that I had before the war. Most of the tenants were single, but some families occupied larger units until suitable housing became affordable. A few of the females that lived in the building visited the shop and knew me. Therefore, it was too risky for Perry to visit under any circumstances. The only private location was the rustic cottage at Lillian, which travel to and from was difficult due to it being so far away. Therefore, it became necessary for me to buy a newer, more reliable automobile. Meetings, occurring at odd, unpredictable hours, would be easier without interference resulting from transportation problems.

Late one afternoon, Perry stopped by the shop and requested a private meeting with Mr. Rutherford. After a brief period, they emerged from the back office and left the shop. I knew the sale was at hand. By 5:00 p.m. Mr. Rutherford returned, and the smile on his face confirmed the deal. However, nothing was mentioned to me. After closing the shop, I headed for my car hoping to hear something from Perry. Sure enough, there was a note secured under the windshield wiper asking me to meet him on Saturday morning at an unfamiliar address. I stopped by a fire station to look at a city map and jotted down directions while wondering what this was all about. Did it have anything to do with the sale of the shop?

The location proved to be interesting. Totally secluded at the end of a narrow road, the address on a vacant house matched the fire station map. A picturesque view of the city was framed on all sides by palm trees, ferns, and tropical plants. A small pond and pool on the secluded west side of the property were shielded from direct sun rays by an iron arbor ladened with wisteria vines. It was a modest, upscale version of a shack in the Caribbean paradise.

"Perry, what is all this about?"

"You and me, of course. Like it?"

"Who wouldn't. It's simply lovely!"

"Good. When can you move in?"

I laughed. "Move in? Are you suggesting that I buy this house?"

"No, it's just for rent."

"Don't be silly! I can't even afford to rent this. I bet it would take a year's salary just to pay for one month's rent."

"Possibly. But with your new income, you will be able to afford this as well as new furnishings."

"My new income? Do you know something that I don't know?"

"Yes, my darling. You see, you are now the new manager of Rutherford's, and I am the new owner. Mr. Rutherford agreed to sell it to me as he is ready to retire. Since the shop is now making money again, I can set your income as high as I would like to compensate for any living expenses that you might incur."

"Some business deal, Mr. Perry Frederick!"

"Indeed, it is. I know that I should have asked you, but I wanted this to be a surprise! Haven't you liked my surprises in the past?"

"Well, of course I have, but nothing has been this ostentatious. This is much too much to accept."

"Tell me you are not turning down a manager's job with an increase in pay? Think of it this way. You will have an excellent job, and I will have a new, lucrative investment. I want my assets to exceed just the lumber and forestry businesses. I want to extend my endeavors to include shipping and real estate. Why not the clothing business, too? As for the house, think of it as an investment for us, more time together. No more traveling to and from this location and that, at least until the owners of this house return to Pensacola."

"And when will that be?"

"At least a year. Maybe longer. The residents moved to the Pacific Northwest for the husband to accept a temporary, higher-paying position. He was an employee of mine, and that's how I knew that the house was going to be available. For right now, he simply agreed to rent until his job is finished in Oregon. I assured him that I knew of someone that would be interested in renting and would be a responsible tenant. Does that explain things a little better?"

"Yes, it does, but this is beyond my wildest dreams. I don't know what to say."

"Say yes? Lorea, this place is ideal. It's near town and totally isolated. Look at this scenery. You can even start painting again."

"You are right, Perry. This place is perfect in every way. The setting is even better than an art studio."

"Is that a yes then?"

"I think it's a very definite yes, Mr. Perry Frederick, master of surprise."

Within two weeks, I settled into the small bungalow. Having total privacy was sheer joy. Plus, I was artistically engaged again, listening to music from the great composers, painting exotic flowers and foliage, writing, and sketching wildlife as well as ideas for evening dresses. It was a haven for creativity, expression, and love.

Ritually, we toasted prosperity and togetherness and

spent romantic evenings by the pond and pool. Delicate fragrances from the flowers, the exquisite taste of expensive champagne, and the soothing sounds of swaying palm trees awakened our senses providing natural foreplay for making love beneath the privacy of the arbor.

Chapter 21

A NEW ERA

A revival of new and returning customers emerged from a dormant war cocoon, creating a metamorphosis into a new era for Rutherford's. Patron numbers tripled the first two years after the war, and an exciting mood developed. Because of this evolution, Rutherford's was fashionably rebranded as Melange.

By 1950, the look of fashion had changed drastically as women celebrated liberation in clothing preferences. Instead of reflecting the image of their mothers, younger women vigorously demanded style, wanting their own unique, personalized flair. A desire to be grown-up and glamorous, emulating influential movie stars of the day, influenced clothing selections. It was a revolution with Dior's latest look leading the charge. Relishing this emancipation, I worked tirelessly to purchase appealing apparel.

Modeling what was in vogue, I oftentimes felt like a walking advertisement. My name was on every guest list in town, which had become a disadvantage in maintaining a sense of privacy that I had once enjoyed. I was grateful that Perry found the house as we were able to meet discreetly whenever possible without fear of exposure.

I corresponded or phoned Mother and Father often but rarely visited. When Mother announced a long, overdue family reunion, a visit home was imminent. I would be especially glad to see my brothers and their families as it had been quite a long time since we laughed about childhood memories and shared stories about our lives.

As I pulled in the driveway, Lori Kate, my niece, greeted me promptly. Born to my oldest brother, Patrick, and his wife Imogene, she was full of spunk and laughter, which permeated her surroundings with a lively ambiance. Escorting me in and thanking me for the new outfit that I sent her for her birthday, she swished around showing off the white nylon dress.

Since the house smelled like a pound cake, I surmised that Mother was baking something for the occasion. David Lee, my nephew, confirmed my suspicions when he raced through the room with chocolate all over his face and slurping his fingers. Red headed with freckles, David Lee greeted each day with an abundance of energy. Born to my youngest brother, Colin, and his wife Ruth Ann, he resembled a tumbleweed, landing anywhere a strong wind took him. It reminded me of his father as a youngster.

"Hey there!" I exclaimed. "How about a hug, please." Chocolate hugs were always welcomed.

"What's baking, Mother? Need any help?" I inquired.

"Yes. I am trying to put finishing touches on this cake and trying to make sure the Roulage makes it to the dinner table, if you know what I mean," she eyed David Lee warily.

"I do. I see you have been entertaining David Lee."

"I don't know if I would call it entertaining, but he has been a frequent visitor in the kitchen, for sure," she looked at me with raised eyebrows.

After greetings and hugs, Mother rang the dinner bell, and we took our traditional positions around the table, adorned with fresh flowers and mother's fine china and silver.

As anticipated, the usual questions about my life surfaced over and over from the entire family. Are there a lot of eligible young men in Pensacola? Are you seeing anyone special? If so, how often? I guess they thought the more they probed they would trick me into revealing something that I had not indicated before. I had become an expert at diverting conversation away from my personal life. Father's store was always an amenable topic that drew interest for everyone. I quickly sidetracked.

"My life is relatively quiet, and that is why it is so good to be home with everyone. I am delighted to be here to celebrate today."

"Lorea, we don't see you as often as we would like, and we miss you. Visits are too seldom, but I understand how hard it would be to run a business if you are out of town" Father said in a melancholy tone.

"I know, and I do miss all of you, too, and wish I could come more often. As you know, Melange is an integral part of my life. Being the manager is more than a full-time job, and the demands on my time are intense. That's why I am appreciative of occasions like this reunion to help me keep things in perspective. However, as you also know, staying busy has always been a strong trait of mine."

"I'll say!" Patrick shouted.

"Hey, let's talk about someone else besides me. Tell me about what is going on in your lives. I am sure it is much more exciting than mine," I deflected again.

Small talk continued as we consumed every morsel placed on the table. As always, Mother was a gracious hostess, and the occasion was festive and entertaining.

Late that afternoon, I found Father sitting alone on the front porch quietly savoring the day. I took advantage of this time to talk with him privately. I knew that he needed reassurance that I was doing well.

"Can I join you?"

"Most certainly. Here, sit with me on the swing."

"Father, I remember when you drove me to Pensacola and stayed with me until I found a job at Rutherford's. I never thought I would be the manager one day. Business has been good, and I must say that I don't have to worry about financial security. It is hard to believe that not too long ago, the world was at war. The economy is improving, and people seem happy once again."

"Yes. I agree with you. Things are going well at last."

"That includes me, Father. I may never marry again, but I do not want you to worry. I have found contentment in my life and enjoy the gratification that comes with that."

He turned his head towards me, and I leaned over and stroked his graying hair. No words were necessary as his warm smile showed understanding. Standing up to knock his pipe tobacco into the shrubbery, he continued with light conversation.

"Hey, speaking of things that provide enjoyment in life, I hear that deep sea fishing is exciting in Pensacola. I think it would be quite an adventure for your brothers and me. It would surely be different than fishing in backwater rivers here. Do you know where we could get a boat for the weekend?"

"No. But since Pensacola is a coastal town, I am sure that rental opportunities are available. However, I am not so sure that it would be a good idea to take a boat out by yourself in coastal waters since the gulf can get very rough at times without warning. Since your experience is limited to fishing the backwaters around Montgomery, I would think that you would want to hire someone to navigate for you."

"Nonsense. Between the three of us, we can manage. You know, we do consider ourselves experienced fishermen."

"I understand. Think about it this way, though. If you have an experienced captain who is familiar with coastal waters, that person will know where to take you to find good fishing beds. Wouldn't that be worth having a local veteran on board?"

The look on Father's face was not in agreement with my suggestion.

"I can see that you disagree with me, but please consider it. Hurricane season is upon us. Weather changes quickly. Promise me you will think about it."

"I'll think about it if that will appease you."

"It does. Now, in the meantime, I'll make the necessary inquiries about boat rental and a captain when I get home and drop you a letter. When were you thinking about coming?"

"Well, I haven't thought that far ahead. Maybe in a few weeks towards the end of the summer. Colin and Patrick can come anytime, but I need to wait until I have a little more time to spare. I am so busy at the store, right now."

"I can certainly relate to being busy with a store! In a few weeks would be good for me, too, as the fall rush won't begin until the weather cools. I do have adequate space for all of you, so please count on staying with me."

"Heavens, no! You wouldn't want stinky fishermen converging on you after a fishing trip!"

"Father, it's not like I haven't been around any stinky fishermen in my life. I can assure you that it will not be a problem. I will be more than happy to host."

"Very well. We will take you up on your offer."

My visit with my family was a joyous one. Sharing old memories and creating a new one had reconnected all of us. It had been especially rewarding for me, providing a sense of renewed stability that had been interrupted during the war.

Chapter 22

TRAGEDY

After inquiries were made at the Pensacola pier, I promptly mailed a letter to Father conveying pertinent information about boat rentals and captains for hire. Within a couple of weeks, Father, Colin, and Patrick joined me for dinner on Friday prior to their Saturday excursion.

"Welcome to my Pensacola home," I joyfully greeted them.

"My, my, Lorea. This is certainly nice. I can see your distinctive touch throughout the house. And look at your artwork. No wonder you are happy," Father commented.

"I told you, didn't I? Maybe now you will finally realize that I have all I need. Hey, let's talk about your fishing adventure. I know you are excited."

"You can say that, again," they responded in unison.

"Why don't we go outside by the pool for a cool refreshment. I have a huge pitcher of iced tea in the refrigerator."

The naturalness of the outdoor setting captured their attention as well as the seclusion of the house. I had to reassure father that the house was in a good neighborhood, and I was perfectly safe. I comforted them by sharing the fact that a neighbor at the entrance of the private road had a big German Shepherd, named Shep, who patrolled the backyard. Shep could sense anyone's presence, and furiously announced arrivals and departures each day, much to the dismay of the postal worker!

"Father, what time tomorrow have you scheduled your fishing trip?"

"We did not schedule anything. According to your information, there are plenty of boats available to rent."

"That is correct, but I thought you were going to schedule something ahead of time. And what about a captain?"

"That won't be necessary. As I have told you before, we are all experienced."

"Father, you promised."

"No, you just asked me to consider, which I did, but we have decided to go it alone."

"Do not do this, please. The weather has been unstable lately, and that affects currents. Experience with navigating rivers is one thing, but these waters are different. I have told you that."

"Lorea. We will be fine. We will either fish in the bay or right offshore in the gulf. That couldn't be any worse than battling river currents during the spring when the floods come."

"It *is* different, Father. Please try and understand. You don't live here, and you don't know how quickly the weather can change, especially during hurricane season."

"Now. Now. Now. You are talking to your old father, here. I remember one day when we were fishing on the Tallapoosa River and got turned around and ended up heading for the fall-line in Wetumpka. We had to maneuver that boat around the rocks and rapids to get back on course. We didn't bring home one bruise or scratch, only bass which was delicious that night for dinner. Tomorrow night, you can plan on the same, only it will be local fish. Just have the hush puppies, beans, and coleslaw ready with plenty of iced tea. We will clean the fish at the pier and fry them once we are home."

"I don't like it, Father. Please promise me that you will check on the weather before you cast off."

"I promise I will do that. Feel better?"

"Somewhat, but I'm still very uneasy about the whole thing."

Before sunrise, I could hear them scuffling around in the house. I had prepared tuna sandwiches, deviled eggs, and pickles for lunch. Father was going to stop and get a block of ice on the way to the boat dock for the small cooler to keep everything chilled. I arose and reminded them to check on the weather and to keep the lid on the cooler securely fastened. Anxious to get the day started, they gathered their hats, bait buckets, and the cooler and kissed me on the cheek.

After they left, I dressed for the market in town. I had to buy the cabbage to make the slaw and cornmeal for the hush puppies. To pass the time, I sketched inside because of the intense heat. Subsequently, I had not noticed the significant increase in wind velocity ripping through the palm trees. Within minutes, pots containing ferns and geraniums overturned, and metal easy chairs positioned on the south side of the pool were rocking as if occupied. Thick, dark clouds suffocated the sunlight. All indications of an incoming storm were present. This is exactly the kind of situation for which I had warned my father and brothers. Surely, they had checked the forecast prior to departure as promised or returned to shore once sinister clouds were visible. Hopefully they were fishing from the shore and not out in the bay or gulf. Since they were being so stubborn about that, I should have checked on weather conditions while in town. The only thing I could think about now was getting down to the pier and finding them.

I could not get there fast enough. By the time I arrived, the fierce storm had engulfed the city and all surrounding areas with no visible end on the horizon. It was electric and violent. For hours, I waited in the car at the pier holding onto the steering wheel and cringing with each bolt of lightning as the car rocked back and forth from powerful wind gusts. Huge waves pounded against the pier. I was terrified.

When the storm cleared, reality set in. My worst fear was sitting on top of my chest like the weight of an elephant. No one was in sight. Eventually, the attendant on duty at the bait shed returned, and I quickly made my way there.

"Sir, I need some information. Did three men come here early this morning? They were going to rent a fishing boat for the day."

"Yes, I remember them. There was an older man with two other fellows. They bought bait from me before renting a boat and heading out."

"Do you know if they returned? They might have come back when the weather looked bad and taken shelter in town somewhere."

"Nope. Boat's not back."

"Oh God. What kind of boat was it?"

"Small one. I wondered about that. Didn't seem big enough for the three of them."

"Do you know if it had life preservers?"

"Can't say for sure, but I don't recall seeing any."

Why? Why didn't they listen to me? And how could anyone be so negligent in renting a watercraft without life preservers? I needed help and quickly.

"Lady, are you ok?"

"No. I'm not. The men you saw are my father and two brothers. I am afraid something terrible has happened," I relayed as I began crying, simultaneously battling anger and fear.

"Is your phone working? I need you to contact the Coast Guard. Can you do that for me?"

Picking up the receiver and holding it to his ear, he nodded affirmatively.

While waiting for him to notify the Coast Guard, I walked to the end of the pier hoping for something and found nothing. I returned to the shed.

"I need to phone someone." My hands, however, were trembling so badly that I couldn't dial.

"Here, ma'am. Let me help you."

I gave him Perry's number with instructions to ask for Mr. Frederick. In a few seconds, he handed me the phone.

"Perry, something awful has happened. I need you to come to the downtown pier. I will explain when you get here if you can come."

"I'm on my way."

After speaking with Perry, I regained enough composure

to make a second phone call to Melange to see if my father and brothers might have taken shelter there. They had not.

By the time Perry joined me, the Coast Guard had arrived. Their brief investigation confirmed the point of departure as well as the failure to return. A search was immediately ordered which included the downtown area.

The news spread rapidly, especially through the radio. Even though the storm had disappeared, the crowds had not. Onlookers jammed the small area on the pier around the bait shed. Individuals with privately-owned boats volunteered their assistance. Between Perry and a host of locals, I was not alone in my vigil.

"Lorea, what can I do to help you?"

"I don't know. Just stay with me if you can. I know that you shouldn't be here, but I don't think I can handle bad news without you. I'm just sick inside thinking about what they may find. What will I tell the family if something tragic has happened? How do you tell them something so horrible?"

"It's hard, and they will need a great deal of comfort. Have you called them yet?"

"No. I do not want to do that until I have to."

Having Perry there in such a public atmosphere created more nervousness than I had anticipated. Guarded in my conversations with him, I tried to lower the risk of exposure. However, he remained steadfast by my side offering words of encouragement and brief hugs.

With support to the Coast Guard from the Pensacola Naval Base, a thorough coastline search followed the investigation. Initially, search results produced only an oar found floating in the water a mile offshore. Later, an overturned boat was sighted and confirmed as the one my father and brothers had rented. Authorities continued searching but ceased their efforts when bodies could not be found. An official report was filed, and my father and two brothers were presumed dead.

The news was devastating. I blamed myself for not checking the weather. Why didn't I rent a big boat and hire a captain and go with them? Why didn't I go to the dock with them and hire a guide? Or surprise them with one? Why? WHY?

The tragedy was unbearable for me, Mother, and my brothers' wives and children. It was more than any of us could endure. Therefore, it became necessary for me to spend several weeks in Montgomery helping with the memorial services and dealing with the grief that consumed us.

I also took over finding someone to run father's business as I had declined a request from mother to move back to Montgomery to be the manager. Since I felt responsible for their deaths, being back in the store permanently would be a constant reminder of the tragedy that I feel I could have prevented. Mother, subsequently, rejected an offer from me to move her to Pensacola as she believed that she would always be haunted by the place where her beloved husband and her sons had died. Therefore, a sustainable plan was needed.

I proposed frequent visits to help her with financial decisions and to support her emotionally in dealing with her grief. I also offered the same for Imogene and Ruth Ann until they could find stability. I was especially adamant about helping Lori Kate and David Lee with the healing process, and I knew that these commitments would forever be an integral part of my life.

* * *

There are usually three stages to a storm. The first whispers with a breeze, tinting the atmosphere with a faint, yellow hue creating a false sense of calmness. Then, tension builds and cracks a whip at the earth with anger and violence. When it is over, invisible arms seize the savage beast, pulling it away, and the earth settles back to normal. Life goes on, forgetting the terrible onslaught until the next one roars in and makes its presence known. Exceptions are not granted to any species, nor the time, nor the place. Survival remains constant with each one, however simple or complex. It is a natural process governed by a higher power.

Chapter 23

NEW AND OLD FACES

Driving back to Pensacola was solemn. The unexpected and tragic loss of my father and brothers severed the reconnection from the family reunion. Life would never be the same again for the McKinleys.

For weeks, multiple visits and conversations with mother regarding the fate of the store consumed our post-memorial time. Her disappointment in my not accepting responsibility for the operation of the store was difficult for her even though she understood that returning to Montgomery would not be in my best interest. She was happy that I had found a new life and supported me in my choice to remain in Pensacola.

Eventually, she agreed to move forward and offered Mr. Johnson, father's long-time assistant, the opportunity to buy the store with a certain percentage of the profits going to her each month until her death. This would provide the financial stability she needed and relieve her of any responsibilities related to owning a business. The decision was the best solution for everyone.

Ruth Ann decided to move back to Louisiana to be close to her mother's side of the family and promised to visit in the summer and during the holidays each year. Her sincere intentions were appreciated yet I knew that being that far away, she would falter on her promise, and seeing David Lee on a regular basis would be difficult.

Imogene decided to remain in Montgomery. Her family lived in Greenville, Alabama, but job opportunities there were limited.

Refusing an opportunity to work for Mr. Johnson as the general manager at McKinley's had surprised us, especially when she announced her intentions to follow in my footsteps and open a dress shop somewhere in downtown Montgomery. I offered encouragement and advice and expressed my appreciation to her for remaining in Montgomery as that would be a source of comfort for Mother. Lori Kate would not be that far away, which would enable them to see each other frequently.

After months of settling multiple issues back home, I eventually gained more time to devote to my life in Pensacola. Perry visited regularly as my sadness and grief had unfortunately rekindled his own personal pain. We often cried and sometimes just sat beside each other in silence. Trying to restore normalcy in our lives was not easy, and I realized that daily life would not get better until I returned to work fulltime.

"Perry, I have severely neglected the dress shop. Even though I am still shattered from everything that has happened, it is time to return to work and get ready for the holiday season. I am indebted to you for hiring Mrs. Narramore to fill in for me during my absence. She is obviously a person that knows how to juggle many things at the same time. I could not have gotten through this without you or her."

"You do not have to thank me. I was glad that I could be of assistance even though what I was able to do seemed quite superficial."

"It was not superficial, Perry. I always knew that you were with me, and that sustained me. I will always be grateful to you for your undying kindness, friendship, and love," I replied as I kissed him sweetly.

"Lorea, you always know how to make my heart dance," he said softly as his fingers traced the outline of my face.

"Speaking of dancing, ideas about the store are doing a tango in my head."

"What's on your mind?"

"I think the holiday season and the coming year could be

the most profitable ever, but I am going to need help. Would it be possible to hire Mrs. Narramore permanently as the bookkeeper? She could also help with customers' needs when the seasonal rush begins. I also need an additional, full-time clerk. I need new window displays immediately, and lots of new and exciting apparel with matching accessories need to be ordered, catalogued, and displayed. What do you think?"

"Welcome back, Lorea. And yes, Mrs. Narramore would be an excellent choice for the bookkeeper. She is quite capable, very trustworthy, and did an excellent job handling everything in your absence. For an additional clerk, you might consider hiring someone much younger to appeal to the newest clientele. Would be a strategic, smart move."

"Mr. Frederick, I like the way you think. I will begin tomorrow with an advertisement in the paper for the clerk's position and offer Mrs. Narramore the bookkeeping job."

"Lorea, there's something else that I would like for you to do."

"And that is?"

"I want you to revitalize your love for painting and sketching. I know that you have created a few pieces of art since you have been in the house, but I have taken the liberty of purchasing several canvases and sketch pads for you. Why not create new pieces and place them in the dress shop? Paint beautiful flowers or sketch fashionable apparel that appeal to women. Showcase your talent with *Originals by Lorea*. It would add another dimension to Melange. What do you think?"

"What heartfelt ideas, Perry. It is exactly what I need as well as the shop."

"I was hoping that you would agree. And if you get an offer from a client to purchase one of your paintings, set your price high."

"If I know you, Mr. Perry Frederick, you will secretly purchase all of them just to make me happy."

"And what would be wrong with that?"

"Nothing. But you have already done so much. You cannot

continue doing so or you will just spoil me terribly."

"The pleasure is all mine, my love!"

At the beginning of the week, Mrs. Naramore accepted the job, and we opened the shop with zest, with me at the helm. I advertised for another clerk in the local paper, and we frantically placed orders for a new line of merchandise as there was simply not enough time to journey to Atlanta on a buying trip. New window displays were created, and existing merchandise was rearranged. It was non-stop at Melange! I was so energized that oftentimes I neglected to eat as we worked straight through until late in the evening. Being busy also helped keep my mind off of the recent tragedies.

During the next few weeks, I found Ethelene to be exactly what Perry had specified. She fit right in and was quite capable of overseeing any assigned tasks. She was mature, divorced, and in dire need of steady employment. Being a little on the conservative side with her dress, older clients trusted her with appraisals of their proposed purchases if they wanted a more traditional look.

As an additional clerk, I hired a young, single girl by the name of Frances Miller, called Francie. She reminded me a great deal of Betty at the boarding house, full of laughter and inquisitiveness. Her wavy blonde hair, worn in a much shorter style than young girls in the 40's, and big blue eyes created a "flirty" look. She interviewed in a pale blue blouse, a tight-fitting brown jacket and full skirt with shoes to match. A smart looking, dark brown hat made of felt, adorned with feathers and netting accessorized the outfit. She carried a silk scarf in her hand with vivid colors of blue, pink, and aqua which did not fully complement her outfit, but it indicated a desire for flare which I liked. I was sure that it cost every penny she had to be impressive for obtaining a position at Melange. She had gone to a great deal of expense, and I was impressed. Once she met Betty, Francie would know everyone in town and know everything about them. The gift of gab would prevail.

With the holiday season upon us, we prepared for

the onset. Francie was in her element, relishing every opportunity to model new and exciting evening and day wear, talking incessantly with customers. My intuition had served me well as she conversed with most of our young to middle-aged clients with tremendous skill. Oftentimes, she could coax them into buying twice as much as they intended by bestowing compliments on them even if the color or style was not totally suited for their figure or coloring. Even some of the older, more daring clients succumbed to her persuasion. She was a true salesperson and was worth her weight in gold!

Late one afternoon, right before the big December galas, an all too familiar client came into the store. Francie quickly embarked on a mission. However, this client required something much more conservative. Someone with more experience was necessary. It was Mrs. Frederick, accompanied by Mrs. Van Mytre. I was shocked that she had ventured out in the unusually cold weather, but with the holiday season approaching, she obviously wanted to shop. Even though we still carried a line of clothing for the older clients, it was always challenging to find just the right clothes for her.

"Francie, I'll handle this one."

Directing my attention to Mrs. Frederick, I extended a cordial greeting.

"Good afternoon, Mrs. Frederick. It is a pleasure to see you again. It has been a while."

"Yes. It has been a long time, Mrs. Hughes. It is still Mrs. Hughes, isn't it?"

"Yes, it is, Mrs. Frederick, and you are looking well," I replied trying to offer some type of compliment to divert her away from personal inquiries about me.

"I am feeling somewhat better these days. Shopping excursions help, you know. And you are doing well, Mrs. Hughes?"

"I can't complain, Mrs. Frederick. The store keeps me totally occupied and on the go."

"A young lady like yourself with good looks and a fine figure needs to attend more parties instead of dressing your clients for them."

"I hardly have the time, Mrs. Frederick, but thank you for your compliments. How can I be of assistance to you today?"

"Mrs. Van Mytre has a list of items that I would like to purchase. While I am here, though, I would like to try on new hats. I am told that you have quite a selection. The ones I have are old and tired, much like me. I need to replace them with the latest colors and styles. I would also like something from your new line of clothing, especially to wear to church this Sunday. I very rarely leave home these days, but I would like to attend some of the special holiday church services."

"Indeed, Mrs. Frederick. We will be more than happy to show you what we have. I am sure that we can find something quite suitable for you. This is Ethelene Narramore. She has been working in the shop for a while. I am not sure if you have met her. She is the new bookkeeper and assistant clerk."

"Since I have not shopped personally in quite some time, I am sure you assisted Mrs. VanMytre," who confirmed with a nod. "Nevertheless, it is nice to meet you, Mrs. Narramore. It is *Mrs.* Narramore, I assume?"

"Yes, and it is my pleasure to serve you."

"I must say, Mrs. Hughes, I was distressed when Mr. Rutherford retired. He was such a nice and polite gentleman, so attentive to his customers."

"He was indeed. I regretted his decision to retire too, but I understand that the family is traveling and enjoying life."

"That's what I hear. And did you purchase the shop from him, Mrs. Hughes?"

I avoided the subject with a quick comment.

"Please excuse my impoliteness. I failed to introduce you to Francie Miller. She is a new clerk in the store."

"Is she the young girl over there?"

"Yes. Francie, could you join us for a minute? Mrs. Frederick, this is Frances Miller. She prefers to be called Francie."

"I see. Pleased to make your acquaintance, Francie. Is it

Miss or Mrs. Miller?"

"I am single, so it's Miss. It is a pleasure to meet you. May I show you some of our new clothing? I know of several things that you might love to take home with you."

"Thank you, Francie, but Mrs. Narramore and I are already assisting Mrs. Frederick."

"Business appears to be good, Mrs. Hughes. The new owner must be pleased, wouldn't you say? And just whom did you mention as the new owner?"

Completely avoiding the subject again, I attempted diversion once more.

"You're right! Business has been very good, Mrs. Frederick. Speaking of business, are you hosting a holiday gala this season?"

"Possibly. It will not be as elaborate as in the past. Only a few very *close* friends are invited. Why do you ask? Were you expecting an invitation as well as an opportunity to tango with Mr. Frederick?"

I gasped at her sharp suggestion as everyone else stood frozen waiting for my reply.

"Why, no. I was not suggesting that at all."

Staring at me with sarcasm in her eyes and voice, she shuffled a laugh towards me.

"Of course not, Mrs. Hughes, of course not. I merely was trying to make it a point to tell you that large socials that we have hosted before are not possible now. We do not engage in large gatherings anymore since the death of our sons."

Still stunned from her direct approach, I smoothed my dress in the front and regained my composure with an apologetic response.

"I totally understand and hope I have not offended you. I was merely trying to make conversation. I apologize for my insensitivity."

"No apologies necessary. Now, do you have plans for the holidays? With anybody special? I am sure that it would be someone that dances, especially the tango. Am I right?"

"Actually, I do have plans. I will be going home to see

Mother."

"Mothers don't tango, Mrs. Hughes!" she stabbed as she belted out a laugh.

"Don't be too sure, Mrs. Frederick. My mother is French and loves a good party with dancing."

"Well, well. French did you say? Then you should have no difficulty in finding a suitable dancing partner well versed in the style and flavor of any dance. French people are such seductive romantics. Am I correct?"

Avoiding another jab, I laughed out loud and claimed a novice posture.

"I don't know about that, but I do know that I would be as rusty as an old nail dancing the tango again."

"Dancing is something that one never forgets, especially if the partner is good. Isn't that right, my dear?"

"I suppose so. However, I mostly enjoy dancing with a pen and a brush."

"A pen and a brush? I am not quite sure I understand, Mrs. Hughes."

"I write and paint as often as possible. They serve as a form of self-expression and attainment of special skills just as one finds when dancing the tango."

"I see. But those means of artistic expression couldn't possibly be as exciting, right?"

"Artistic beauty means different things to different people. Now, I believe that Mrs. Narramore has your order prepared. I will be more than happy to assist Mrs. Van Mytre in getting the parcels to your car. You have made some wonderful selections. I am sure that everyone in church will be envious!"

"Envy is a sin, Mrs. Hughes, just like other things. I do not wish to be a sinful person."

"Of course not. Will there be anything else for you today?"

"No, nothing else at this time. The day has proven to be an interesting one, indeed."

"Very well. It has been our pleasure to serve you. We look forward to seeing you again soon," I replied as we moved towards the front door of the shop.

After she left, I began thinking. Either her comments were totally innocent, just exaggerated in my mind by guilt, or either she was as shrewd and astute as a private detective. Either way, it was most uncomfortable. I would have to share this with Perry as soon as possible.

"Begging your pardon, Mrs. Hughes, but that was one snooty and difficult lady," Francie appraised, placing her hand on her hip.

"Now, Francie, be kind. Mrs. Frederick has been ill for quite some time, now. Not only is she in poor physical health, but she also lost her two sons during the war. I am sure that she means well. She has always been a loyal customer."

"Loyal customer or not, she sure leaves a bitter taste in one's mouth. Pardon me for saying so, but if I didn't know any better, I would think that she just came in to be nosy and rude. She's the type that likes to gossip and stir up trouble. I am glad you waited on her and not me. What do you think, Mrs. Narramore?"

"I would have to agree, Francie. And that Mrs. Van Mytre! They are both well suited for each other. But I must say, Lorea, you did an excellent job in derailing her apparent inquisitiveness about matters of which are no concern of hers."

"I'm not so sure that I did handle the situation that well, Ethelene. But there is one thing I know for certain."

"And what is that, Mrs. Hughes?"

"She'll be back."

I immediately contacted Perry to tell him what happened, and we made plans for dinner the next week as he was out of town on business. In the meantime, I would keep busy in the shop and not think about what just occurred. However, her visit continued to plague me. I could not shake it off.

Prior to her visit, weeks of hard work and late nights had fatigued me more than I realized. Since my appetite had decreased and healthy eating had become null and void, my physical health was depleted. The incident at the shop only compounded the current state of my well-being. The day after her visit, I became nauseous and weak and fainted.

When I woke up in the hospital, Ethelene was sitting by the bed. She explained that I had collapsed and was rushed to the hospital. A visit from the attending physician confirmed that I was severely malnourished and physically depleted. After blood tests, multiple examinations, and private consultations, the attending doctor ordered indefinite bedrest, possibly as long as six months with no work allowed or visitors permitted due to my physical and emotional state. A private nurse was consigned to attend to my needs.

Chapter 24

LILLIAN

As predicted, Mrs. Frederick did return to the shop and quite often while I was convalescing. Ethelene and Francie sent messages that she became more inquisitive with each visit regarding my whereabouts. Perry eventually shared something that he had been hiding from me. Mrs. Frederick had witnessed the whole ordeal at the pier, and our demeanor towards each other created suspicion. He had learned that when the storm engulfed the city, she was shopping at Melange with Mrs.Van Mytre and remained there until it was over. During that time, I called the store searching for my father and brothers. Ethelene shared the news with them, and on the way home they stopped by the pier. Unbeknownst to us, she watched everything from a distance.

Eventually confronting Perry, he explained that he had heard about the missing fishermen and drove to the pier to see if he could help with rescue efforts. He doubted that she believed him, but she never pursued the situation further.

Therefore, when I returned to work after being gone for several months, I spent most of my time in the back of the shop attending to incoming merchandise and updating inventories. I avoided social events, being conveniently out of town or committed to prior engagements. I commissioned Francie to fill in for me at said parties, which thrilled her as it created opportunities to rub elbows with many of the town's elite and catch up on local gossip. She delighted in being able to select apparel from the latest merchandise in the store. This was a good business move as she truly brought in increased business from the younger clientele.

Late one Saturday afternoon, right before the shop closed, Perry phoned. He wanted me to meet him at the old unfinished hotel at Perdido Beach where we picnicked often because it was secluded and quiet. Construction began in the 20's and was halted with the onset of the Depression, and construction never resumed. After years of sitting silently, the old structure represented economic devastation. What was proposed to be the grand hotel on the Florida panhandle was changed by fate, like so many things in life.

When I arrived, he quickly escorted me to his car and headed towards Lillian.

"Ok. Something is up. What do you have up your sleeve, Mr. Frederick?"

"Your questions will be answered very soon, my dear."

Within 30 minutes, we crossed the bay bridge and turned down the scenic road that would carry us to the cottage. Memories returned about the first time we were there in the small rustic cottage on the bluffs after we had been apart for so long. The second occasion was the post-war celebration with just the two of us. The vivid memory of both remained steadfast in my mind as they were major turning points in our relationship.

Now, we were returning, again. I contemplated the purpose of this visit. Parking the car beyond the grove of old pine trees on the sandy road as usual, we walked the remaining distance to the cottage carrying our picnic basket and blankets. The smell of the pine trees and blooming magnolias, combined with the beauty of the landscape, created a unique welcoming atmosphere. The location was one of the most beautiful settings in the area.

"I was not expecting this since you mentioned the beach. This place brings back wonderful memories. We certainly have had enough sad ones. Promise me, Perry, that we will preserve the good ones."

"That's why we are here. We are going to keep the good ones and make new ones. Welcome to Escondido Cottage."

"Escondido Cottage? That's Spanish isn't it?"

"Yes, it means 'hidden'." It is perfect for us, and I want you to live here. I hope you will say yes. Please."

"You want me to live here? Who owns it?"

"Well, let's just say that the owner wishes to remain anonymous. However, I have exclusive rights to live here and renovate it. If you like it, you might want to even live here year-round and open an art studio. Either way, this will be our place. No more beach house rentals, no more hiding in secluded spots away from Pensacola just to have a picnic, and no more confrontations with Eleanor. What do you think?"

"Perry, I am at a loss for words. You never cease to amaze me. This tops anything you have ever done. What can I say?"

"You can say yes! How about it?"

"Well, it's not really livable."

"Yes, I know, but I'm going to take care of that. It needs new plumbing, new wiring, a new roof, lots of paint, and steps leading down to the water to get to a boat dock, just for starters."

"Steps? Boat dock?"

"Yes, my love. I am going to build steps going down the bluff so that we will have easy access to the boat."

"What boat?"

"A boat called the Rendezvous."

"You are going to buy a boat called the Rendezvous."

"Not going to. I already have."

He ecstatically explained that he had purchased a boat that was anchored at a nearby location. When he visited, he would come by boat providing the secrecy and privacy that we needed. He was giddy with excitement. I had not ever seen him this happy.

"Well, Mr. Frederick. You really outdid yourself this time. What if I say no?"

"Then I guess I'm stuck with a cottage that needs repairs that comes with a boat that doesn't need repairs."

"Perry, you are just too much. When will the cottage be ready for occupancy?"

"As soon as possible after I get a yes from you. What will it be, my darling?"

"Well, this offer is hard to refuse," I responded as the huge smile on my face confirmed my acceptance.

Perry immediately began repairs on the cottage anticipating occupancy by Christmas, However, our excitement had to be tempered because of weather related delays and problems with the extent of the needed renovations, which proved to be more than anticipated. Perry had even drawn up plans for an art studio, a greenhouse, and a pond. Therefore, it was the middle of June before I could move in, and by the end of July, Lori Kate and David Lee visited.

For two weeks, Perry, the kids, and I cooked out, went crabbing, cruised the bay on the Rendezvous and bought a dog that we named Scout. Lori Kate and David Lee especially enjoyed stocking the pond with huge goldfish. David Lee would sit for hours and just watch them swim around in their new home. He named all of them. His favorite was No-Winker. He said that he named him that because he never blinked.

Lori Kate, on the other hand, started a shell collection. She painted faces on the big ones, and we made wind chimes. She would giggle and say that they talked when the wind blew. It was fascinating to watch them experience simple pleasures and gratifying to see Perry enjoying their company. I sensed that he was beginning to heal from the devastating losses from the past few years. The kids were his own remembered.

The art studio was the center of activity at the cottage. At the end of two weeks, each child had completed one canvas. David Lee captured Scout's likeness in a rough-like caricature using oil pastels. Lori Kate tried her hand at reproducing a Van Gogh using mounds on top of mounds of oil paints. Not being familiar with using these mediums, some of their shirts and shorts were permanently stained. I would be sure to tuck money away in their luggage for my sisters-in-law to replace the damaged clothing. They would not be pleased that I had been so careless, but I didn't care. During the two weeks that they were with me, I wanted to give them something that they could keep forever, and I had. Before they left, we made plans for the next summer. Escondido Cottage had come to life.

Chapter 25

THE MEMORY KEEPER

The summer after I moved to Lillian, mother passed away. Aunt Irenee could not make the journey for health reasons, and Camille was her only caregiver. Therefore, Imogene, Lori Kate, Ruth Ann, David Lee, and I represented the family at the funeral along with a host of friends and acquaintances.

Condolences continued for two days after the funeral, and I was surprised by an unannounced visit from none other than Finley Hughes. We exchanged polite greetings and well wishes. His demeanor had not changed at all. Stuffy and formal still characterized his disposition. The only thing that had changed was the fact that he had two children. I was sure that dinner conversations around the table focused on manners and proper etiquette. If he knew what my life had been like over the years, he would have choked in his stiff collared shirt. I chuckled to myself as I pictured Perry and I swimming nude at Pensacola Beach. Even though Finley had children, I was sure that the only image of him even partially nude was only seen by the bathroom mirror.

Since I was the only living child, my part of the inheritance was enough to provide a little security for me for a few years. However, I was worried about the part of the estate that mother had given to Imogene and Ruth Ann. I would have thought a substantial trust fund for Lori Kate and David Lee would have been appropriate, but mother was a benevolent person and trusted Imogene and Ruth Ann to do the right thing. Since both daughters-in-law had remarried, I knew it was just a matter of time before their inheritance would be gone.

When the dress shop did not materialize, Imogene remarried an Air Force officer stationed at Maxwell Air Force Base in Montgomery and eventually moved to Keesler Air Force Base in Mississippi. Ruth Ann remarried a car dealer from New Iberia, Louisiana, divorced him within a year, remarried again, and relocated to southern Florida to work in hotel management. In hindsight, I should have talked with mother about her will after father died, but it never occurred to me that she would leave anything to her former daughters-in-law after they remarried, rather than directly to the grandchildren. That's how inheritances disappear.

The house was sold along with many household items. A few treasured pieces of furniture were given to Imogene and Ruth Ann. For me, I inherited Mother's old divan and antique pine chifforobe. Both were in dire need of restoration.

Leaving Montgomery for the last time closed a major chapter in my life. With one last visit to the cemetery, father's store, and Union Station, I recorded final memories in my journal and bid farewell. In no time, I was back in Lillian with Perry. I felt strangely desperate.

It was one thing for me to move to Lillian, but to completely dissolve my involvement in the dress shop was a hard blow for Ethelene. I was the only person even remotely close by that could be considered family to her. Therefore, I was not surprised when she announced her retirement and began looking for property in Lillian, protectively declaring that it was just too unsafe for me to live out there all alone. Within a few months, she purchased a small house not too far from the cottage. It was a good decision as there were times during hurricane season when a close neighbor was needed.

Even though I missed the dress shop, I loved my new life in Lillian. To occupy my time, I once again painted madly. Ethelene and I took day trips so that I could purchase new canvases and hats, which I began collecting. It seemed quite odd that I had worked in a dress shop for years and left with only a few. I searched for unique ones from the 20's, 30's and 40's. I even built shelving in the large dress closet where I kept cocktail dresses, ball gowns, and jewelry. Several times I had thought of donating most of it to charity, but Lori Kate loved to play *dress up*. During her first visit to the cottage, we pretended to be guests at a grand gala called *Moonlight Ball by the Bay* which I predicted would become a tradition.

On Tuesdays and Thursdays, local artists used the studio to paint, shared their expertise, and conversed about anything pertinent to the art world. It was especially gratifying when someone sold their first painting. For these special occasions, we celebrated with wine and champagne, much like christening a new ship for its maiden voyage. Most of my paintings were sold at art shows in and around the Lillian area, but I saved the special ones.

Perry was particularly fond of an oil painting of two of us sitting on the bench in the garden overlooking Perdido Bay artistically created in tones of black, white, and cream. He loved the fact that I included his hat and boots in the painting. We hung it over the mantel in the sunroom. On an adjacent west wall, I hung one of my favorites that I completed the first fall right after moving to Escondido. It was a typical sunset with rich colors of orange, red, aqua, and brown that added a warm ambience to the room during crisp autumn nights.

By far my favorite, though, was something far more risqué than anything I had ever done. It was a painting of me sitting on the divan with Perry. My beautiful shawl was the focal point and the only thing I was wearing. Since the nature of the composition had a seductive and sensual flair, I appropriately hung it in the bedroom along with two other pieces of art, a watercolor of *The Pond at Escondido* and a composition of people in a tropical setting in the style of Gauguin.

Perry and I especially looked forward to the summertime when Lori Kate and David Lee joined us at the cottage along with a neighbor's child named John who helped me occasionally with gardening. He was Lori Kate's age, and they were infatuated with each other.

Perry, David Lee, and John especially enjoyed fishing excursions on the Rendezvous while Lori Kate and I made costumes, attended ballet performances, or dabbled in my French perfume while listening to classical music and dressing for the *Moonlight Ball by the Bay*. Picnics were always a part of our seasonal agenda, and the location was always the old unfinished hotel at Perdido where we collected hundreds of shells. Evenings at Lillian were spent sitting by the bluff listening to classical favorites and sharing special moments from the day. It was a daily routine that we ritually observed during their visits.

* * *

At the end of the 50's, we enjoyed a grand celebration for the positive productivity and ease of living that had returned after the war. Each year, especially during the summer season, new memories were created, reflecting the joyous times of the decade.

As time passed, we watched the kids grow up, and what we knew would eventually happen did happen.

David Lee graduated from high school and thought about joining the Army, but he never committed. Instead, he drifted from town to town, from job to job, and never married. Most of the time, his whereabouts are unknown.

Lori Kate, on the other hand, went off to college, graduated, and accepted a job in pharmaceutical sales in Jackson, Mississippi. Even though I corresponded with her, regular visits diminished.

John moved away with his adoptive parents to South Carolina as his father was transferred from the Pensacola Naval Station to the Charleston Navy Shipyard to repair and refit combatant ships and submarines. To our dismay, communication with them was lost after they relocated.

When I look at Escondido Cottage from the water, it reminds me of a sentinel, a silent guardian maintaining a constant vigil on the bluffs, watching over us and providing safety and shelter to things valuable and priceless. It was indeed a protector of memories, just as I had become. With those sentiments, I penned the following on a small canvas that I framed and placed on a table by the divan. It was a message to all who entered. It read:

Memories only survive by those who treasure and preserve them. Never let them die.

Chapter 26

SUMMER LOVE

The sound of a car racing down the sandy road, tires spinning madly, caused me to jump out of bed and part the drapes covering the French doors in my bedroom. Immediately, I heard Ethelene's screaming voice as she wheeled the car into a parking space by the greenhouse. This was totally out of character for her. Something had lit a fuse and caused an explosion. I opened the doors and yelled back.

"What on earth is going on, Ethelene?"

"Crazy tourists. They need to get out of Lillian. Couldn't even get gas because the car line was backed up halfway down the bridge highway. Who invited them here, anyway?"

"Now Ethelene. You know this place is growing, and you know how bad the traffic is during the summer season. Come on in. Let's make some coffee, or maybe you need something cooler to cool you off."

"Crazy tourists," she continued to balk. "They are everywhere, littering the beaches and crowding all the shops, and not just in Lillian. And don't give me the lecture about needed revenue for this area. We were doing simply fine without them. I refuse to put out a welcome sign and won't be inclined to venture out much for a while. At least until I see their taillights heading out of town."

I laughed as I placed the lemons on the table for our iced tea and filled our glasses with ice.

"Well, I guess our day trips are off during the next few weeks. Huh?"

"You've got it. It's too hot anyway."

"My, my, Ethelene. And I just thought that the weather forecast for this summer would be the only thing sizzling!"

She was right. Lillian and the surrounding areas had ballooned with tourists. I was glad that Perry and I had privacy at the cottage. When it was possible, we cruised around Perdido Bay on the Rendezvous as the temperature on the water was less intense than on land. Sleeping on the boat at night was a special treat, and evening dips in the cool bay water were invigorating.

By summer's end, sunsets were breathtaking. I could have painted hundreds of canvases capturing their beauty. All were uniquely different, much like fingerprints. No matter what the occasion, light dinners were prepared to avoid the double of summer humidity and heat in the kitchen. After dusk, we listened to classical composers or impromptu concerts provided by a chorus of katydids and bullfrogs that mesmerized their audience and served as a tonic for relaxation or an aphrodisiac for making love.

Perry came when he could, always on the Rendezvous, always at dusk. Oftentimes, I watched for him sitting on the garden bench overlooking the bay. The vigil was reminiscent of times long ago when women would wait on the shore for a loved one to return home after a long voyage at sea. Each time I saw the approaching light from the boat, and he sounded the horn, my heart was overjoyed. It never changed, no matter how many times he came. The excitement was there as well as the desire to be touched and loved by him.

Parting, on the other hand, was an entirely different emotion. At dawn he would leave, and I never knew how long it would be before he could return. It was always a struggle to let go, especially after our intimacy.

My journals reflected my memories. Sitting on the garden bench drinking coffee, walking on the shoreline at dawn enjoying the water nibbling at our toes, cutting fresh flowers from the garden, harvesting aromatic herbs from the greenhouse, sipping champagne, celebrating beautiful sunsets, and squeezing fresh oranges for breakfast were typical journal entries as the simple pleasures stayed with me. However, recollection of intimacy lingered longer with much more emotion. Smelling his Old Spice aftershave on my pillow after he had gone, remembering his soft, provocative expressions of love in my ear provoked reactions of satisfaction as well as sadness.

I had hoped that over the years we would eventually have more time together. Neither of us, however, wanted this at the expense of another person. Perry's devotion to the care of Mrs. Frederick was unwavering, a character trait that I admired greatly. Since her overall health had declined since the death of her sons, I respectfully stayed in the shadows, supporting Perry in what we both considered a necessary obligation and responsibility.

I dare not pretend to be the heroine, though. Sometimes, frustration invaded rational thinking. But I did not want to jeopardize our relationship by sharing my innermost thoughts, even though I knew he would understand. Confiding in him might create unneeded pressure and tension which we never wanted to have again. So, I stayed busy during his absences, painting, writing, and gardening, especially caring for my beautiful orchids.

For the entire month of September that year, Perry was completely absorbed in his business endeavors. He had announced his retirement and was in the process of transferring the management and ownership to Board members and various employees. He had resisted the change since his work provided a sense of accomplishment for him just as managing the dress shop had been for me. However, it was time to move on, and he knew it. Maybe this change in life would afford us more time together, and my wish would at long last come true.

One evening, arriving much later than usual, he blew the horn from the boat and made his way up to the house. Anticipating a quiet evening at home, I was surprised when he entered and announced different plans. Taking me in his arms, he joyfully proclaimed a daring getaway far away from Lillian.

"Get dressed, my darling! We are going out for an evening on the town."

"But Perry! We can't do that. What if we are seen?"

"What if? What if? What If?"

"Well, yes. I moved here for the seclusion we needed. Remember?"

"Don't worry. Our destination is a secure place. You will see. We need some adventure, and I want to celebrate retirement. Will you trust me?"

"Yes, of course."

"Then let's go. Let's dance. Let's tango. Let's forget about everything but us! Dress for the dance, my love. The night is ours. Wear something soft and sensual that captures the wind."

With that, I donned the most romantic garment I had in the closet. Wearing a loose-fitting, pale pink crepe dress, accentuated with my Parisian shawl, we drove to Pensacola Beach in my car. Within an hour, we were standing in the doorway of a little open air bar. Perry requested a table in the front corner overlooking the beach. The clientele appeared to be locals who lived in and around the area. No one acknowledged our entrance except the bartender. Perry had anticipated that champagne would not be available and wisely brought our own bottle. We laughed while drinking our very expensive champagne from beer mugs!

The Japanese lanterns and orange candles provided the only sources of light except that which came from the kitchen area. A variety of old pictures and different types of paraphernalia of every kind were tacked onto the walls. An old pair of cowboy boots dangled from the ceiling with a picture of Hank Williams close by. Not being a white tablecloth establishment, patrons selected their own seating based on availability. Tables varied from wooden to metal with unmatched chairs. Booths had café style seating. Instead of replacing worn out seats, thick tape was used to cover torn places and to secure broken frames. The only décor on tables consisted of ketchup and mustard bottles, salt and pepper shakers, and tin napkin holders. A juke box provided the music. Selections could be made from miniature boxes found on each table. When the music stopped, customers would drop a coin or two in the coin slot for more, always selecting the same, easy shuffle tunes, over and over.

"Well, what do you think? It is a unique place, right?"

"I'll say. It will definitely be one of my most interesting journal entries yet. How in the world did you find out about this place?"

"From a restaurant owner in Pensacola. He described it as having a raw appearance with great crab claws and good cold beer. He explained that it was hard to find, and only local beach dwellers claimed the spot. He told me that no one would bother you if you minded your own business. It sounded perfect."

"Well, I can definitely see that keeping to ourselves won't be a problem."

The smell of salty air and cooking spices set the tone for our meal. Feasting on a large bowl of crab claws with bread, coleslaw, and our bottle of champagne, we agreed that they were as tasty as the restaurant owner in Pensacola had described. Dessert consisted of what little champagne was left as we serenely enjoyed the sound of the pounding surf and the sultry breeze coming in from the gulf.

"Lorea, after all these years, you are more beautiful than ever."

"What a nice compliment, Perry. Guess it's the company I keep that keeps me young. That sense of excitement when I'm with you works on me like a tonic."

"Well, speaking of tonic, shall we dance? I am sure that our brand of music is not a part of the selections on the juke box, so we may have to improvise and dance the tango to the beat of a western two step."

I chuckled. "I'll dance to anything as long as it is with you."

"Then let's swing it, old gal!"

The dance floor, protruding from the center of the open-air bar, was simply a square concrete slab with an iron railing around it. A sign with an arrow directed dancers to an area called *the boogie box*, but no one was dancing. It was vacant as the meager crowd was preoccupied in the bar area laughing and consuming beer. Lazy, slow songs played on the juke box in the background, and we quietly made our way to the boogie box and began a slow, rhythmic dance to a tune that we did not recognize. No one noticed. No one cared, especially the two of us.

The intensity of the wind increased, and the strong breeze from the gulf blew my hair wildly. The bottom edge of my dress swirled up to my upper thighs, and Perry caught the hemline and slowly slid it back down touching my hips and thighs. Passion engulfed us. Sensing that, Perry gathered my shawl, paid the cashier, and drove to a small cottage on the beach. I recognized it immediately as the one we rented for the summer before the war. It had not changed and brought back wonderful memories.

"It's still a rental property, and it is ours for the night."

"You think of everything, Perry. No wonder I cannot resist you."

Once inside, Perry lit candles, turned on soft music, and opened the big double doors leading to the small veranda on the beach side of the cottage. Taking me in his arms, he kissed me sweetly. Slowing unzipping the back of my dress, Perry's hands teased my arms and back. In a soft velvety tone, he whispered words of tenderness and love while gracefully swaying me over to a chaise lounge.

Age had not deprived Perry the art of seduction. His face and body, although naturally weathered and worn, created an aura of strength. Time on the Rendezvous had tanned his upper torso which was still slim and firm. I desired him more than ever.

After satisfying our desires, he kissed my forehead, cheeks, and stroked my hair, creating the calming sedative that we both needed to stabilize our emotions. Covered with a large afghan, we drifted into a peaceful sleep with our bodies entwined. Only the dawn interrupted our serenity.

Before leaving for Lillian the next morning, Perry placed a small box in my hand.

"What is this?"

"I hope you will accept it was a token of my enduring love for you as well as my appreciation to you for the gift of companionship and unconditional love that you have given me over the years."

The emerald cut diamond ring was breathtaking. Two large diamonds, framed with onyx, were set in a filigree mounting.

"Perry, this is exquisite. I do not deserve ..."

"Yes, my darling, you do."

"It looks vintage. Where did you find it?"

"In an antique shop. It was made in 1936, the year we met. The store bought it from an estate sale. It is meant for you. Do you like it?"

"Of course. It is extraordinary!"

Kissing the back of my hand, he placed the ring on my finger.

"I love you, Lorea."

Chapter 27

THE DEADLY STORM

Seasonal bad weather moved in quickly two days after we danced in the boogie box and spent the night at Pensacola beach. Dark skies and heavy rain signaled the approaching storm. Since the practice of maintaining a supply of water, food, and candles was imperative for coastal residents, preparation was not a last-minute thing.

High winds created havoc in the area, and skinny pine trees, anchored in sandy soil, toppled like toothpicks. Power outages were vast as phone lines snapped preventing emergency calls. Being in a remote area, I knew that immediate restoration of electricity and phone service would take days. The worst of it all was that I had no means of communicating with Perry.

Once the storm cleared the area and daylight appeared, I covered my hair with a bandana and put on my garden overalls and boots to begin the process of inspecting for damage and removing debris. The sound of a truck coming towards the bluff diverted my attention. Could it be the power company coming so soon? The insignia on the side of the approaching vehicle indicated otherwise. It was a delivery truck from a garden shop in Pensacola. A young male driver emerged from the front seat removing his wide-brimmed western hat and wiping his brow with the sleeve of his sweaty-looking blue shirt. His brown pants and cowboy boots were covered in mud and dirt. His black hair, combed to a point on his forehead, dangled over his thick eyebrows.

"Howdy there ma'am."

"Good morning. I was hoping you were the power company. Obviously, you're not. You look lost."

"I may be. I'm looking for someone by the name of Lorea Hughes."

"I am Lorea Hughes. Pleased to meet you. And you are?"

"Harold McCoy's my name, but everyone calls me Hank. That's my rodeo name, you see. I go by that mostly other than when my boss gets mad and calls me Mr. McCoy like he's going to do if I get back to town and ain't made this delivery. I've been driving around here since early this morning. There's stuff in the road everywhere."

"I am sure, judging by the looks of my own property."

"Yep. Even had to move a big limb all by myself. It had the road completely blocked. With so much stuff on the road, I wasn't sure I could make it anywhere. That was some powerful storm went through here! Must have been a tornado."

"I'm not sure. I lost power immediately, and I've not been able to listen to the radio nor phone anyone to get any information on just how bad the storm was."

"Well, ma'am. I did hear that there was a terrible accident on one of the county roads close to here. It was on the radio news this morning."

"Well, let's hope no one was injured. Now, you said something about a delivery.

"Yep. Right here in the back of the truck."

"What a beautiful rose bush. Who sent it? Is there a card?"

"Yes, u'm there is. It's somewhere. Yep. Here it is. It was ordered yesterday with instructions to be delivered today."

He handed it to me, and I immediately recognized Perry's handwriting. The message read:

> *Enjoyed our boogie. As always, my heart is dancing.*
> *Perry*

"Thank you, Hank. Wait. I need to give you something for

your trouble."

"Nope. My boss said that had been taken care of. No charge, ma'am."

"Very well, then. Please take care driving back and watch out for downed power lines."

"Thanks, ma'am. Now you take care, and I hope you get your power and phone service real soon."

Looking at the card, my thoughts drifted back to our night at Pensacola Beach. However, the sound of dueling car horns interrupted my thoughts. Ethelene and the delivery boy were having a standoff coming and going on the small road which was not wide enough to accommodate two cars. If one pulled off to the side, getting stuck in the sandy shoulder would occur. Ethelene, used to traveling in and out of the sandy road, backed out to the entrance, enabling the truck to pass. I knew she was angry as she gunned the gas pedal leaving a trail of flying debris behind her. If a tornado did not come through this area during the storm, it was surely happening now.

As soon as the car slid to a stop and the door opened, I heard her disenchanted proclamation.

"That fool! He almost ran right over me. What in blazes did he want anyway? He's not from around here. Bet he's a tourist."

"No, Ethelene. Didn't you notice that he was driving a delivery truck? He delivered this rose bush to me. Look at the unusual lavender color. What do you think? It's from ..."

"I don't care who it's from. I don't care if it's from Heaven above! Doesn't help the situation at all."

"Ethelene, please calm down. There are more important things to worry about. Come in and let me make you a strong cup of coffee to ease your nerves."

"Got anything stronger than that? I do need something to improve my nerves, and you need something to prepare you for some bad news, Lorea."

"Bad news?"

"Yes, I have some really bad news about an accident that

happened last night on one of the county roads close to here."

"Last night? That must have been the accident that the delivery boy was talking about. Did it involve someone around here?"

"Not exactly. Not anyone around here, but someone we know."

"Ethelene, what does *not exactly* mean?

"Let's go inside, Lorea."

"You are scaring me now. What is it?"

"The automobile accident the delivery boy was referring to involved Perry. It is already in the paper and on the radio."

I stood motionless. I could not process the horror of what she was saying. It couldn't be true. He is safe in Pensacola.

"Lorea, did you hear me?"

"I did, but it's a mistake. He's in Pensacola."

"No. It's not a mistake. I got here as soon as I could."

I walked over to the bench beside the garden and just sat there for a minute before I replied.

"If it's true, I must go to him. Right now!"

"You can't see him, Lorea. He is in critical condition in Pensacola General."

"I don't care. I'm going. He will need me to reassure him that everything will be ok. I must talk to him. Don't you understand?"

"Lorea, I don't think you understand. He is in very bad shape. He doesn't need anything to upset him right now. You need to know that he is not expected to live."

"That's ridiculous. I'm not going to accept that. You know how things like this get exaggerated. I am sure he may be bruised with maybe some broken bones, but I can't believe he's not expected to live. He is so strong and has to be okay. I know he will, but I need to leave right now to go to the hospital."

"I'm going with you, then. You certainly can't drive yourself under the circumstances. But prepare yourself. It's not good."

"It may not be good, but he won't die. I know that. He won't die," I screamed as I looked down at the ring that he had given me.

During the drive in, Ethelene shared information about the accident.

"Ethelene, what was he doing out in such bad weather? That's not like him. He knows better."

"The account in the paper said that he was headed in this direction on a back road. Of course, the papers did not have an explanation for that."

"Headed in this direction? God, Ethelene. He was coming to the cottage. He has always worried about me being out here alone during bad storms, especially after what happened to my father and brothers. Surely, though, he would have called before he drove out here in a severe storm or possible tornado."

"Lorea, you are not thinking clearly. Remember, this area lost power right before the storm hit because of the winds. And you don't know for sure that he was coming here."

"Yes, he was. He couldn't reach me by phone, so he was trying to get here. I should have tried to get word to him not to come. I would have never thought, though, that he would have ventured out in such severe weather."

"But you couldn't have contacted him. It was impossible, and you don't need to blame yourself. That will not change what has happened."

"I know that, but if I had just thought about it and acted quickly, I might have been able to stop him. Do you know if he was able to talk to anyone after the accident?"

"The news account focused on the cause of the accident. A large tree fell in front of the car, and he swerved to prevent a collision causing it to spin out of control and flip over several times. Being thrown from the car, he was found several yards away. As of this morning, he still had not regained consciousness."

"How did you find out, Ethelene?"

"I went to Pensacola yesterday to shop and visit with Francie.By the time I was ready to leave, it was too late. The storm had already moved in. I had to spend the night with her. I tried to call and check on you, but the call would not go through. When I stopped for gas, I heard the news in the gas station, and then saw the morning paper. I got here as soon as I could. Lorea, at his age ..."

"His age?" I abruptly interrupted. "The man is incredibly strong. He's been through so much and survived. He will survive this, too."

We remained silent during the rest of the drive into Pensacola. What usually took an hour took much longer because of detours caused by fallen trees and flooded streets.

The waiting room in the hospital was still and somber. I didn't see Mrs. Frederick, and I was glad as I had no idea what I would say in my present state of mind. Ethelene found out that she had gone home to rest but would return in a few hours. I needed to see Perry as soon as I could before she returned. However, visitation was restricted to family members only, so I lurked in the corners of the hall waiting for the right moment to quietly move to his side undetected.

Pretending to be a distant relative, Ethelene talked with the nurses, but information was limited. Even though he had regained consciousness, his injuries were life-threatening. The one that I didn't expect was paralysis. His spine had sustained injury, and he was immobile from his waist down. A punctured lung impaired breathing, and one eye had been severely damaged from flying glass from the front window shield. It was worse than I expected.

Shift changes at the nurse's station eventually provided an opportunity for me to see him without anyone noticing. Bandages, protecting cuts and bruises on his upper torso to the top of his head, made him hardly recognizable. Bewilderment stunned back tears of hysteria as I sat quietly by his bedside listening to mumbling sounds and rubbing his cheek. He was in a living Hell.

"It's Lorea. I'm here," I whispered.

"Lorea, go. No. Can't see me like this. Painful," were his only discernable words.

"Don't be silly, Perry. Pain is not being together. Remember?

In no time my love, we will be on the Rendezvous enjoying a swim in the cool water. But for now, you must rest. I'll be close by. I love you."

After what seemed like an eternity of pacing the floor and hiding in the corridors, Ethelene suggested that we get coffee. I knew her real reason was to get me away from waiting areas to avoid a confrontation with Mrs. Frederick as she was due back any minute. When we returned, she was coming out of his room and my presence was unavoidable. Our eyes locked. The intensity of the moment rivaled the storm. Not breaking eye contact with me, she addressed the doctor in a cold, grim voice.

"Dr. Baldwin, since it is only a matter of time, now, I have spoken with my husband. He has requested no visitors under any circumstances except for me. As his wife, I am also prohibiting visitation from anyone. Therefore, I have arranged for nurses to be on duty around the clock. See that they carry out our requests."

And with that said, Ms. Van Mytre rolled her wheelchair directly past me. With her eyes still fixed on mine in a stern, unbroken stare, she disappeared down the hallway. After speaking with a friend of Ethelene's that worked as a volunteer at the desk on the same floor where Perry was located, we left the hospital.

The drive back to Lillian was a blur. The cottage seemed so far away, so empty and desolate. Not being able to see him again before we left was excruciating. I just sat in silence on the bench by the garden overlooking the bay, fearing the worst yet hoping for a miracle. The stages of dealing with the death of a loved one once again hovered over me as I dealt with shock, denial, anger, and depression. If he died, I was sure that depression would remain with me until my death, but I would not let any guilt about our friendship and extraordinary love cloud my memories.

Eventually, a phone call from the volunteer at the hospital broke the silence. Ethelene's expression conveyed my worst fear. Perry was dead.

A despondent stillness took over my body. My sorrow and grief had only begun. He was gone. After years of being together, we had parted, for the last time. Our voyages were over, and my screams of agony echoed across the bay as I had lost my beloved friend and the love of my life. My world was shattered.

Part III

Chapter 28

THE WIDOW

After Aunt Lorea's death, I packed away her manuscript, journals, and pictures and stored them in my attic. After more than a decade, my grief and animosity towards her and the situation had diminished. Aunt Lorea and Escondido Cottage were gone, and I finally accepted that and got on with my life. However, occasionally attending art shows catapulted me back to Lillian. Memories there lingered deep within me like a dormant virus.

When the pharmaceutical company I worked for announced Perdido Bay as the location for the summer convention, a sojourn to Lillian was imminent. The idea of returning intrigued me, although I knew things would be different as Ethelene died soon after Aunt Lorea as well as all of the friends that attended the memorial service.

I was sure that building construction had changed the complexion of the area and contemplated what I would find. Had the old unfinished hotel on the beach where we enjoyed picnics, survived years of enraged hurricanes or new land developments? Even though the O'Neal's were deceased, would the old store still exist under new management or did new land development encroach there, also?

If Bayside Café was still in operation, eating there would be pleasurable. I immediately started to salivate remembering house specials like their grilled cheese sandwiches, french fries, tart lemon pies, and chocolate-cherry cokes.

Thinking about riding down the scenic road leading to the

cottage brought back memories of my first driving adventure one summer in Aunt Lorea's new Cadillac before I was old enough to drive. I can still hear her laughing like she was watching a comedy show.

Did the dress shop, The Occasion, where she purchased so many of her hats survive the influx of strip malls and outlet stores? Memories were vivid of how Aunt Lorea and Ethelene would constantly talk about their buying trips and joke about 'frivaloot' money.

And of course, what about Escondido Cottage? If visitation was possible, rubbing my hand across the weathered cornerstone bearing the name would be a physical and mental postscript that I needed. It would be a symbolic sense of finality, relinquishing everything to the current owner which I never got to do.

The weekend before I left, I needed to find beachwear stored in a container in the attic which resembled a flea market as no semblance of order existed. I would have to search high and low for one small, under-the-bed plastic storage box. Reshuffling old chairs, hanging garment bags, boxes, seasonal decorations, and a host of discarded household items would be necessary.

Stumbling upon the boxes containing Aunt Lorea's manuscript, pictures, and journals, I questioned the purpose of their residency in the current location. A thought surfaced. Why not burn them and lay the ashes to rest with her in Lillian? Because time heals, I realized that I was prepared to let go of these personal possessions that still linked us together. They needed to rest with her and not me. But there was one thing that I wanted to do before offering them a more appropriate place of rest. I was going to read everything from start to finish which was something I had never done.

I read nonstop. None of her entries were hugely significant until the very last one. The entry page said:

REFLECTIONS AND LAST WILL AND TESTAMENT

What is this? Was it truly her Last Will and Testament? If so, it has existed all this time. Surely, this would not have served as an official document, but the location of official ones might be listed. Like a child ripping through wrapped packages at Christmas, I mentally raced through the pages of the leather-bound notebook, finding multiple last entries from her.

Perry died in an automobile accident. His premature death has left me emotionally barren, and I am beyond grief. I feel responsible for this tragedy, a burden that I can't endure. His refusal to let me be with him at the end will forever haunt me. I have packed away his old boots and hat that he wore when we worked in the garden. The sight of them is unbearable, just as my life is now.

Perry found this place in Lillian, Alabama overlooking Perdido Bay, far away from Pensacola. The name Escondido Cottage was chosen because it means "hidden" in Spanish. A cornerstone was appropriately placed to ensure eternal remembrance.

Escondido Cottage was our hideaway from the world. The secluded location was perfect as Perry could come to me by water unbeknownst to anyone. Needless to say, we spent many wonderful years together here in our private world by the bay. I have no regrets, and I cherish the friendship and love we shared together, even though sadness now consumes my soul.

I have no knowledge about the bill of sale

and the deed to the property other than they are "protected" documents. This was guaranteed to preserve anonymity. I do not know with whom Perry entrusted these documents, but he assured me that I would be taken care of until my death, even if his death precedes mine. Therefore, the cottage and the land are not mine to give, and a will is not necessary as I have nothing except for my personal possessions and my memories.

One day, someone will eventually come forward to claim the property. However, Perry does not want disclosure of any kind until all relatives and close friends are deceased. He was adamant about preserving our secret relationship as it would cause pain and suffering to those left behind. Thus, I live here, alone and in secrecy, hidden away from the world, until my death.

Memories only survive by those who treasure and preserve them. Never let them die.

I was beyond astonished. Even though I had figured out some things surrounding her life, the full story was now revealed. The last entries succinctly encapsulated everything. After Perry's unexpected death, her loyalty to him and their previous agreement dictated her actions. When both were deceased, the land and the cottage would at some point in time go to someone else.

Ironically, the answers had been hiding in my attic all this time. I should have stopped and read everything, when I was in Lillian trying to oversee the estate. However, I don't know that it would have changed anything had I made this discovery, even during the probate process. It all makes sense now, though. Finally, after all this time, I am going back with the answers to an unsolved mystery.

A new emotion evolved during my drive to Perdido Bay. A haunting aura filled the space around me suggesting a mission of resurrection. It was strange and unsettling.

Once there, I began my quest by searching for the old hotel. What I remembered to be the approximate location, did not reveal the same structure. I surmised that it had been torn down to make way for new construction. I stopped in a convenience store nearby what I believed to be the old site and asked for information.

"Could you help me, please. I am looking for the old hotel that was here years ago. With new buildings and rerouted roads, I can't pinpoint the exact spot."

"You're a little late, lady. Sorry. Construction crews demolished it about a year ago to make way for the multi-tower complex that is there now called Perdido Dunes."

"Oh, well. I speculated as much. A '*day late and a dollar short*' as the old saying goes."

I wondered if this first disappointment would carry over for the remainder of the day and sadly proceeded towards Lillian. Time and progress had taken away one special memory already, and I hoped the same would not continue.

I felt relieved at my next stop. The Bay Bridge Café was still there. However, the basic turquoise structure was now just an empty, dilapidated shell. The faded cafe sign, once located above the entrance, was leaning against the waterfront side of the building. It was obvious it had long since fallen from its prominent position over the entrance. An unshaven, older man with ragged clothing was sitting in a rattan chair under a palm tree on the side of the café overlooking the bay. He stood up, slipped on his beach sandals, and looked at me as if he wanted an explanation of my presence there.

"Good morning. My name is Lori. I used to eat at Bayside Café when I was younger. I am just passing through and reminiscing."

"Oh yeah. Well, welcome back. I don't see many people these days that remember the old place. I'm the current owner, Charlie Whitt."

"Nice to meet you, Charlie. I must say that I was looking forward to a meal, here, but obviously that is not possible."

"Not anymore. It's been closed for a long time."

"Yes, I can tell. That is sad. I remember the specialties, especially the lemon pie. It was so good."

He nodded his head but refrained from commenting. I immediately engaged in a subject change.

"Do you mind if I take a picture or two?"

"Nope. Go right ahead. It might not be here this time next year. New construction always moving in you know," he said as he looked down, kicking the sandy soil with his weathered beach sandals as he walked away.

The coastal smell was familiar. I could hear Aunt Lorea's laughter when I would say, "*You can just smell that Florida smell.*"

Busy with the photography, I failed to notice Charlie's return until I felt a tap on my shoulder. He handed me a postcard, one of those souvenir Florida cards from the fifties. It was a picture of the café in its heyday. The narrative on the back indicated its location, carried a brief description, and stated the name of the owner, Clarence Whitt.

"That's my father, Clarence Whitt. He kept the cafe up and running for years, but he gave it up when the new restaurants started popping up in the beach areas. Just didn't have the business anymore."

"That must have been hard for him, and I'm sure that probably happened to many small restaurants in this area."

"Yes 'em it did. Seems like it happened overnight, too. Hey, miss. You can keep the postcard. I have plenty."

"Thank you. I appreciate this special souvenir. I have a couple of questions that I think you could answer for me. I am looking for an old store that used to be close by. O'Neal's Store. It has been so long, though, that it is probably no longer there."

"Nope. There's a Texaco station there now. O'Neal's Store has been gone for quite a while."

"That's what I thought. What about a dress shop close by called The Occasion? Is it still in business?"

"Nope. The big outlet mall and several strip malls put 'em right out of business."

"Why am I not surprised? And I will probably have *more surprises* by the end of the day. Well, Charlie, thanks for your time and the postcard."

"Nice seeing and talking with you ma'am."

The ride down the small, scenic road leading to the cottage was unchanged. Still dense with old trees with Spanish moss clinging to low-lying limbs, it was obvious that the major hurricane that smashed through the area several years ago and eroded the bluffs, had not ravaged this area too badly. I pulled over to the side of the road and inhaled the peaceful and still moment, escaping big city traffic and noise. Memories of Aunt Lorea driving down this road in her Cadillac were vivid.

Escondido Cottage was just around the last turn of the scenic road which came to a dead end at a small intersection. Memories flooded my subconscious. I instinctively turned left and took an extra breath as the exhilaration overcame me, somewhat comparable to the first few seconds before a wild roller coaster ride.

The sandy, dirt road entrance to the property would not be far, only down the road a hundred yards or so. As I approached, I found a one-story white clapboard house with green shutters blocking what used to be the primitive car path to the cottage. So, where was the cottage? Maybe new construction had claimed it or a destructive hurricane. The only indication that some type of residence might still be there was a graveled entrance about fifty feet up the road that obviously led back into the woods. A *No Trespassing* sign on the open, gated entrance was posted. Dare I venture in?

The new road was wider and void of sandy pits. A construction crew was building a two-story structure which explained why the gate was open. I cautiously proceeded into the house. Someone working on an electrical outlet at the top of the stairs looked in my way. I quickly made my inquiry.

"Excuse me. I am looking for Escondido Cottage that used to be somewhere in this area. Do you possibly know ..."

"Yep. Can't see it from here, but it's right around the corner. Just hang a right. Can't miss it."

Each footstep echoed loudly, competing with my heartbeat. Please let it be there. Tears came as the cornerstone became visible. I touched it softly and let the memories slide in and out of my mind as I cried for someone and something that I knew did not exist anymore. However, this experience was long overdue, and I had to let it play forward.

Jingling wind chimes diverted my attention to a screened porch filled with colorful furniture. Continued searching took me to the site of the pond which had been located between the porch and the art studio. It was gone. That's when I noticed a wide-open space beyond the pond that had not been there the last time I was here. It was the site of the art studio. It was gone, also. Only a slab foundation remained.

I stood frozen as if I had been immediately tossed into a sub-zero meat locker. It took a few minutes for me to thaw. Did I really think that time would have stood still all these years, and nothing would be different?

I was not bold enough to walk over to the bluff as too many memories rushed me all at once. Pushing my limit about being on the property without permission, prompted me to knock on the door and state my business for being there.

A friendly face greeted me at the door. Her warm smile and gracious reception suggested that I would not be arrested or questioned for trespassing. Her delightful British accent was immediately obvious.

"May I help you, love?"

"Yes. My name is Lori, and my aunt, Lorea Hughes, moved here in the early 50's. It's been years since I was here last. I assume you are the current owner?"

"Yes, I am. My husband and I have lived here quite a few

years. Might I ask what brings you here after such a long time?"

"I am in town for the week to attend a convention. I just wanted to come by and see the place since I have not been here since my aunt's memorial service and the estate was dissolved."

"Well, this visit must be very meaningful for you, and I am so glad that we were here. Please forgive my manners. Do come in."

"Thank you. I promise I won't stay long. I really don't want to impose on you like this, unannounced and all. I just had to see the cottage."

"No imposition at all. I would love to know more about Escondido Cottage. Please join me in the sunroom."

I turned and walked a familiar path. I could see Aunt Lorea sitting in her chair listening to classical music by the indoor pond. I was quite overwhelmed.

"Please, do sit down and make yourself comfortable? I am certain you enjoyed this gorgeous view many times."

"Yes. I did. It's still the same only some of the trees are taller."

"You said your aunt lived here in the 50's?"

"She did. Not only in the 50's but for many years after that. It seems like it was just yesterday. Things were wonderful back then, so simple. I took many pictures with my Kodak camera and actually brought some of them with me."

"How lovely. I would love to see them. Oh, for goodness' sake! How rude of me. I did not introduce myself. I am Margaret Thompson, and my husband, Philip, and I live here most of the year. Just call me Maggie. We are about to leave for our home in England in about two weeks, so your timing is incredibly good. Now, I have just put the kettle on. Would you like to join me for afternoon tea? Or since this is a special occasion, would you rather have a little wine or champagne?"

"Champagne? Oh, my. That was my aunt's favorite beverage. Talk about memories. Yes, Maggie, I think champagne would be nice, and it may calm my nerves. It is not every day that

I invade private property. Plus being back here, what can I say?"

"Say no more, love. Champagne coming up."

Maggie was the type of person that shone with warmth and hospitality through her humbleness and genuine personality. My being a stranger as well as a trespasser had not altered her reaction to me, whatsoever. She was a perfect match for my vision of the owner and caretaker of the cottage. She had short auburn hair, just like Aunt Lorea and was slim and dainty, also like Aunt Lorea. Her smile was friendly and welcoming, inviting friendship.

While she popped the cork and poured the champagne into etched champagne glasses, I glanced around the room and noticed the abstract garden painting over the mantel was still there. The sunset painting remained in its original location on the west wall as well. I was glad the paintings had not been sold or removed over the years. I would have to tell Maggie all about them.

"I hope this champagne meets with your approval. I always keep some on hand for special occasions."

"Yes, of course. Here's to special occasions," I said as we toasted.

"Good. Before we sit and talk a bit, why don't I show you around?"

"If you have the time."

"Oh my, I have plenty of that. My husband and I are on holiday right now away from business back home. We work with Crown Publishing. Philip is a sales executive, and I am a book editor. Time here allows for more reading and editing. Our jobs consume our time, and that's why we truly love coming here to rest and visit with relatives. Philip is originally from Pensacola, you see."

"Well, that's interesting," I replied as I breathed deeply. I wondered if his family knew the Frederick family. How uncanny would that be? But I dare not ask.

"Come, Lori. Let's look around, shall we?"

The large, picturesque windows on all three sides were

void of any window treatment which provided a panoramic view of the bay. Different groupings of furniture were strategically placed around the room to enjoy sunrises and sunsets. Although the style of the furniture was different, the same peaceful mood prevailed. The only thing missing was the inside water fountain. Since Aunt Lorea loved the sound of flowing water, she had installed one on the wall that now housed a fireplace.

The colors in the room were tastefully done in blues, greens, and soft browns, vastly different than the glaring turquoise and pink colors of the 50's. A driftwood collection adorned the shelves around the fireplace, and shells of every kind were on coffee and end tables. Books about gardening were stacked in a basket by an easy chair. A pole lamp provided soft lighting, creating a comfortable place for reading. A big white paddle fan emulated the breeze from the bluff. Large European throw pillows and soft blankets in coordinating colors were placed in front of the fireplace, perfect for those winter evenings on the bluff which could be quite chilly.

"Well, what do you think so far, Lori?"

"I think Aunt Lorea would certainly approve! How long did you say that Philip and you have lived here?"

"We have been here about ten years. We had to remodel and repair quite a bit after we moved into the cottage. It was our understanding that a developer purchased the cottage a few years before we bought it, but nothing materialized. It just sat here aging. Therefore, renovation was necessary to make it comfortable for us and to accommodate our needs."

"That is interesting. I did not know that. I must say, then, that you have done a wonderful job with restoration, and I am grateful. How totally distressing it would have been for me to have come back found the place uninhabited and in disrepair."

Maggie shared that the rest of the cottage had undergone extensive renovation except for the small guest bedroom that was quaint and unassuming with two twin beds, a dressing table, and a closet. White louvered shutters provided privacy instead of curtains. Patchwork quilts in patterns of yellow, green, and blue at the foot of each bed were color coordinated with the seafoam green color on the walls.

The long, skinny hallway that connected the front part of the house to Aunt Lorea's bedroom in the back had been enlarged, and one familiar art piece hung beneath recessed lighting. It was the Gauguin-like painting of people in a tropical setting. A slight tug on my heart occurred as I saw Aunt Lorea's distinct signature in lower case letters at the bottom of the right-hand corner.

"Do you recognize this?"

"Yes. I remember it well along with two in the sunroom. When the cottage went up for sale, some of her paintings were designated as part of the estate exclusively to remain here. There was one exception. I kept one painting of a woman wearing only a shawl. I am so glad the ones designated to be part of the estate did not disappear. Maybe because the cottage sat vacant for so long, explains why they are still here. Thank you for not selling them."

"They are simply lovely, and I would not have considered it. I have always wanted to know about them. How many did you leave behind?"

"I think four."

"Well, there are four still here. There is another one in the main bedroom. *The Pond at Escondido* had been reframed and hung over an antique table that had a French flair. It was the first thing you noticed as you entered the room.

The décor was centered around the serene colors in the painting with soft light streaming from hand painted, vintage lamps. I immediately noticed the hat closet that Aunt Lorea built within the dress-up closet. The slanted wall next to the bathroom where her dressing table was had been restructured into a straight wall, consumed with a large, antique chest of drawers. The greenhouse, which had been located in close proximity to the double bedroom doors to the outside, was gone, but construction materials for a new one was stacked neatly in the same location.

"Is it anything like it used to be, Lori?"

"With the paintings still here, it feels like the old place, but you have added a great deal of charm and refreshing appeal. As I mentioned, she moved here in the 50's, and Escondido Cottage was established just for Aunt Lorea and her lifestyle. Some things are different, but the unique flavor of the cottage is still here. I see you are planning to build a greenhouse. Aunt Lorea maintained one for as long as I can remember. She loved orchids."

"We do have plans for a new one. The old one had to be torn down, critters living in it, you know. I am anxious to get the new one filled with tropical flowers and herbs. I have never grown orchids, but I just may have to try my hand at that. Speaking of growing things, I want to show you the garden area by the bluff."

As we passed by what used to be the art studio, I paused. Pinching the bridge of my nose halted forthcoming tears. Maggie sensed my mood change and immediately put her arms around my shoulders.

"Lori, is something wrong?"

"This was where the art studio used to be. What happened to it?"

"I regret that it was destroyed by high winds from one of the hurricanes. The roof blew off during the storm, and the interior was ruined from the rain and flying debris. We just tore it down last year. We plan to resurface and make a patio for outdoor cooking."

The thought of roasting food over memories from the past somehow seemed unthinkable, but Maggie and Phillip were not hostage to memories of the cottage like I was.

The garden area was lush with flowers, and at every turn, there was an abundance of different varieties. She explained that with every season, there was something aways growing.

"Maggie, you have done an amazing job with preserving and enhancing this area. You might be interested in knowing that Aunt Lorea and I spent hours sitting on the bench, smelling the flowers, and looking out over the bay. This was where we buried her dog, Scout. It was our make-believe garden ballroom where we dined and danced at *Moonlight Ball by the Bay.* It was where I experienced my first kiss from a boy named John. This was where we held the memorial service for her and cast her ashes to the wind."

"Such memories, love. Thank you for sharing. It just adds more meaning to the place."

Between the champagne, reminiscing, and knowing what I learned from Aunt Lorea's last journal, I was dazed with emotion, so the moment was not appropriate to approach Maggie with the idea of burning the journals, pictures, and manuscript and spreading the ashes over the bluff. For several seconds, I tuned out everything. Her voice eventually brought awareness back to me with a startling statement.

"You know, Lori, I do love this garden, too. It is so much a part of my English upbringing. The gardens are lovely in England, and my home there is no exception. However, winters are harsh there and not conducive for gardening. With the hot, wet summers and mild winters here, I can grow almost anything I want which gives me great pleasure. I spend a considerable amount of time working in the garden and harvesting seasonal blooms. I am so tired after hours of weeding and planting that I make it a habit of sitting right here on the garden bench at the end of the day to rest. That is when I have this strange feeling."

"Strange feeling? About what?""

"I feel as if there's always someone here in the garden with me. There seems to be a presence of some kind. Oftentimes, I look over my shoulder to see if someone is here."

"Hold on. You are saying that you sense a presence of someone here after you have been working in the garden?"

"Yes, and quite often, too."

"Do you have a vision of what this person looks like?"

"Not really, but I have thought many times that it's a man wearing a hat and boots. Do you know of anyone that it could be?"

Her description zapped me like a stun gun.

"Lori, did you hear me? You do have a strange look on your face. Is he familiar to you?"

"Maggie, you are suggesting that Escondido Cottage has a ghost. I don't believe in ghosts."

"I didn't either until we moved here. Now, I am not so certain. You do seem rather upset. Are you sure you are, okay?"

"Can you give me a minute? I am going to the car to get something. This may be quite interesting. I'll be right back."

It couldn't be Perry I thought as I sprinted towards my car like a marathon runner. Surely Maggie was not toying with me. *Why would she do that?* She had absolutely no knowledge of Perry and Lorea. Ethelene had died soon after Lorea as well as other neighbors and friends before Philip and Maggie bought the place. I yanked my tote bag from the trunk and dashed back to the garden bench.

"Maggie, I have many photos. Some were taken in Montgomery before Lorea moved to this area. Some were taken in Pensacola at various residences there. Some were taken of my cousin, me, and our friend John during summer visits here. I don't know if you'll find a likeness, but I want you to look at them and see if you recognize anyone."

She studied them carefully and finally answered.

"Not really. My vision of the presence I feel is not that clear. So, it is hard to say. However, this one sort of grabs me because of the hat and the boots."

It was Perry. I felt an arctic chill on my neck. I turned around. Was someone there?

"Now, my dear, you look as if you have seen a ghost!"

"Maggie, are you sure this is the man?"

"Well, not really. But you obviously know him, or you wouldn't have a picture of him. Who is he? Her father? Husband?"

"No, it couldn't be Aunt Lorea's father. He died before she even moved to Lillian. If there were such a thing as ghosts, there would be no reason for him to haunt this place. Paranormal creatures supposedly don't haunt places they have never been. But, yes, I do know him. He was a special friend of my aunt's."

"Oh, she fancied him, did she?"

"I didn't say that."

"Well, it may not be what you said, but your reaction says otherwise. Come, we need to go back inside. Maybe both of us need more champagne."

Maggie was right. I was a little shaken. I did not believe in ghosts. It was nonsense. But I did feel a chill, didn't I? If spirits existed, it would make complete sense for Perry to be the one that was visiting the garden. It was their place. Since their parting was so painful, it was logical for one to believe that he could return in some way to be with her.

"Lori, are you listening?"

"No, I'm sorry. What did you say, Maggie?"

"Nothing, actually. I was just chatting away. I am sure all of this means nothing. I am probably just imagining things. I am sure if this place were haunted, you would have known about it. She worked so hard to develop and maintain Escondido Cottage all by herself since she was a widow. That's why I thought it might be a loved one returning to check on her."

"Wait a minute. Did you say widow?"

"Why, yes, but we really don't know much about that. Nothing seems to be on record anywhere about Escondido Cottage. However, when we moved here, the company that sold us the place shared that the lady that originally lived here was a deeply saddened widow who chose to live mostly in seclusion. As the story goes, she died of a broken heart."

"A widow, huh? Is that all you know?"

"That's it. Historical information is really sketchy as most landowners in this area died before we moved here. All we know is what I just mentioned and that she was referred to as the widow. Quite legendary around here, you know."

I sat there mesmerized by this new discovery. Everything was swirling through my mind much like a windstorm. I knew that I had to leave to collect my thoughts and sort them out. I graciously thanked Maggie for her time and hospitality and headed for the door.

"Maggie, I feel like I should leave now."

"You are definitely upset. Won't you please stay for dinner? We should talk further about your aunt and the cottage. There is still so much that I don't know about this place, and I would love to hear about your summers here and learn more about your talented Aunt Lorea. Who knows when you will return to Lillian again."

Turning to her, I cupped her hands in mine in a gracious manner.

"I am not upset with you. I was just caught off guard a little with our conversations about your garden visitor and the 'widow.' I appreciate your hospitality and your invitation, but I have plans for the evening with people that are down here for the convention. Tell you what. If it is okay, I will come back tomorrow as soon as my meetings are concluded. I have a proposal for something I want to do here for 'the widow'."

"Splendid! May we count on you for dinner tomorrow night? Come a little early so we can continue our chat."

"Will do, and thanks for the invite."

That evening, I sat on the balcony outside of my room and chuckled at it all. Just when I thought the entire mystery was solved, new ones surfaced. Secrets at the cottage, indeed! So, everyone thought she was a widow. She must have told them that to preserve the secret, and Ethelene backed her up and probably assumed a widow role as well. Interesting. I knew that being divorced in their day was shameful, so assuming widow status created a different image of a poor lady, all alone, living in a small cottage minding her own business. She would have been considered an upstanding citizen with no questions asked about her personal life. Total privacy achieved. It was a masterful plan, establishing a solid reputation and living as a recluse to avoid scandal. They lived happily until his death. If indeed Perry had returned to the garden as a ghost, he was there to console her until she joined him in another garden. End of story.

Still pondering everything, I thought about her message to me taped to the bottom of the strong box.

> *I know that one day you will find these pictures, my journals, and my manuscript. When you do, I hope that you will understand and appreciate the beauty of a special friendship and love that few ever experience in a lifetime. There's a wonderful story here. Do with it what you may.*

With that, I knew what needed to be done.

The next afternoon, I drove back to Lillian. Maggie was on the porch having tea.

"Lori, how lovely to see you again. We are delighted that you are joining us for dinner. We still have so much to talk about. While I am thinking about it, I wanted to bring up someone that you mentioned by the name of John that was here when you were years ago. Your 'first kiss' guy."

"Yes. He came around often when my cousin and I visited in the summer. I don't know much about him, though. Why do you ask?"

"About three years ago, a man showed up at the door, much like you did, and said that he used to visit here in the summer when he was young. His name was John. He explained that he had moved away and had never returned. He claimed that he knew the owner of this place and the lady who lived here long ago. He was visiting the Naval Air Station and decided to check out Escondido Cottage before he returned home."

"Really? That's very interesting. Did he mention his last name?"

"He said his last name was Frederick."

"What? He said his last name was Frederick? Are you sure?"

"Yes, quite sure. Lori, you seem somewhat taken aback by this."

"What you just said has totally caught me off guard, once again, and I'm a little stunned. What a jolt! I just need a minute to process what you have shared."

My mind was racing with disbelief. Couldn't be *my* John. I don't think. Or could it be? No way. Wouldn't I have known that or was that something else that was hidden? What is it about this place that continues to be a source of mystery and surprises?

"Did he leave any contact information with you?"

"No, and I didn't see any reason to ask him for that. I am so sorry. Looks like it's a dead end. But speaking of surprises, I have one for you."

"Maggie, I'm not sure if I can handle any more surprises," I sighed.

She smiled and disappeared, returning with the painting *The Pond at Escondido.*

"It's yours. I want you to have it because of the sentimental value. I think you should be the rightful heir."

"I don't know what to say. This is such an unexpected, generous gesture. I appreciate this more than you will ever know," I replied as my voice quivered and tears welled up in my eyes.

"Oh my, now I have upset you again today. I am dreadfully sorry."

"No need to be sorry. I promise, you have done nothing wrong. Actually, you have given me two gifts. Yesterday you helped provide closure regarding Escondido Cottage and today the gift of the painting. And now, you have given me the name of someone that I *must* find named John Frederick."

"I'm not quite sure I understand."

"You will, Maggie. I brought a bottle of wine to enjoy during dinner, and I have champagne. You get the glasses and open the bottles while I unpack several boxes. We will sit back and relax as we will be here long into the evening hours."

"Long into the evening hours, you say?" she responded inquisitively.

"Yes. You see, I have some things that belonged to the

'widow' that I want to leave here. Plus, you said that you wanted to learn more about the history of the cottage and the woman that lived here. I have a story to tell which begins with the man in the hat and boots in the painting over the mantle sitting beside *The Widow of Escondido*.

MEMORIES ONLY SURVIVE BY THOSE WHO
TREASURE AND PRESERVE THEM.
NEVER LET THEM DIE.

About the Author

Emme Rocher

Linda Maxwell (pen name: Emme Rocher) has always loved writing, spending her childhood summers writing and performing plays with neighborhood friends.

"Wooden crates became the stage floor, and scenic backdrops were painted onto old sheets and taped to walls and fences. Before an adoring audience of parents and neighbors, we created colorful characters with rich dialogue ... the ultimate experience in writing."

A retired educator, Linda was both an elementary school teacher and intermediate school principal. While earning a doctorate from the University of Alabama and UAB, she fostered writing experiences for her young students with a weekly *Author's Chair.* Later in her career, she created *The Lunch Bunch Writing Club* where parents were invited to school for an hour each week to write with their kids and enjoy the *Author's Chair* experience, a practice published in a national educational magazine.

The Widow of Escondido is a novel she began writing three decades ago.

"A published writer once told me to always be a literary kleptomaniac by listening to the rhythm of spoken and written language, studying movie characters and themes, and watching performances of any kind. Over the years, I did just that."

Linda's favorite hobby is river and ocean cruising with her husband, Joel.

Acknowledgements

To my husband ... Your support of and belief in me throughout MANY years as I created "The Widow" has been unbelievable. Thank you for the hundreds and hundreds of hours listening to my ideas, advising me when revisions were needed, and providing countless trips to Florida for me to "dance with the pen." Most of all, thank you for your patience and love. You have made a difference in my life. My heart dances.

To my family ... Thank you for believing in me as a writer and helping me keep the faith so that seeing life and the world through words was possible. Thank you for your celebrations when the big moment finally came. You have helped this dream come true by encouraging my colorful hands and inspiring me with ideas.

To Debbie, my sister ... Thank you for helping me "grow" this story over many years and being the constant gardener.

To my personal and professional friends ... I cannot express my appreciation enough to ALL of you for the encouragement I received on this "voyage" to publication. So many of you volunteered your time to read paragraphs, or pages, or chapters. A special thanks to all of my colleagues at Oak Mountain ... our profound theme ... the extra degree ... 212 ... has stayed with me.

To Anne Glass for introducing me to Bob and Hidden Shelf Publishing House. Without her, Widow would still be "hidden" in a three-ring binder. Also, to Bob ... Writing this acknowledgement is finally possible because you gave me a chance. I am forever grateful to you for this opportunity. This is truly a colossal "author's chair" for me. And to Kerstin ... her patience has no limits. Throughout the editing process, she was there for me with unwavering support.

Explore the Hidden Shelf